EMERALD FLASH

EMERALD FLASH

CHARLES KNIEF

THOMAS
DUNNE
BOOKS

ST. MARTIN'S PRESS
NEW YORK

THOMAS DUNNE BOOKS.
An imprint of St. Martin's Press.

Library of Congress Cataloging-in-Publication Data

Knief, Charles.
    Emerald flash / Charles Knief. — 1st ed.
    p.   cm.
    ISBN 0-312-19866-3
    I. Title.
    PS3561.N426   E46   1999
    813'.54—dc21   98-43784
                                                          CIP

First edition: April 1999

10 9 8 7 6 5 4 3 2 1

For Ildiko.
The day I found you should be a national holiday,
the day I married you, a sacred one.

Emerald Flash: An atmospheric phenomenon that rarely occurs, even on those extraordinary days when there are no clouds all the way to the horizon. As the last infinitesimal part of the sun slides below the edge, there is a brilliant emerald flash. It blooms, blossoms, and vanishes so quickly your brain records its presence after it has already gone, leaving only a memory that something beautiful has happened.

The first time I saw Margo Halliday she was stark-naked, running for all she was worth down a Honolulu alley in the middle of the night.

A big man chased her. Every thirty feet or so he'd stop and fire a round from an automatic pistol. The woman was in more danger of stepping in broken glass than getting hit by a bullet. The big guy's heart wasn't in it. Unsteady on his feet, just tipsy enough to be overcautious, he would come to a complete stop, carefully aim way to the right or way to the left, and pull the trigger. He'd watch the bullet powder brick on either side of the alley, then start chasing her again. It reminded me of a cat chasing a mouse. A lot of fun for the cat, sure, if he felt sadistic, but the mouse would just as soon prefer to be otherwise occupied.

This time neither party appeared to be having fun. The man cried as he chased her, mouthing unintelligible words, tears streaking his cheeks, his nose running. He looked like a wounded man, the way a man can only be wounded by a woman. And for all his pain he looked grimly intent on inflicting pain of another kind on the source of his misery.

I'd just left the back room of Chawlie's Chinatown restaurant, where he'd beaten me once again at Go. That made it about twenty-five gazillion to two, and I was very proud of those two.

The big man jogged past and I dropped him with a flying kick. He went down easy but refused to let go of the pistol, so I broke his wrist and he gave it up. All the fight went out of him. He deflated like an octopus brought up on a lure and dumped into the bottom of a canoe, when it knew it was going to die.

I released the pistol's clip and eased back the slide. A bright brass 9-mm cartridge popped out. The gun was a Glock, one of those new automatics that carry half a box of ammunition. Load it up in the morning and shoot all day. It was good for those unsure of their marksmanship, or for those loonies who imagined themselves facing hordes of enemy lurking between their homes and the corner 7-Eleven. I stuck the gun, safed, in the hip pocket of my shorts.

"Is he dead?"

The naked woman had returned. She stood near the big man, who lay curled against Chawlie's back wall. Hip slung, she presented an explicit representation of female anatomy.

"Not unless he's had a heart attack." I squatted and felt the big neck. The slow, strong heartbeat was reassuring. "He's okay," I said, looking up. She had moved closer and my face was now in direct proximity to her sex.

I stood and pulled off my sleeveless SKI THE VOLCANO sweatshirt and handed it to her. The sides gapped, but if she kept her arms down it would cover her. She was not a particularly small woman, but it was an XXL.

She silently accepted the sweatshirt but held it against her thigh. She stood naked in the filthy Chinatown alley, as still and as beautiful as a Grecian statue. And as unremarkable. All flesh is equal, regardless of its age or condition. Her body was one I could admire as I would admire a work by a master sculptor, but like a statue, no heat radiated from it, and I was not drawn to her.

"Put it on," I said.

"Oh." Her eyes focused suddenly. She had been far away, but she came back from wherever she'd been and shrugged the shirt over her head.

"Thank you," she said, her voice shaky. Now she looked scared.

"You know this guy?"

She nodded, her arms wrapped around her body, long fingers gripping the gray sweat cloth. "He's my husband. Or was. We're divorced. Have been for years. But he keeps coming around, making demands."

"Come on," I said, reaching for her. She flinched away.

"Where?"

"In here. It's a restaurant." I pointed to Chawlie's back door. "There are people in there. Other women. They'll take care of you. Get you some clothes. Then you can decide what to do."

She nodded again. "What about him?"

I looked down at the man. He still lay against the wall. I couldn't tell if he was unconscious or if he was faking. It didn't matter.

"What about him?"

"He's hurt," she said. "Shouldn't we do something for him?"

"Why?"

She thought about it. Then she nodded again and I knew she was going to be all right.

John Caine. You only man I know who can walk out the door and come right back with naked woman," Chawlie whispered, his smile large and generous, his eyes twinkling.

We lounged at his bar sharing one more beer. His bar girls had taken charge of Margo, wrapping her in silk and taking her back to Chawlie's private quarters. Eventually one of the girls returned with much ceremony and giggling to present me with my sweatshirt.

"Anthony checked man in alley His arm broken, he no move. Next time he look, man gone. You do him, eh?"

"He was chasing the woman and shooting at her with this." I pulled the automatic from my hip pocket and handed it to Chawlie.

"Grock."

"Yeah. A Grock. He was shooting, but he didn't mean to hit her. He aimed wide."

"This her husband?"

"Ex-husband."

Chawlie shook his head. The lack of clarity and the vagaries of haole relationships were alien to him. He offered me the gun.

"You keep it," I said. "I don't like those things."

He laughed. "You old-fashioned."

"A nine's too small," I said.

"You like what you like. Forty-five your gun." Chawlie examined the automatic again. "Expensive," he muttered, and put it away behind the bar. "You know this man? You recognize him?"

"Who? The woman's husband?"

"Yes."

"No. Do you?"

"Never saw him before," said Chawlie, sipping his Tsingtao. "Just wondered. All you haoles look alike to me. Especially in the dark."

"Funny, Chawlie."

"You see bruises on young woman's face? Or you just looking at her tits?"

I hadn't seen any bruises, but it was dark in the alley.

"So what you going to do, John Caine? You going take young woman home, be her big hero? Hope to get lucky, or what?"

"Somebody's got to take her home."

"I send girls and a couple of my people. She feel safer that way, I think."

Chawlie was trying to get rid of me. That meant there was something he could use to his advantage. And he didn't want me involved.

That Chawlie would send the woman home with his girls was certain. He might be a criminal, he might break the law, but unlike most of those who craft the laws, he is a man of his word. Although I didn't know her name at the time, Margo Halliday was safer than she'd ever been in her life. Whatever advantage he might gain by assuming the responsibility for the woman's safety would not adversely affect her in any way.

"I'll take that hint," I said, sliding off the barstool, "and go home."

"Leave by front door this time."

"Good night, old friend."

"Good night, John Caine. If you find any more strays tonight, you keep them."

That was the first time I'd ever seen Margo Halliday. It would not be the last.

The next time I was aware of her was seven months later, when news of the murder was the *Advertiser*'s lead story, her photograph prominently displayed on the front page, her features instantly recognizable, bringing back the events of that warm summer evening. Her ex-husband had been shot to death in her Hawaii Kai condominium. Police wasted no time in charging her with a variety of crimes, curiously excluding any of those indictments that can be brought when one human being takes the life of another. The crimes were all misdemeanors and minor felonies and she made bail with the help of a high-priced defense attorney from Bishop Street.

The paper reported the sanctioned police statement that they were investigating and would have further announcements. It didn't look good for the woman I'd briefly met in that dark, dirty alley.

I remembered her. In great and specific detail. Curiously, I was not aroused by the memory.

I read through the newspaper again and found a related story. My old friend Lieutenant Kimo Kahanamoku was in charge of the case. It made me feel better. Regardless of the facts, Margo Halliday would get a fair shake. If she didn't do it, no harm would come her way. If she did it with malice aforethought, Kimo would bring her to justice. If it had been done in self-defense, he'd see to it she would be released without further charges, and possibly drop the ones already in place. Kimo had a wife to whom he was strictly devoted, and he didn't like wife beaters.

The paper built its own case, reporting of two restraining orders out on Halliday, one here in Hawaii and one in California. The orders would have been explicit, carefully drawn by expensive attorneys and approved by well-meaning judges. Yet it looked like Halliday was dead because she still had to defend herself with a gun.

The article continued, describing Halliday's business activities in Hawaii and on the Mainland. He'd had some modest successes and he'd had some spectacular failures, one of which concluded with Mr. Halliday's spending a little downtime in a federal correctional institution over what his attorney had described as "a few minor bookkeeping oversights." He'd had more ups and down than an elevator, but it looked as if he'd just pushed the UP button before he'd been killed.

In recent weeks Glen Halliday had received a humanitarian award from the Crippled Children's Fund and been feted at a Cancer Research dinner for his generous support. A photograph showed him shaking hands with the President and the First Lady, and mentioned he had been one of those heavy campaign contributors who had once spent the night at the White House. That was a difficult picture to harmonize with the man I'd fought in the alley, the mean drunk waving a pistol, chasing the naked ex-wife through a dark and humid night. Kimo wouldn't be surprised. He was good, one of the best. He'd cut through the crap, and eventually my name would crop up.

So there was no surprise when Kimo came to visit a few days later, clumping down the dock in his size 14 double-wide sandals and 3XL Aloha shirt. *Olympia* settled noticeably when he came aboard, climbing over her teak railing. Light dimmed as he eclipsed the sun, peering down into the engine compartment access hatch, where he found me.

"Hey, Kimo," I said, looking up from my tight little space, wedged between the diesel engine block and the hull, "come aboard."

"I'm already here."

"I noticed. You're supposed to ask permission, and then I say 'Sure, come aboard,' and then you climb up there and say hello and then I offer you a beer. I was just trying to bring you up to speed." I held up my hand, covered in grease to the elbow, but he waved it off.

"Where's the beer?"

"Ah, a man with a mission. In the fridge. Help yourself. I'll be finished in a minute."

His brightly hued bulk disappeared from the engine hatch. When he reappeared he held an Edelweiss Dunkel.

"Your boat's broke?"

"Just maintenance. It could get kind of inconvenient if it breaks out there on the deep briny."

He smiled. Kimo was a waterman, too, sprung from a long line. "Crank up the iron sail, huh?"

"When I need to." I finished tightening the last nut, checked for loose tools and foreign objects, and backed out of the engine compartment. I was sweating, soaked from head to toe from my hours in the hot, tight space. I wiped the grease from my hands with a rough rag. The breezes flowing off Pearl

Harbor's placid surface felt good and I wanted to stay outside. Kimo beckoned me to the cabin and I reluctantly climbed down into the lounge.

"Here." Kimo handed me a cold beer as I slid behind the table.

"Thanks. Buy me one of my own, eh?"

"I'm a policeman. Can't afford this kind of luxury."

"With ten kids, who could?"

"Got two at U of H, one over at Stanford. Lucky they all on scholarships; I'd be destitute." He glanced out the porthole, darkened by the shadow of the concrete structure overhead. "Doesn't the new bridge bother you?"

While I was in-between boats, the Navy had built a bridge to Ford Island almost directly over my slip. I'd been afraid that the traffic might make too much noise but, like everything else, it quickly assimilated into the background. Pearl Harbor was a peaceful place, regardless of the massive war machines and the constant preparations for war that required their existence.

While I'd been gone they also moved in the USS *Missouri* and berthed her next to the *Arizona* Memorial, just across the water from the Rainbow Marina. Pearl Harbor was rapidly becoming a tourist attraction.

"Not anymore. This about Halliday?"

He nodded. "Heard you met the happy couple."

"A few months back."

"You and that Chinese criminal."

"I don't remember, Kimo."

He shook his head. "You got a better memory than that, Caine. I know you hang out with Chawlie. What I want to know is how he knew Halliday."

The conversation had moved into dangerous territory. Kimo wasn't making mere conversation.

"Don't know," I said, which was the truth. I wouldn't pretend to know everything and everybody Chawlie knew.

"Information I got was that Mrs. Halliday was escorted like royalty by some of his goons. Everywhere she went."

"Got that from the condo doorman?"

"Lots of people recognized the car, knew the driver, who he worked for."

"And were willing to talk to the police about it. This happen a lot?" I drained the bottle, replenishing my fluids, not wanting the big cop to see my face.

"From what I hear, Mrs. Halliday and the crook had a regular thing going. Your friend seems to have a lot of energy. That's the rumor."

"It's a small island."

"And folks have big mouths. Except you, John Caine."

"Aw, shucks," I said.

"You know something," said Kimo in his cop voice. "You working the case? Or hope to?"

"Not working at the moment." I didn't need to. According to this morning's paper, Petersoft, Ltd, topped 38-1/4 in trading on the NASDAQ and was expected to top forty before an anticipated split. Claire's little bonus had been sweet. I had to admit being intrigued by this case, but Chawlie's presence was enough to keep me out of it.

"You and Chawlie are pretty tight. You helped him a couple of times. But I don't think you know what you're into."

"I'm used to it." I wasn't into anything yet, but there was nothing to be gained by useless denial. Kimo wouldn't believe me, anyway.

"I think Choy had Halliday killed. I think he had some business dealings with him on Kauai. I think he had something going with the ex, and Halliday became too big of a pain in the ass."

"Interesting. And you don't think Mrs. Halliday killed anyone."

"That's—" He cut himself off, placing a big hand over his mouth. "Forgot who I was talking to."

"Save it, Kimo. I really don't want to know anything. Depending on what I already knew, I might tell you just to help you out. And you're right. Chawlie's a friend. But this time I'm a blank."

"You broke Halliday's arm. That's not relevant?"

"Not really. And Chawlie didn't hire me to kill him."

"Not that you wouldn't."

"I'm mellowing. It's not like that."

The big cop pursed his lips, concentrating on the teak bulkhead.

"Anything else?" I asked.

"No." He drained the last of his beer, got up and started for the ladder. "But if I think of anything else I'll let you know."

"You're my friend, too."

He paused on the ladder and looked down at me, a hard stare, the cop look. "The first time we met, you were a suspect. You got involved with a good cop who was killed when she got between you and your quarry. You might have saved her, but you waited until you were sure you could kill the guy. I never forget that."

He shook his head sadly. "I'm never sure just where you stand, Caine. I'd hate to have to stake my life on it."

2

One of the reasons I like you, John Caine, is that you ask few questions. Why you try to mess that up?" Chawlie sat across from me in his customary orange plastic chair in the foyer of his restaurant. I'd come unbidden and unexpected, something I rarely did. Old friends in the traditional Asian sense, our friendship had structure, based upon mutual trust and expectations. When I appeared out of sequence or schedule it tended to strain the trust. And now, for the first time since the death of his son, I began pressing him for information, another unwelcome intrusion.

"Remember the night I brought Margo Halliday here?"

"That question. That no answer."

"Kimo paid me a visit today. He thinks you had something to do with Halliday's death."

"Kimo?" Chawlie knew exactly who Kimo was, but his feigned ignorance gave him some small time to collect his thoughts.

"You know the big policeman, the one who helped us both a couple of years ago?"

Hard black eyes stared at me, hardly a ripple in the deep pool of emotions flickering across the face. I waited for a response and got nothing. I gave nothing, either. We sat like two mute statues until I spoke.

"I didn't tell him anything."

Chawlie grunted. "Nothing you can say. Let it alone."

"That sounds like an order."

"Just advice."

So this time he either didn't trust me or felt he couldn't if I knew the truth; another old friend who refused to stake his life on me.

"Who is this woman, anyway?"

"Enough!" Chawlie sat upright, glaring at me. The last time I'd seen him this angry he'd put out a contract on my life. "This does not concern you. Nobody ask for your help."

"I'm offering."

"What do you think you can do?"

And there it was, the pertinent question, itself the answer. Irreducible tides were running here. The best I could do was to flow with them.

I stood up. "I've wasted your time, old friend. Forgive me."

Chawlie nodded, his black eyes cold as polished pebbles.

"You know where to find me," I said.

He gave me no response. I left the restaurant, feeling a little more empty than before. I'd tried to interpose myself between two friends in conflict and had been bruised for my efforts. Neither man appreciated my effort. Clarity had not been sought. Other agendas were operating, something I sensed, but grasped no understanding of their structure.

Blessed are the peacemakers, for they shall be confused.

Sometimes we have to find the grace to step back and let nature take its course. We can't solve all the world's problems. As I got older I began to understand some of these things. Had I understood them earlier in my life, I'd have avoided many of the scars on my body and my soul. I decided to let Chawlie have his way. My offer had been made and rejected. John Caine could happily bow out of this one.

The night was balmy, with a full moon riding billowy clouds over Honolulu Harbor. Gentle, warm breezes rustled the palms lining the Nu'uanu Stream that flowed along River Street. I'd parked my Jeep on pier 11, a short walk from Chawlie's place. The stroll helped clear my head. The end of another hurricane season had passed without incident. The weather changed, not much, but dropping a degree or two, becoming more temperate. Hawaii has only two seasons, but they're ruled by the winds, not the calendar. It's either trades or konas here. Thankfully, it's mostly trades, gentle, cooling breezes that blow from the east. When the konas come, the air gets still, humidity soars, the murder rate climbs.

I'd recently returned from California, a flight of six hours, a simple feat that had become habitual. I felt like one of those birds that fly across the ocean to mate. Once a month I'd pack a bag, hop a red-eye, and arrive in San Francisco at six in the morning California time. I'd linger no more than a week, reveling in the hospitality and the charm that only a warm, intelligent woman who loves you can bestow, and then I'd head home, winging my way back to my personal Paradise.

My last trip had ended only days before and a question had come with me this time, something inevitable, something that could not be avoided.

"Why don't you stay?" Barbara Klein had asked, walking me to the gate. "It isn't so bad here, is it?"

San Francisco was beautiful, but it wasn't where I belonged. The woman was sweet and loving, the conversation stimulating, the nights silky. Time spent with Barbara was comfortable. We truly seemed to enjoy each other's company. And every night back home, when I crawled into bed alone, the same question popped into my consciousness: *How long have you got left, old buddy? How much longer can you cling to this existence? And do you really want to keep on doing it alone?*

To this there had been no answer. I'd been careful to avoid excitement lately, refusing to take those cases that looked dangerous, I enjoyed my rainbows and my sunsets and felt greedy. I wanted as many as I could get. With Barbara Klein twenty-six hundred miles away working on penetrating the glass ceiling of the large bank, I had never considered exchanging my place in paradise for a different kind of life in San Francisco.

"I'll think about it," I had told her, immediately feeling the chill.

"You can bring *Olympia* back in the spring. I'll find her a permanent slip. I know of some over in Sausalito. And we'll find something for you to do here."

When my reply was less than instant, unqualified enthusiasm, Barbara's good-bye kiss matched, as if my indecision had forced her own resolve. Faced with a choice, this proud woman would choose what was right for her. If I didn't fit the equation she'd write me out of it. And out of her life.

Barbara's offer was enticing. At this stage of my life further tilting at windmills seemed ludicrous, another way of prolonging my adolescence. But somehow I could not see myself living away from the Islands. Hawaii was where my soul felt free. I loved the eternal summer, the trade winds, the smell the breezes carried down the mountains, full of spices and moisture and the warm, rich earth. Hawaii fit me like a second skin. It was where I saw myself living out the rest of my days. I couldn't see slipping the lines and sailing to the Mainland to live, regardless of the enticement. I was an Islander. I felt comfortable here. I felt safe. I was home.

Was I as set in my ways and stuck in the mud as all that? It was something that demanded examination. I needed some time to think about it.

"I'll call you. This is a big step," I said to her. "I need to think this over."

She looked me in the eyes, disappointment written on her lovely face. "You do that, John Caine. And call me when you make up your mind."

There were many things I could have said, I suppose, to have softened the blow, but I couldn't think of anything to save me. I suppose I might have contrived something to make her feel better, but I couldn't. Not then. No flip phrase could salvage the moment. And I wasn't interested in playing heart tag with this lovely woman. She deserved the truth. All the time and every time.

"Good-bye, sailor," she said at last, ending a long and painful moment of silence.

"Good-bye, Barbara."

She hugged me, but turned her face away when I kissed her. Without saying another word she walked down the concourse, leaving me with a large group of strangers and a question to ponder.

That had been several days ago and I was still pondering the question, hoping it was the right question. Back on Oahu the situation seemed less complicated. Trade winds blew. Waves fell upon shining white sand beaches. Palm trees swayed like hula dancers. Rainbows graced the flanks of the emerald mountains. The moon shone brightly in the heavens. Why would I want to be anyplace else?

The answer, you fool, said the little man in the back of my head, is that you are *here* alone, and she is *there* alone, and you seem to be in the process of missing a once in a lifetime opportunity.

Still pondering questions and possibilities, I climbed into my old Jeep beneath the lighted clock of the Aloha Tower, turned onto westbound Nimitz, and followed the moon toward Pearl Harbor and home.

Olympia had been visited in my absence, during my talk with Chawlie. All her invisible laser alarms were triggered, every sector violated. Someone had been on her deck and somehow managed to get inside. Or still was there.

I don't like surprises. I like trespassers even less. Some people think I'm merely just a pleasant fellow, a boat bum living aboard his sailboat, coasting through an easy life in the sun. Others have expended serious funds and considerable energy trying to end my life as expeditiously as possible. I've made as many enemies as friends over the years. Some are still alive. I didn't know who was below, but the probability was high it wasn't the Nobel Committee, here to award me this year's Peace Prize.

I retreated to my Jeep and unlocked the stainless-steel watertight compartment welded below the dash and removed my Colt Cadet. A .22 automatic loaded with ten Stinger hypervelocity rounds, the Cadet's bull barrel would substitute as a cosh if I didn't have to shoot. I jacked a cartridge into the chamber and crept back to my boat.

A shadow moved inside, passing between portholes, a darkness moving within darkness.

Getting aboard *Olympia* is fairly easy, but boarding any boat without shifting its balance in the water is difficult. She is a large craft, but I'm a big man. Any motion I made would alert my intruder.

I suppose I could have waited until my intruder got hungry, or bored, or seasick, or grew old and died, but unless I wanted to stand around all night outside of my own home, the only way to get it done was by frontal attack.

I didn't think it over, just jumped the rail and charged the cabin, flung open the hatch and dived inside, headfirst, arms outstretched, my body following the Colt. I slammed onto the deck, landing ungracefully on my stomach and elbows, flattened against the teak and rolled beneath the lounge table, smacking my head painfully against the table support.

The overhead light came on, competition for the shooting stars and skyrockets going off inside my head. It had not been the best of entries, about a two on the ten-scale, only a little less painful than walking in and having my visitor bonk me on the head from behind, if that was on his agenda. I forced myself to keep the focus of my attention on what lay before the gun, peering over the cushion, tracking everything from behind the pistol's sights.

A woman stood framed against the doorway, one hand poised on the light switch, the other covering her mouth, her eyes wide, fixed on the gun barrel.

"Don't shoot," she said.

I lowered the pistol, recognizing her voice and with it, her identity: Margo Halliday. Her face had been somehow familiar, but it was her voice that brought it all back. Chawlie had been right, that night in the alley. I had not paid much attention to her facial features.

"Mrs. Halliday."

"Margo."

"Good evening," I said, standing up, unloading the pistol and tucking it away in my shorts.

"Do you always come in like that?"

"Didn't know just who I might find aboard. How did you get in?"

"Chawlie told me where you keep your spare key."

I found that fascinating, seeing as how I'd never revealed its location to him or anybody else. "Chawlie also tell you where I live?"

"He took me sailing a couple of times. Once we sailed Pearl Harbor. We passed this marina and he pointed out your boat."

"Why?" It was uncharacteristic of the old man. He must have felt expansive. So it was true. Chawlie and Margo did have something going.

"He told me that if I ever got into trouble I could come to you and you'd help. He said you could help if he couldn't. You already saved me once."

That was partially true, but it didn't mean much. It had only been a minor alley scuffle. Her story didn't ring true. I didn't believe it. Something was going on here and I wasn't catching it. But then, that wasn't extraordinary.

"And he can't."

"He sent me here tonight. You were gone when I got here, so I hid. When it got dark I didn't turn on the lights. I just hid inside until you came home."

"Tonight," I repeated, calculating cause and effect, time and distance. He must have sent her before I went to see him, if what she said was true. Chawlie may have been angry with me because he'd dispatched the woman and I wasn't there, had come to see him, our paths crossing on the highway. But why didn't he tell me? Chawlie has his own agendas, most of them obscure to anyone else, but I'd offered my help and he'd flatly refused. "Tonight?"

She nodded, warm, soulful eyes watching mine. She was sending signals, trying to establish some form of alliance, but I wasn't receiving. My tuner was turned off. She was lying. I could feel it. And the little guy in the back of my mind, the one who's in charge of my well-being, the one who's supposed to keep me out of trouble, he was waving a red flag for all he was worth. On the flag were big white capital letters that said: LOOK OUT, FOOL!

"I'm making some coffee," I said. "You want some?"

"I'd rather have a real drink."

"How about Keoki Coffee. I've got some Blue Mountain here."

The woman shrugged. "Jim Beam would be nice. Over ice." She looked around the cabin. "If you have any."

"Liquor cabinet is over there. Refrigerator's there." I pointed out *Olympia*'s hidden compartments. Everything aboard has to have its own place. A boat must be organized. Otherwise it would quickly fill with trash. To an untrained eye it just looks like a bank of teak cabinets. "Help yourself."

I went to the galley and started the coffee perking while she packed crushed ice into a rocks glass and filled the glass to the brim with amber. It seemed a familiar ritual. I wondered what kind of relationship she had with Chawlie, and why she felt she had to hide from him. The more I thought about it, the more certain I became that Chawlie had not sent her to me. I figured the two of us—old Jim Beam and me—would help the truth find some avenue of escape.

She didn't seem too eager to keep it all in, anyway.

The aroma of percolating coffee filled the interior of *Olympia*. I busied myself in the galley, choosing my coffee mug. There are four to choose from, all white china, all identical. While I pretended to play with the mugs, the woman occupied her time studying the rows of books on the shelves on the opposite bulkhead. I noticed her lips move as she read the titles.

When the coffee finished perking I filled my mug and sat across from her and then immediately got up and refilled her glass. The way things were going, I'd get more alert and she'd probably get sleepy. John Caine, the perfect host.

"So tell me," I said, handing her the Jim Beam, "what does Chawlie think I can do for you?"

"He said things were getting too hot. He wants you to hide me. He said I have to get away from Oahu until things are better."

"He say where?"

She shook her head. "He said you'd know."

There was an ongoing police investigation into her ex-husband's death. The lady was out on bail, the money presumably fronted by Chawlie. If she disappeared, the bail would be forfeit. I'd told Kimo I wasn't involved and that I knew nothing other than what I'd related about that first night. Well, that had been true when I said it.

"Do you think you're in danger?"

She nodded.

"Did you get threats?"

"Someone tried to kidnap me."

"When?"

"This evening. I went for a walk on the beach. Two men followed me. I ran. They chased me. A police car drove by and they stopped. I got away."

"That's it?"

"They had guns."

"They shoot at you?"

She shook her head. "They lifted their shirts and showed me the guns. That's when I ran."

It still didn't sound like a kidnapping. A mugging, maybe. "You ever see either of these two men before?"

"No."

Something about the curtness of her answer and the tone of her voice made me wonder again if she was telling the truth. Or all the truth. Whatever the case, I wasn't taking *Olympia* anywhere tonight.

"Why would somebody want to kidnap you?"

"I don't know. Why would they kill my husband?"

So she was admitting nothing, not even a distant knowledge of any possible motives. No wonder Kimo was frustrated. This woman didn't need an attorney. She knew how to keep her mouth shut.

"You have a change of clothing?"

"I packed two bags. They're in . . ." She turned and pointed to the nearest stateroom behind her . . . "in there."

"Okay. We'll stay put tonight. Tomorrow I want to check a couple of things, talk to Chawlie, see if we can go where I think we can go. Then we'll go cruising. You get seasick?" I watched her reaction when I mentioned talking to Chawlie. She went pale.

"No!"

"Good," I said, smiling, the big, dense beach bum, not reading her obvious alarm at the mention of Chawlie's name. "It gets pretty rough out there between the islands and you're going to get bounced around. If things work out we'll sail to another island. I've got friends there. They'll take care of you until it's safe to come back. Okay?"

"I meant don't talk to Chawlie! He doesn't want . . . to be traced . . . dragged into this."

I nodded, intentionally amiable and dense, trying to draw her out. "Why not?"

"He doesn't want anybody else to know where I am. Only him. Only you. He says there are people after me and there may be someone in his organization who's feeding them information. He doesn't want any leaks. You call him and it could get sloppy. He'll be angry. Can you understand that?"

"I guess so."

"I thought we could leave tonight," she said, suddenly changing gears. My sudden capitulation turned her, making her less wary. I played the dumb game too well, sometimes.

"It's too late. And it wouldn't help. You're safe. That's why Chawlie sent you here. Because I can protect you."

"Okay."

"You find the bathroom?"

She nodded.

"You can stay where you stashed your bags. I'll lock up and set the alarms. Do not open the hatch for any reason or the alarm will go off and I'll come out quick and aggressive and probably still asleep. It's dangerous to get in my way when I'm in the attack mode. Understand?"

She nodded, her face a blank. I didn't know if my macho act worked on her and I didn't care. All I wanted her to do was go into her stateroom and leave me alone. An unwelcome burden, she annoyed. One man close to her had already been killed and I was getting the feeling that she had somehow taken advantage of Chawlie and was now running for her life. Regardless, I didn't want her to misread the situation.

"I understand, Mr. Caine. Can I take a shower?"

The only shower aboard *Olympia* was in the master stateroom. That was mine. "Of course," I said. "I'll wait out on deck until you're done. Fifteen minutes?"

"Half an hour would be better."

"Okay." A half-hour shower might deplete the freshwater tanks, but I didn't say anything. I'd refill them in the morning. "You need anything else?"

"No, Mr. Caine. I'll be fine." She went into her room and came out carrying a small bag. She glanced at me over her shoulder and gave me a look I probably was supposed to understand, but didn't, and then entered my cabin and closed the door behind her. I dug one of the last special-run Cohiba Esplendidos from my humidor and climbed up on deck to watch the night sky.

Pearl Harbor constantly bustled with building and shipping activity, yet it never seemed to change. For a military base it is as peaceful as it gets. I had been here on the fiftieth anniversary of the Japanese attack, and I recalled reading Gordon W. Prange's great books about that day and the unreality the defenders felt in the very beginning, coming as it did on that quiet Sunday morning. Tiny warplanes droning across the sky seemed out of place, anomalies that lulled the defenders into a dangerous complacency until the first bombs began exploding among them. It just wasn't natural. I had those same feelings this night, with gentle tropical breezes wafting across the calm surface of the water, pleasantly riffling my hair and caressing my skin. Something stirred in the back of my mind, an alarm bell to go with the little man still furiously waving his big red flag. He was waving it, all right, but now he also wore a look of disappointment, as if he knew he was being ignored.

The woman wasn't bright, but she knew something, something whose importance she might not completely comprehend. And she was frightened, not only of the two men with the guns below their Aloha shirts, but also of Chawlie. When I mentioned speaking to him she nearly became hysterical.

I could kick her off my boat and allow her to find her own way, or I could play along, take her to Ed Alapai and put her on ice until I found out what was going on. I could let Chawlie know, if I thought he wouldn't kill her. Depending on what she had done to him, he might do just that. Loyalty was fairly high up on Chawlie's ladder of importance, disloyalty ferociously discouraged. Given her intimate access to the man, she would have had the chance to learn enough to really hurt him.

That was why the old man wanted me out of this particular picture.

And that was why she wanted off this island.

So she had come to the man who'd saved her once, and who introduced her to Chawlie, the tall, bearded stranger who could bring down a big man with one kick, the one who owned the big boat casually pointed out during a lazy afternoon sail.

Feeling confident the woman would have completed her shower, I finished my smoke and checked the lines and secured *Olympia* for the night. There would be plenty of time to work it all out in the morning. And the lady would tell all, given enough time and enough Jim Beam. She thought of me as an ally and in a way she was right. I just didn't know how far I would have to go this time.

Light pooled on the corridor deck from under her cabin door. I carefully trod the teak to avoid making a sound and sneaked into my stateroom, undressed, and crawled into bed.

My cabin smelled pleasantly of hot steam and lavender soap. I lay in bed, staring at the overhead and listening to the sounds of the night. The woman made noises moving around her cabin. She seemed restless, a stranger uncomfortable in alien surroundings. I sympathized. No matter where I was, I always felt that way.

Minding the warning of the little man with the flag, and remembering I was baby-sitting a woman with a price or two on her head, I slipped my Colt .45 from its hiding place in the bookcase and eased a round into the chamber, locked the safety in place, and laid it on the mattress within reach. The .22 would go back to the Jeep in the morning. I left it on the locker wrapped in my shirt.

I fell asleep listening to the woman and thinking of other ladies on other boats, of other nights in other harbors, wishing that my current stowaway could be magically transformed into another incarnation, knowing it wouldn't happen, and if it could it probably wouldn't be for the best.

For either one of us.

The sun rose at five-seventeen and so did I, creeping through the murky gray interior of my boat, feeling like a thief, not wanting to awaken my guest. I climbed on deck and sat on the stern cushions to put on my running shoes, treasuring the golden warmth of the new morning.

I had expected the woman to come to my cabin during the night. It would have been her way of formalizing whatever contract existed between us. If she and Chawlie had anything at all, it would have centered on that kind of exchange: his protection and gifts for sexual favors, her only currency. An age-old compact.

But the woman didn't make the attempt and I was glad she'd stayed away, saving me from having to make the noble refusal.

Having a houseguest is uncomfortable when you don't know or particularly like that person. When the intrusion happens and your personal living space is already cramped, as it is aboard any boat, and when you're used to living alone, the discomfort is felt immediately. But *Olympia* was all I had, and the woman apparently had nowhere else to go. In a way I'd asked for this. I couldn't very well snivel since my request had been answered.

If my living accommodations were strained, my morning run was a disappointment. It gets more difficult every year to maintain the same level of fitness I've taken, for granted all my life, forcing me to work twice as hard for lesser results. Some mornings everything still falls into place. That morning I felt creaky and old, my legs seemed to be tree stumps. There was no resiliency to my step. Still, I struggled through the six-mile round trip at nearly my best pace, evidence that my dragging was merely mental.

Cars and trucks streamed across the bridge above my slip, federal workers and uniformed personnel heading over to Ford Island to begin another day of whatever they do over there. One of the advantages of my chosen profession was my erratic schedule. No nine-to-five for old John Caine. I choose my time and I cherish my freedom. As I watched the federal workers driving toward their jobs I cherished it even more. I'd see them again at three-thirty, fleeing their offices and shops like lost souls released from the depths of hell itself.

Not having a schedule means I can pick my cases and work when and for whom I choose.

Yeah, sure.

The woman waiting for me at the gate to my dock didn't look like a client.

Another unwanted intrusion, she was young, but worn and raw-boned, somewhere on the far side of skinny, a farm girl, daughter of the Great American Midwest, carrying a golden-haired child that I thought might be a girl. Cute, with a pixie face and turned-up nose, the child clung to her, tiny pink fingers clutching a faded blanket. The woman stood her ground in front of my gate as I approached, searching my eyes for an opening.

"Excuse me, Mr. Caine? Are you John Caine?"

"What's left of him." I tried to smile and catch my breath. My T-shirt was black with sweat. Salty beads kept running down my forehead into my eyes.

She tossed her head in frustration, mousy bangs falling away from her eyes. Her hair looked self-cut. "And you are the private detective? I was told you are a private detective. I need you . . . your services."

"And you are?"

"Karen."

"Just Karen?"

"Karen Graham, Mr. Caine. The police gave me your name and told me where you lived. I'm looking for my husband, Billy."

"Your husband is Billy Graham?"

"Not that one. Billy is missing." When I opened my mouth to respond, she pressed on. "My husband came to Hawaii two months ago to work construction. He's here someplace. I know it. And I need to find him."

"Who did he work for?"

"I don't know. He never told us. Billy came over to work the eggs-and-bacon wages here at Pearl Harbor. He's a journeyman electrician and he's good at it. Once he got here he never wrote, he never called, he never . . . he never sent money like he promised. He just . . . vanished." The child peered at me from behind blond curls, huge blue eyes regarding me gravely. I smiled. She ducked back behind her mother's shoulder.

"Are you sure he came here?"

"Oh, yes. I put him on the airplane. It didn't land anywhere else." The certainty of her feelings held a forceful urgency, a potent argument in her favor.

"Well . . ." I didn't need another client. Although, when I thought about it, I wasn't sure what Margo's status really was. She hadn't offered to pay me, and I hadn't asked. This woman had a stray husband, another construction worker come to Hawaii to work the Pearl Harbor base and get the highest mandated wages in the country, the Davis-Bacon wages. I didn't do husbands, missing or otherwise.

"Don't say no. You can't say no until you've heard what I have to say."

"Let's hear your story."

"I can't pay you. I mean, I can't pay you *now*, but I *will* pay you when . . . how much do you cost?"

"Whoa! Wait a minute. Let's sit down over here." I led her to a bench on the shaded lawn outside the Marina Restaurant. Because she appeared out of nowhere, immediately after Margo's sudden appearance with her brush with murder and tales of assassins, I would not bring this woman and child aboard *Olympia*. Whatever their problems, I could not take the case. But Karen Graham had come to tell her story and the least I could do was listen.

"Don't you have an office, Mr. Caine?"

"No."

"What kind of private eye are you?"

"The best kind," I said. "I'm so good people beat a path to my door."

"But you have a gate."

"That's why." When she didn't respond, I continued. "You were referred to me. I don't advertise."

"I tried looking on the base, but they wouldn't let me on. A guard at the gate sent me to the base police station. When I told the sergeant . . . the woman there, is she a sergeant? She's sort of blond, but I think she's really not."

"She's a chief, but go on." I couldn't place the person from the description, but the sailor in charge would have been a chief. It didn't matter, but I found it interesting that the location of my personal residence was being handed out to just about anybody who asked. I don't like being that popular.

"When I told the lady my story she told me about you and how to get here. Julia and I took the bus from the airport to Pearl Harbor, but I walked over here to find you. I got lost a couple of times, but people are nice here and someone gave me a ride the last mile."

The distance from the base police station at the Makalapa Gate to the Rainbow Marina was about three miles as a mynah bird flies, but more like six as the roads wandered around the edge of the base, up and down the little molehills. Getting lost would have added. And the woman walked it carrying her child because she had no car and no money for a taxi.

"Did you just get here? On the island?"

"Last night. We started looking for Billy this morning."

"Where are you staying?"

The question caught her off-guard. Her Midwestern pride blossomed, then faded, as she wrestled with the answer. "We spent the night at the airport and came out here when the buses started running."

"You have no money?"

"If you're worried about your feet, don't. I can pay you! I just need to find my husband!"

Julia pulled away from her mother's neck and looked at me again, this time with the intense, direct stare devoid of guile that only a small child can achieve, soaking in all of my being. She studied me for a long, unblinking moment. Then she burst into tears.

"Hush, Julia," said Karen gently. "Hush, girl."

The child murmured something I couldn't understand.

"Not now, honey," said her mother.

"Hungry!"

And I realized then that the woman had spent most of her cash for the plane tickets and she had no plan, no idea how to find Billy Graham. If they had not eaten since last night she'd be hungry, but Julia would be starving.

Beyond brave, bordering on either the desperate or the stupid, she'd taken her child and jumped on a flight to Honolulu, most likely with the perception that Oahu is a small island. It is, but there are nearly a million people living here. Tens of thousands work at Pearl Harbor, and searching for one person requires thought, a knowledge of the local conditions, and at least a starting point. It also requires time and money. Hawaii is a fine, gentle place, with a perfect climate and a better-than-average economy. It attracts thousands of people who think they can make a living here. What they don't know is that Hawaii has a hellish cost of living, especially for those itinerants trying to get one of the choice jobs that pay the federal Davis-Bacon wages paid by the big contractors working at Pearl Harbor. And Hawaii is no place to be if you know no one and have little money.

"Why don't you come down to the boat? We're about to have breakfast. Would you like to join us?"

I'd expected a prairie rant, an assertion of independence, claims that they could cope with the problem, but the depth of Karen's desperation must have been enormous because she burst into tears, too. So there I sat, feeling helpless, with two crying females, unsure what to do until Karen Graham saved me with her acceptance.

"Thank you," she said, wiping her nose with a pale blue tissue. "I know I shouldn't, but Julia's hungry and thirsty. We haven't eaten since the flight." She had her fists balled tight around the tissue. She squeezed her hands so tightly together her knuckles were white.

"Come on," I said, knowing that breakfast would spill over into lunch and then dinner, and tonight I'd be making up the bunk in the third stateroom, hardly believing I was doing what I was doing. Yesterday I lived happily alone, just me and my sailboat, the aimless beach bum living under the tropical sunshine. Last night I'd started collecting strays, a bad habit I'd continued through the morning. "I live right over there," I said. What the hell, it seemed the right thing to do.

"Promise me you'll find Billy. I appreciate your feeding us, but I will pay you."

"Don't worry about the money."

"You will be paid. Promise me you'll find Billy. Julia needs her daddy."

"I promise," I said, wondering if I should raise my right hand.

"Here." She dug into her purse, extracting a lonely and crumpled twenty-dollar bill.

"That's about right," I said, taking the bill and handing it back. "But you pay me only if I find him. If I don't, it'll be no charge."

"John! John Caine! Who is that?"

The woman, the child, and I turned to see Margo Halliday calling from the deck of *Olympia*. She was loosely wrapped in a white robe, my white robe, and from the plunging neckline exposing large portions of unrestrained white flesh, she didn't appear to wear anything else. Margo's face was puffy, evidence of a losing wrestling match with sleep.

"Is that your wife?"

"No."

A look of disapproval crossed Karen Graham's face as the possibilities filtered through her Midwestern mind. Margo represented the kind of female Karen Graham detested, but I felt no need to explain. "She's hanging out," she said, observing the open condition of Margo's robe.

"John!" Margo was insistent.

"Take a shower! You've got fifteen minutes. We've got company."

Margo shielded her eyes against the sun, watching us. She shook her head and crawled back into the boat, exposing as much of her chest as possible.

"I live down this way."

"Who is that woman?"

"A client."

Karen gave me a sideways glance, an openly concerned appraisal, as if she were troubled about bringing her child into my floating den of iniquity. But she followed me down the gangway and I helped them over the railing. Karen held tightly on to her child as if she were the most precious creature that had ever existed.

I invited them down to the lounge and searched the cold locker for milk and eggs while they occupied the teak table. Thinking they were both hungry and thirsty, I poured them each a big glass of milk, demonstrating my abysmal ignorance of children. The little girl took two gulps from her glass and spilled the rest, swamping the table and the carpet. I was on my hands and knees helping Karen sop up the mess when Margo joined us.

"John! Who is that person? Who are these people?"

"This is Karen Graham, and that"—I pointed toward Julia, busy working on her second glass of milk and staring solemnly at Margo, the same wide-eyed stare she'd trained on me earlier, except this time she wasn't crying—"is Julia. They are clients. Karen, meet Margo Halliday. Also a client."

"Pleased to meet you, ma'am."

"You didn't understand anything I said to you last night, did you?"

"Margo and I were heading for another port of call this morning," I explained to Karen, who looked up from her chore to study the woman Chawlie might have hung around my neck. "I think she'd have preferred to have my full-time interest."

"Well, what's wrong with that?"

"It isn't like that, Margo. You're safe here. Karen has a problem that I think I can solve before the end of the day."

Karen started, turning toward me, as if she'd heard indisputable evidence of the proof of God.

"I'm going to try, anyway," I continued. "You stay aboard until I get back, or you can leave. If you're here when I get back, we'll go. If you're not, then I'll consider myself fired."

To her credit she waited the full count before she answered. Reviewing her options, she made a quick decision, pasted on a smile, crossed the lounge in three long strides and stuck out her hand. "I'm pleased to meet you, Karen. Hello, Julia."

Julia took one hand from her glass and waved at Margo, nearly losing control, but catching it before disaster struck again.

"Can you help with breakfast, Margo?" I asked. "I need to take a shower. I stink."

She smiled. "I took a quick shower."

"You're learning. I'll need to fill the tanks after I shower."

She smiled again, either out of amusement or defiance, I couldn't tell and I didn't care. "There's no water left. Did you know that?"

I smiled. When I smiled I gritted my teeth.

It didn't help.

5

It took over thirty minutes to fill *Olympia*'s water tanks and less than five to take my normal Navy shower. I rushed getting to it and the water was cold.

Sweat had dried to white swirls of salt by the time I got my shirt and shorts off. I rinsed them and hung them over a towel bar, judging them too filthy even to drop into the dirty-clothes hamper.

By the time I dressed, my guests had already finished eating. My single gallon of milk and the dozen eggs, both usually good for more than a week, were depleted in one meal. I made a mental note to stock up at the Safeway before taking *Olympia* to sea.

That thought brought related chores to mind: Calling Penny, a neighbor of Ed Alapai, and asking her to let him know we were coming. Ed, Kimo's cousin, lived on the slopes of Anahola Mountain, up on the north coast, without a telephone or any other connection to the nineteenth century, much less the twenty-first. I'd spent some time there a few years back recuperating from injuries, and Ed had made it clear that I could return whenever I wished. I'd come back on occasion, but always called a neighbor first, not wanting to strain the relationship.

I still had a few associations yet undamaged.

"I'm hungry," I said to my guests, noting that the women had formed some kind of alliance, as grown-ups tended to do when faced with the tyranny of a small child. "Anything left?"

"Plenty of food in the galley," answered Margo. "What's your pleasure?"

"Anything but eggs." I loved eggs, but could see there weren't any.

"You like cornflakes? You've got cornflakes. Oh, wait, there's no milk."

"I'll cut some fruit," I said, heading for the galley.

"You have fruit?"

"Bananas, strawberries, grapes, lemons, watermelon—"

"That sounds good."

"Which?"

"Bananas, strawberries, grapes, watermelon . . ."

I pointed to the cabinet above the refrigerator. "Help me."

Margo retrieved an old Gerber blade from the knife block and pulled half a watermelon from the cold locker. I worked on a basket of fresh strawberries and a couple of South American bananas.

"You don't seem to mind having all these women," she said, cutting into the watermelon, surprising me by her response. She looked up from her task. "I know it must be hard, having us here. You live alone, don't you?"

"Yep."

"I'm sorry." She looked up from her task, keeping her voice low, so Karen wouldn't hear. "I hoped you wouldn't try to come into my room last night. I locked my door but I knew you'd have a key. I had my speech all prepared, and a gun in case you didn't listen to reason." She kept her gaze on her fingers wrapped around the knife while she cut carefully, as if she wasn't certain of her skills. "But I didn't need any of it. When I decided you were probably going to stay in your room, I relaxed. Finally, when I was sure of it, I slept."

"Not easy for you, I guess." The thought that we both had been equally apprehensive of the other's intentions made me smile.

She finished cutting the fruit and put four plates on the lounge table. I retrieved a loaf of French bread I'd picked up fresh the day before. "Do you remember the night I met you?"

"Of course."

"You were a total stranger and you rescued me when you didn't have to get involved. I see now that you do that kind of thing on a regular basis." She looked over her shoulder toward the lounge table, where Karen was helping Julia finish her eggs. The girl was well-behaved, better than I'd expected. Having no experience with that kind of creature, and reminding myself that she'd burst into tears after carefully studying my face, I stayed away from her. She scared me.

"You frightened me, the way you broke Glen's arm," Margo continued. "It looked so easy and I know it wasn't. He always seemed so huge. He terrified me." A shiver shook her, so slight I doubted she felt it. "I hoped you still were the same kind of gentleman, but the rules change once a woman is inside a man's home. I didn't know how you'd react. Some men might take it wrong. But Chawlie said you would take care of me and you wouldn't hurt me, and he was right."

"I can't resist a damsel in distress."

She gave me an appraising look. "So. Where are we going?"

"Nawiliwili Harbor."

"Kauai?"

"It's far, about a hundred miles away, with a good harbor and a nearby resort full of strangers coming and going, so you'll be anonymous. I've got friends there. We'll put you up with a local family. They live rough, but comfortable. You'll be safe."

"How long will I have to be there?"

"I was hoping you could tell me."

"A month, perhaps longer." She looked amused, as if some stray thought had passed across her frontal lobes, something she would not share—wanted to, would love to, but couldn't.

"Think things will blow over by then?"

"Yep," she said, the secret smile still in place despite her struggle to contain it.

And then I knew. I didn't *know*, but I felt the tug of her thoughts, understanding her plan, not *knowing*, but getting a glimmering, beginning to think as the woman thought: She would run as soon as I'd disappeared from the far shore. She would use me to get out of town, to get to somewhere safe, where no one knew her. She would use Ed Alapai as she had used Chawlie. As she was using me. It meant she had resources of her own.

"I must find this Billy Graham before we go. Stay put. It should only take a few hours and then, after I reunite the happy couple, we'll take off."

She nodded, clearly displeased, but having accepted the reality of Karen and Julia and their helplessness, she was not willing to cross me because of them. "How do you find someone like that?"

"Several ways. When he came to the island there would have been ads in the paper for rooms to let. It's standard. Guys like him don't stay in hotels, they rent rooms by the month, living in private homes until they get on their feet and can afford an apartment. I'll look at the ads from back then, call everyone to see if they rented to a Billy Graham. Don't think they'd forget a name like that, eh?"

She shook her head.

"The second way takes longer. I'll go visit a couple of job trailers on the base and see if he's an employee. They don't have to tell me, but they will. People love to talk. Especially if somebody's interested in what they have to say."

I stood while I ate, savoring fruit that tasted as sweet as

candy. Margo began cleaning my little galley and I wondered what she really thought about the situation. In many ways she surprised me, but I felt she was still a little off-balance discovering where she'd ended up on her run.

Margo was running from Chawlie just as certain as she was running from the law. She held secrets that were more deeply embedded than I'd suspected, and more firmly secreted. I knew now that she would run once she was clear of me. Or try to. Ed Alapai was a man who would keep her, if I asked him, regardless of her intentions.

"Do us both a favor. Keep Julia and Karen occupied until I get back. Go look at the submarine museum just down the way. Nobody will bother you there and you'll be safe. Visit the *Arizona* Memorial. Buy them lunch up at the Marina. Take some money—you have money?—and buy the kid some toys or something in the gift shops over there. I'll be along, but it will work best if I'm alone. All I need is a recent photo of the young man."

"I've got one right here," said Karen, pushing a color photograph of one Billy Graham into my hand. I had not been aware she had been listening, and I hoped I hadn't embarrassed her or myself by my words.

"You've been awful nice, Mr. Caine," she said. "But I don't want to burden you any more than necessary. I know Mrs. Halliday wants to get going, and I don't want to hold you here any longer than you should. If you don't find Billy, then maybe he's already left and gone back home."

Other possibilities seemed more likely, but I didn't want to explore them in front of his wife.

"I'll find him. It won't be difficult," I said, hoping my words would be prophetic.

I looked at the picture. A round-faced country boy looked out at me, a broad neck and workman's arms bulging a thick plaid hunting shirt, lever-action deer rifle in the crook of his arm, leaning against a snow-laden tree. Nose and ears reddened with cold, he smiled a frank, open smile, appearing almost as guileless as his daughter: Something happened to young Mr. Graham once he hit the islands, something either very, very bad, or very, very good. So good he didn't want to think of home again.

His picture told me it was either/or with this guy. There wouldn't be any middle ground. Shades of gray did not inhabit this man's territory.

Almost as if she'd read my thoughts, Karen sighed and said, "I know he looks innocent, but he's lain with other women before. In town, when he went there, he went to massage parlors. I know I'm not much, but he is my husband, and he is the father of Julia and I do want him back, Mr. Caine. You'll tell me, won't you? If you find out he's living with another woman?"

When the lie stuck in my throat, refusing release, she smiled a sad, knowing smile. "I have this feeling. He's here. He's somewhere close. And he doesn't want me anymore, I guess. Nor his daughter, either. You'll tell me, won't you?"

I nodded. "Yes."

"Promise?"

"Promise."

"Thank you, Mr. Caine. I shall wait here with Julia and Mrs. Halliday. I think it will be nice to see the submarine. Don't worry about us. We'll be fine."

Of course they would. Nothing to it. I'll just go out and track down the husband. He won't want to come back. He'll resent me finding him and there will be a nasty scene. I might have to hurt him. Something vicious inside of me wanted to hurt him, anyway. Maybe I'd egg him on, make him mad and make him make me hurt him.

"I'll try the newspaper first. It won't take long. If that doesn't pan out I'll try the contractors. I'll be back before three."

"Good luck."

"Yeah."

I went up on deck and jumped over the railing, heading for my Jeep, wondering which one of us would have the luck, and what, exactly, that meant. I'd find the man. That much was certain. But I wasn't sure if it would be good luck or bad.

Or for whom.

6

Most things are either harder or easier than you anticipate, depending on the way you look at them. It was easier to find Billy Graham than I expected, but much more difficult to get him to talk to me.

It only took the better part of an hour to find the newspaper ad the young man had answered to find a rented room. The technique was mostly pure research, going back through the advertisements found in back issues of the *Advertiser* and the *Star-Bulletin* and placing calls and telling the truth to whoever answered my call. I didn't try to get cute. I just said that the man's wife was trying to contact him on a family matter. I had neither the time nor the inclination to talk story, and the people I was depending on to tell me what happened would not be amenable to lies. Once caught in a lie I would be unable to go any further. It wasn't a question of honor. It was just the best way to do business.

The owner of the house, a Filipino woman whose family owned an import-export company near the Aloha Stadium and rented out four of their five bedrooms for additional income, had let a furnished room to Billy Graham two nights after he came to the islands and she was happy to talk to me. He had paid a month in advance, plus the security deposit, and remained the two months, burning off the deposit in the second month. He left owing nothing, but had not cleaned out his room, leaving clothing and some other personal items behind. She didn't mind if I came over and looked at what he'd left behind and I did, making the drive from downtown in twenty minutes.

She had stored everything in a cardboard box, explaining that in such circumstances she usually kept the orphans for six months, discarding them if the tenant didn't return by then. The clothing was a collection of heavy wool and cotton shirts similar to the one he wore in the photograph, garments hardly appropriate for the local climate. The personal items were collections of *Hustler* and *Penthouse* and other, more explicit, sex magazines, stacked ten-deep in the box, quite an accumulation for a man not there two months. Billy seemed to have an insatiable appetite. And it didn't look as if he planned on returning to cold weather.

The woman had no idea where Billy had gone, but one of the tenants, a curly-headed blond Gen-X-er with a lazy, tropical manner, a man on Hawaii time who seemed to have retired in his twenties, said he'd seen him move out. Billy didn't own a car but a woman had driven him here to get his stuff.

''He ever talk to you about a woman?''

''Hell, that's all he did. But not just *a* woman. *Lots* of women. He was always going down to the clubs on Kapiolani, the Korean bars, the topless joints. Billy had money to burn and he spent it on what he liked.''

''You ever see this woman before? The one who helped him move?''

''Like I told you, man, not just one woman. It was his hobby. I never seen her before, but he had a different one every other day. He didn't always bring 'em home.'' He snickered. ''Hell, he didn't always *come* home.''

Behind him, the landlady clucked her tongue and nodded disapproving agreement.

Some guys surf, some collect shells. Others put ships in bottles. It sounded as if Billy had his own interests. It wasn't something I could take back to his wife. Not that it wasn't something she didn't already know.

"Tell you what, though; I know where he works."

I stared at him. He wanted to help, but he didn't want to be too helpful in case it might get him into trouble. Coasting along at the bottom of the food chain, he would be careful about causing problems that could come back at him. In a second, careful examination, Billy's face in the photograph, the one treasured by his wife, had traits of meanness seared through it. Billy Graham looked like one of those good old boys with a chip on his shoulder, a man who could get worked up real fast over small slights, real or imagined.

"Okay," I said, keeping my stare leveled at him, making certain he understood that he already had problems he couldn't avoid.

"That big contractor over on Salt Lake, near gate seventeen. There's a job trailer just inside the gate. He works out of there."

"You sure?"

"Sure. Drove him down to get his paycheck once. Over a thousand dollars take-home for one week. We cashed it and went bar-hopping. He damn near spent it all that night. Crazy fucker. I made that much money, those Davis-Bacon wages, I'd buy a house in Kahala."

"His job is on Salt Lake Boulevard?"

"Yeah. Down to the Fast Stop, turn left, go down a ways, about a mile. There's a trailer. Big white one, just inside the gate."

"Thanks."

"You won't tell Billy, will you?"

"About what?"

"That I told you?"

"You told me what?"

He smiled, a wry grin. "Okay. I get it. Thanks, man."

"Thank you," I said, turning to the landlady. "And thank you, ma'am, for your time. I hope you have a very good day."

"I hope you find him. For his wife. Billy Graham is not a nice man. I don't like such peoples in my home."

"I don't blame you," I said, wondering just how much trouble Billy Graham was going to be once I found him.

He sounded like a man whose interests lay close at hand, whatever he could see or touch or feel at the time. Images of his wife and child became two-dimensional when he arrived in Paradise. I imagined how it had hit him, once he got off the airplane and took a look around. It's different here in Hawaii. And it's not just the climate. Billy may have found something here that drove him mad—the air, the heat, the sound of the palm trees, the sensual touch of the breezes as they wrap themselves around you. And the high wages at the federal projects could have turned him. He made a lot of money and spent it just as fast. On himself.

I found gate 17 at the bottom of a shallow hill on the dry side of Pearl Harbor between a military family housing area and the Public Works Center. A separately fenced enclosure, the contractor gate was unlocked and unguarded and I drove right in and parked below one of the trailer's windows. Painted wooden steps led to a door at each end, temporary affairs that looked as if they'd served many years of constant use. All the windows and both doors were open. INTELCOM INTERNATIONAL, INC., a sign said, affixed to a trailer. A mongoose, one of those dirt-colored weasels that had been brought here in the nineteenth century to rid the islands of rats, scurried from a corner of the yard to its hiding place beneath the trailer.

"Help you?" A man appeared in one of the doorways. A big, red-haired man with a dark red beard grinned at me. Everything about him looked tough and competent, from his faded blue-and-white Aloha shirt to the tips of his scuffed steel-toed boots. He would have looked like an unfriendly bear but for the twinkle in his eye.

"If you're looking for work, we might have an opening. What are you? Electrician? I need a good estimator."

"Not looking. I'm working. My name's John Caine."

"Chuck MacDonald," he said, extending his hand. "I'm the project manager. Saw you park and wondered about you."

"Don't get many visitors?"

He shook his head. "Get plenty, but I know most of them. What's your story?"

"You have an employee named Billy Graham?"

"The preacher? Sure."

"The preacher?"

He laughed. "About as far from a preacher as you can get. His mother must have had some sense of humor, naming him that. Or too much hope. That kid's nothing but trouble, and he's a cock hound. If he wasn't such a crackerjack electrician I wouldn't waste my time on him, but he's very, very competent. He knows his way around the job. Made him foreman last month when the other one got island fever and quit on me to go back to the Mainland."

That was a lot of information to give a stranger. It made me suspicious. "He still work for you?"

"He's out on Ford Island, preparing for a transformer, a big one. We're getting delivery tomorrow. It's arriving on time, which is very weird, since everything takes so damn much time to ship, hardly anything ever gets here when it's supposed to. Naturally, we're not ready. Billy's pushing the crew so the crane time won't be wasted tomorrow. Why you want him? You a cop?"

"No. His wife's here. She hasn't heard from him since he got to Hawaii and she hired me to find him."

"Oh." MacDonald squinched up his face, adding smile and frown wrinkles simultaneously, more lines to an already deeply lined, weathered face. "That could be a problem."

"So now you're going to ask me to leave?"

"No. You don't look like you're going to cause me any trouble. Of course, few people do." He grinned at me, and I understood that he'd been to a few of the same places I'd been, and I wondered if I'd ever run across him before.

"You ever in the military?"

"Back when I didn't have much of a choice. Got drafted right after Tet, applied for officer's school and the fools accepted me. Did my tours, got out after that."

"What unit were you in?"

"Different ones, here and there. Who's asking?"

It was an expected question. There are enough guys around who brag about their service time without having been there. We were two of a kind, I could see that, and it made me smile.

"Take a look at my windshield."

His eyes flicked to the stickers in the top center of the Jeep's windscreen, especially the officer's blue band below the white Department of Defense sticker.

"Thought so. You're *that* John Caine."

"Well, that's my name."

He laughed. "There's only one on this island. I know about you. You were in Vietnam and Grenada, and a lot of other places from what I heard."

"Yep." I didn't need to tell him any more than that. It was unnecessary and would have taken the conversation into different dimensions, places I didn't want to go. I didn't know where my name had been discussed, and I wasn't here for old home week, and although I might like a man like Chuck MacDonald, I didn't have the time. In the back of my mind I worried about the women I'd left behind on *Olympia*.

"Come on in," he said, retreating into the trailer. I climbed the wooden steps and found myself inside a large empty space with photograph murals covering the walls and a vinyl composition tile floor. Old metal desks covered with printed schedules and blueline drawings were pushed up against the walls.

I followed him to the only enclosed space, a ten-foot-square cubicle in the far corner. Photographs of Wake Island and Guam and dozens of other out-of-the-way places adorned the walls, imperfectly framed by careless hands. Memories of far-flung adventures, of working Department of Defense bases like a modern-day Indiana Jones.

"It's not much, but it's my office," he said, when I followed him into the room. "This year, at least. Close the door so we can talk in peace and take a seat and tell me how we're going to solve this problem we got."

I did as he asked and sat in an uncomfortable straight-backed metal chair facing his desk. "We have a problem?"

"Yeah. You want to talk to Billy Graham, and, as his employer, I'm not supposed to let you. The law says we're supposed to protect his privacy. I'm not, say, supposed to tell you that Billy always stops at the Monkey Bar for a cool one every day after work. You know the Monkey Bar?"

"Pearl City Tavern," I said. Everyone in Pearl Harbor knew the landmark bar and restaurant in Pearl City. It had been there since the opening days of World War II, and hadn't changed much.

"And I'm not supposed to tell you that he gets off at three o'clock, and that he'll be there by three-thirty. He drinks beer and eats popcorn covered with Tabasco until six or six-thirty, then he heads down to Waikiki for a look at the girls."

"And you're not supposed to tell me where he lives?"

"That's right. And I won't."

I studied him. I could get to like the guy if I had the time. "Why are you telling me this?"

"Like I said, I've heard of you. Good things. I heard the story about you losing your yacht a couple of years back, lost it sailing into a hurricane to rescue some detective. I heard about what you used to be. I hang out at the Marina Bar and

I hear people talk about it. They talk about you like you're something out of some kind of movie, although from looking at you I wouldn't think you're any kind of leading man. I don't have any love lost for Billy. He's a good worker when he works, but at times he's a pain in the ass, and I don't care for guys like him. I won't protect him. You say his wife is here; I can't think of another reason why you'd come around asking questions. So I can tell you where he usually goes after work. I won't do anything that will get me in trouble, though. Know what I mean?"

I nodded. "Thanks, Chuck. It's been a help."

"You still living down at the marina? You were gone for a long time, and then you came back. With that new boat."

"Yep."

"She's a beauty."

"She sure is. Thanks."

"Could I see her? I might stop by sometime. I eat over there a lot."

"Come on by," I said, knowing I'd be gone again for a while, and hoping he'd stay away. I wasn't looking for a relationship with this guy, regardless of his history. "I've got some good beer you might try."

"Fine."

"Well, thanks a lot." I got up to leave.

"Mr. Caine!"

"Yes?"

"I need that boy working tomorrow. Don't hurt him too bad. We'll need him first thing in the morning for when the transformer comes in."

"What makes you think I'm going to hurt him?"

"That's what I'd do, I was in your shoes. And you might have to. Just don't make me sorry I told you anything."

"Sure."

"You promise?"

"I promise," I said, regretting the fact that he'd asked,

knowing I wouldn't hurt the kid so badly he wouldn't be able to work.

He had a lot of people depending on him to punch that time clock.

I leaned against the doorjamb. "Not a leading man, eh?"

"You're no Pierce Brosnan."

"Not even Bruce Willis?"

"You're kind of a type like Bruce, but I was thinking more like Willie Nelson."

"I can settle for that."

"I didn't mean it. Forgive me."

"At least you didn't say Lassie."

7

It had been years since I'd visited the Monkey Bar. It was a four-mile turn-around destination on my northern Pearl Harbor run. I'd transited the parking lot many times but hadn't gone in. When I first arrived in Honolulu I was fascinated by the glass wall behind the bar shielding an enclosure filled with tiny South American spider monkeys, but once too often I'd seen a sad little guy with his feet wrapped around a doorknob, staring off into space and masturbating to give himself some small comfort.

It reminded me of the human condition.

In essence it's what we all do, either alone or with somebody. I watched the wretched creature and decided that whether we call it love, or lust, or infatuation, or magic, what it really is is the seeking of temporary comfort, a pathetic attempt to prevent the inevitable from becoming reality. We are alone. We arrive alone and we check out the same way. And in every millisecond in-between we try to bridge the gap between ourselves and others. The sex act is the closest we can get, merging our bodies the way we long to merge our souls. Beyond the intimacy, the touching and the closeness of another human being, there's the simple atavistic longing not to be alone.

Whether those thoughts arose from the eerie resemblance of those sad little primates or the alcohol sailing through my system or the weird combination of the two, I didn't know and didn't care. I quit going there to drink. I didn't want to look at the monkeys anymore.

It was hard enough just looking at the people.

The Monkey Bar was off to the left as you entered the restaurant, a dark cave in an otherwise ordinary room. It's a big place, two-storied, full of memories and bonsai trees. I walked inside and found a spot at the end, facing the entrance. A couple of marines from Kaneohe occupied the far end, young privates, not long out of boot, out seeing the sights. Just them and me. It was too early for the business crowd, and tourists came in the early evening.

I ordered grapefruit juice from the bartender and got comfortable. Three-thirty would come soon enough, and with it, I hoped, Billy Graham.

He arrived right on time, coming in the door the way Hitler invaded Poland. I watched him shove barstools away from his chosen spot, fixing The Stare at the two young marines to keep them at bay, wrap long blue-jeaned legs around his own perch, and plant bare meaty forearms on the edge of the bar, his long-sleeved khaki work shirt rolled up past bulging triceps. He didn't so much sit down as claim territory, extending to a couple of feet of space on either side. Billy was a brawler and a bully, a spoiler. When I considered him in all his resplendent glory, it came as no surprise that he would marry the most vulnerable woman in his community and, once she had become totally submissive, burdened with a child, abandon her.

I sipped my grapefruit juice while he ordered boilermakers, and waited while he consumed enough to fog his brain and slow him down some. Billy Graham was a big man and had about twenty years on me, and while I knew well how to defend myself, I was also old enough to know my limitations, carefully picking my fights when I could. Billy didn't look like a man who would listen to reason, drunk or sober. As long as he was voluntarily consuming enough alcohol to slow down a charging rhinoceros, I thought it prudent to let him. It would make my plan easier to execute.

Billy drank and watched the monkeys.

Contrary to some of my mishaps in the past I did have a plan, and I added refinements as I watched him drink, noting that the bartender knew him but handled him with indifference, the way he would treat a regular customer who regularly neglected to tip. There was also a tinge of fear there, just a hint, and the reason became evident when a sailor in whites came in and sat next to him, moving his barstool closer than the imposed limit. Billy snarled at the man, who got up and moved to a table across the room, not looking for the fight that was certain had he remained where he was. That gave me the idea.

I left a twenty on the bar and went upstairs to the men's room. When I returned I chose one of the barstools next to Billy, ignoring the warning glare that he shot me when I sat down. After ordering another drink I intentionally edged my stool closer to the man's territory, violating his space, receiving a long, unbroken stare as my reward. I ignored that, too, watching the glass behind the bar, where I could see the reflections of two men, one giving his full attention to the other, the second man blissfully gazing straight ahead.

When I didn't respond to the stare I received a sharp nudge. I looked down and saw a steel-toed boot positioned on the rung of my barstool, the leg cocked, ready to push me over. I looked up at Billy Graham, who continued scowling at me. I smiled, nodded agreeably, and turned back to watch the monkeys.

I had to catch the edge of the bar as my stool was shoved violently to the side. Watching the glass, I saw him rear back and I hung on to keep from falling over, setting one foot down to retain my balance. No harm done, I silently righted the stool and sat back down without reaction, reached over to retrieve my glass of grapefruit juice and took a long sip, once again ignoring the angry young man on my left.

The bartender watched, openmouthed.

I winked at him, took another sip, and moved my barstool closer to Billy by a couple of feet.

"Hey!"

I turned lazily, as if I had no appreciation of the imminent danger. "Hey, yourself, sweetheart."

He was fast, much quicker than I'd expected. His arm snaked out in a lightning strike, slamming a big meaty fist against the side of my deltoid muscle. It had been aimed at my face. I managed to get my shoulder up to block, but the force of the blow sent me sprawling off my seat to collide into the stools next to mine. As I went down I saw the bartender reaching for the telephone.

"Don't do that," I said to the bartender as I regained my feet, but it was too late. He had already dialed 911, and once dialed, those calls cannot be terminated without some kind of official interest coming around to question the source and the reason, especially when the call was disconnected. I'd planned on taking Billy out back and having a Come-to-Jesus Meeting with him, but now it was too late and I'd have to revise.

And do it while he came in, swinging another fist the size of a coconut at my head.

Revise I did. I'd seen Billy as a brawler, not trained, but big enough and fast enough to bully his way through a fight without ever having to train. Once I got him outside I would finesse him with aikido, letting him take all the punishment, wearing him down until he was tired, and doing it without truly hurting him. When he had exhausted himself trying to cave in my skull, I could then tell him why I had been dogging him. It made sense, and would satisfy all the promises I'd made on this particular quest. Because law enforcement was now involved, and because this had started inside the bar, I'd have to move fast.

I knew only one way to do that and still fulfill my promises to his wife and employer.

I edged out of the way as he swung again and missed, wordlessly shuffling toward me, each attempt accompanied by a toneless grunt. I tried to stay back, mindful of those steel-toed boots that he would undoubtedly use if I gave him the opening. So far he'd only connected with the first swing. As long as I could move, he would have to get very lucky before he hit me again.

I began moving toward the entry. If I could get him outside before the police arrived I still might be able to bring him back without either one of us getting hurt or going to jail.

He grunted and swung again. I got my hands on the outside of his arms as they went by and, using his own strength and momentum, pushed him into the wall. He connected with the teak paneling, did a slow push-up off the wall and came back at me, keeping himself low, arms out in front, trying for a tackle.

I kneed him in the shoulder as he went down and sweep-kicked his arms away so he fell to the floor, absorbing another rap to his forehead. I danced away on sandaled feet, toward the entry, hoping he would follow.

He did, rushing the door.

I fled outside.

Back out in the bright sunlight, I put my original plan to work, but with some urgency. I needed to get him into my Jeep before the cops arrived.

One nice thing about the brain is that no matter the stress, it usually works when you really need it. While Billy Graham chased me through the parking lot I remembered the handcuffs I kept in the glove compartment of my Jeep. I keep them as a memento to remind myself how dangerous it can be to get careless. I got them several years ago, donated by a serial killer who also strapped a weight belt around my waist and threw me into the water some eight miles at sea. He died shortly afterward when I put a knife through his heart.

I headed for my Jeep so I could conclude this pas de deux as quickly as possible. Billy followed, grunting and swinging, hurting himself a little more each time, slowing down a little more, too. Following me around the nearly empty lot, he started mumbling to himself, a monotone rambling monologue, issuing a slang catalog of female body parts and scatological assemblies, all punctuated with his standard "Oomph!" each time he swung one of those big fists my direction.

By the time we got to my Jeep he was panting, still mumbling epithets and expletives, and still trying to beat on me for violating his space. The alcohol and the heat and the exertion had finally done what I'd intended without hurting him. It was time now for me to act.

I turned and faced him.

The human nervous system is a wonderful and extremely complicated piece of biological engineering. Scientists are only just now beginning to discover how it works. That it works, and that it is connected so perfectly with all parts of the body, has been known in Asia for thousands of years. They did not study it because they had advanced knowledge of medicine. They studied it because they wanted to know how to use this wonder to control an opponent quickly in single combat. The way to do that, they found, was by finding places where nerves connected, distribution points that created intense and immobilizing pain when touched in a certain way, using a specific pressure. It causes instant paralysis and pain, and although the effect is only temporary, it enables the practitioner to do whatever he wishes with the victim for a short time.

Thinking I had finally stopped running from him, he got a second wind and closed on me, punching his fists together and scuffling his boots along the asphalt, readying for an all-out assault with fists and feet.

I let him come, waiting until he struck for the last time.

When he did, swinging at my chest with a big roundhouse right, I turned him, windmilling his body out of control. He tried kicking me as he went by, but his balance was gone and it only added to his problems and he bounced against the Jeep and crashed to the ground, landing on his face.

I straddled him and put my hands on his neck, my fingers finding two of those special locations, giving him something to remember for years to come. The pain was instant and so intense he could not react. He could not, and did not, move.

I pulled out the cuffs and snapped them on his wrists behind his back before he recovered, hauled him upright and herded him into the passenger side of the Jeep. I wrapped a seat belt around him and cinched it tight so he couldn't fall out, hurried around to the driver's side and started the engine.

We drove out of the back parking lot just as the first blue-and-white entered from Kamehameha Highway. I steered the Jeep through an alley and back around a side street and turned onto Kam Highway, heading toward Pearl Harbor.

"You okay, Billy?"

He turned and looked at me, bleary-eyed, not comprehending yet what had just happened.

"The pain's getting better. Isn't it getting better?"

"Wha—? Who—?"

"My name's John Caine," I said, keeping an eye on the rearview mirror, looking for police pursuit. There was nothing behind us.

"Who're you?"

"Your wife hired me. She wants to know why you haven't called lately."

B illy looked at me, his mouth open. "She's here?"

I downshifted, turned off Kamehameha Highway and wandered through the warren of narrow side streets in the hills above the Aloha Stadium in case the police got a description of my Jeep. It was unlikely. I thought we got away clean, but I wanted this finished as fast as possible. Official police presence would ask too many questions I didn't have the time to answer.

"Yep," I said.

"You tracked me down, beat me up, handcuffed me, kidnapped me—for *her?*" His voice, already a high nasal twang, got higher when he strained it.

"Julia, too."

"I won't stay. I'll talk to her, but I won't stay."

"That's your choice, but either way you owe me twenty dollars."

He stared, his mouth gaping like a fish long out of water.

"That's my fee," I explained.

He struggled against the seat belt, but couldn't budge the buckles and straps. I'd tucked him in good and tight so he wouldn't fall out or get stupid ideas. The Jeep had no doors and I didn't want anybody getting hurt.

We turned again and went down another hill and I rec-ognized the neighborhood where Billy used to live. When we passed his old street I saw him take a quick glance up the hill toward the boardinghouse. I ignored it, hoping he wouldn't put two and two together and come back for some vengeance.

"We're almost there," I said, turning onto Salt Lake Bou-levard, toward the marina. "Take it easy. Talk to your wife, or"—I risked looking directly into his eyes—"more important, let *her* talk to you. Get it settled between you two—what you want, what she wants—make some arrangements for support. And then you can do what you want."

"You some kind of family counselor?"

"Not hardly. But your wife hired me. You know she came here with no money? Because you didn't call or write or any-thing since you got here. So she spent all her cash getting here, hoping to find you. When that didn't work out, someone rec-ommended me. So you're going to speak to the lady and my job's done. Can you be reasonable?" I took my hand off the gearshift and flexed it to remind him what being unreasonable would do for him.

"Yeah."

"Yeah, what?"

"Yeah, sir."

"No, Billy. Can you be reasonable for an hour or so? Get it all worked out? Let us all go on with our lives?"

I parked in the marina parking lot next to a bright blue half-ton, four-wheel-drive pickup truck. I stared at him while he thought it over, considering his alternatives. He truly did not want to face his wife. He must have felt like a small child being dragged home to Mom, who had been caught doing something wrong; but he'd been on a two-month bender in Paradise and it was time to face reality. I didn't feel sorry for him. There was no male solidarity. We're not all alike in that way. Some of us take our promises seriously, regardless of the circumstance, regardless of the price.

"If you promise to behave yourself, I'll cut you loose from those cuffs. If not, you keep on wearing them, face your wife and child like that."

"I'll talk to her."

"All right, stand up." I unbuckled his seat belt and he slid out of the old leather seat and turned around. I unlocked the cuffs and put them away, turning my back on him, giving him the chance to run or attack me. If he was going to do either it would be here, behind the big truck, and I figured it would be less embarrassing for him to get it over with now, rather than in front of his family.

But Billy knew when he was whipped. When I closed the glove box and turned around he still stood there, flat-footed, rubbing his wrists and staring across the parking lot toward the bright surface of Pearl Harbor.

"Follow me," I said, starting toward the boat dock. Without hesitation, he followed.

"She's here?"

"I've got a boat," I said. "She's aboard, with someone else, another of my clients. A woman," I said, interpreting his look as one of jealousy, something I found inexplicable. "They spent the day together while I looked for you."

"Who are you?"

"Just a private detective. You're a case. I guess I can say you're a closed case, now."

"My wife hired a private detective? I thought you said she didn't have any money."

"That's why you owe me twenty dollars."

"That's your fee?"

"For hard cases I charge more." We reached the gate and I unlocked it, watching my sarcasm passing harmlessly over his head. Billy Graham wasn't paying attention to me anymore. He had more urgent problems in his immediate future.

It looked like a party in progress on board *Olympia*, with more people on deck than I'd planned. When we got closer I recognized that the crowd was just Kimo, dressed in a bright red Aloha shirt, drinking another of my Edelweiss Dunkels and talking to Julia, who sat on his lap. Karen and Margo sat on the cushions near the wheel, talking earnestly, their heads close together.

Margo looked up and gave me a significant look, and then went back to her conversation with Karen.

Women seem to be the cooperative members of the species. Men are always competitive. Whether they come from totally different backgrounds, whether or not they like each other, women seem to form some kind of bond when thrown together. Even when they cannot stand each other. Men, on the other hand, are always comparing something, always competing, always jockeying for the top position. Maybe it goes back to the days of hunter-gatherers, when the females had to band together and do the gathering in a coordinated group, while the males hunted, sometimes alone, sometimes in a group, all time locked in grim, unwritten but universally understood competition. The best hunter got the best cuts of meat, the best place to sleep, and the pick of the females.

Nothing's changed. These days I have noted that all the really big yachts—the multimillion dollar oceangoing vessels that require an all-ocean-licensed captain and a competent crew—those yachts all come with hot-and-cold-running playmates. In any port, in any sea, I've watched the big boys come and go, and aboard every one of the big party boats the party girls are there, as though they came with the furniture.

I climbed aboard *Olympia* while Billy held back, unsure how to address Reality now that she sat not ten feet from where he stood. I watched out of the corner of my eye, certain he would run, but he didn't.

"Drinking my beer again, Kimo?"

"I can come by every day for this," he said, smiling, as if his previous angry words had never been spoken. He gave a knowing glance at Margo, then at me, and I knew I'd been busted. "You got a minute?" He handed the child back to her mother and stood up.

"In a minute. Have another. If there's any left." I looked at Karen, who sat and stared at her husband with a look that combined hurt and relief and anger and love and understanding and betrayal all rolled into one expression, another ability women have that men will never, in this or any other millennium, have a clue how to achieve. "I think you two should be alone."

Kimo saw what I saw and nodded. He silently followed Margo into the lounge. I wondered what kind of conversations they'd had while I was gone. Margo ignored me, as if she blamed me for still being on Oahu so she had to endure more questioning by the police.

Well, she was right.

"Daddy!"

Julia saw her father and ran to him, throwing her tiny body at him. He caught and held her awkwardly, silently accepting the child's kisses, never taking his eyes off his wife.

In that moment, I almost believed they would make it, nearly forgetting what I'd learned and what I'd seen.

"Down here, Caine." Kimo's voice drifted up from the cabin below. I wanted to go down there as much as Billy wanted to be on deck. Below lurked Kimo and Margo, not the combination I would have hoped for, knowing I was responsible for their coming together again, knowing Kimo would think that I lied to him about knowing of her whereabouts. Could I get away with telling him that at the time I said those words it was the truth?

Probably not.

Only one way to tell.

"You going to be all right?" I asked, the question directed to anyone who cared to answer.

"Billy and I have lots to catch up on, Mr. Caine. You

brought him to me just like you said you would. We'll be okay now."

"Uh-huh." Sometimes it is best not to allow your imagination to run wild. Sometimes it's best to be guided by faith.

"I'll be below," I said, not knowing if it was a warning or an assurance.

"Have a beer," said Kimo as I climbed down the ladder into the gloom of my lounge. Margo and the big policeman faced each other across the table. He had a big sappy smile on his face. Margo slouched against the sofa bench, pointedly not looking in my direction.

I opened the cold locker and took one of my steadily diminishing supply of Edelweiss. You can't easily get them here in Hawaii. I have them shipped directly from California. I don't drink American beer. Our laws make the brewers water it down so much it tastes as if they should pour it back through the horse. I like German and Austrian beer. They invented it and they've had about six hundred years to get it right. I met Pa, the retired literature professor who imports it to the United States, a few years back and he introduced me to Edelweiss. It was love at first taste.

"So you seem to have found Mrs. Halliday."

"She found me, Kimo. Last evening, after you came to see me."

"Nice how you rushed to a telephone to let me know."

I looked at Margo, then back at the big cop. "She came here because she was frightened of everyone else. She needed refuge, a breather. She had nowhere else to go."

"Came here because you saved her? Or because Chawlie sent her?"

"Why don't you ask the lady?"

"I did. She said it was because you'd saved her that night in the alley."

"Then there you go."

"Uh-huh." Kimo didn't buy the story, but he'd fed me her

answer so I wouldn't get stupid and give him a different one. This wasn't an interrogation. He'd already made up his mind and I wondered when he would get to the point.

Getting to the point would have to wait. Topside, Billy Graham's voice shouted something unintelligible, but full of passion, and the clear heartbreaking sound of a fist smacking flesh immediately followed. I beat Kimo to the hatchway, but he was right behind me on the ladder and once on deck I found myself shoved aside as the big policeman lifted the young man off his feet and tossed him far out into the oily waters of Pearl Harbor.

Kimo fished Billy out of the water while Margo rushed to comfort his wife and child. He kept me away from the young man, waving me off, shielding him with his huge body, slapping handcuffs onto wrists where another pair had only recently been removed. It took a moment for me to understand that I had reached for his throat, my hands moving as if they had minds separate from the one I carried in my head. Or tried to.

"Back off, Caine!" he snarled at me, bringing me back from the black hole my soul had entered.

While Kimo secured his prisoner, he informed him he was under arrest for assault, battery, and for making terroristic threats, one misdemeanor and two felonies, and then he read him the laundry list of his rights the way he was supposed to. Careful to make no error that would give any court an excuse to allow Billy to slip away from his responsibilities, Kimo treated the man gently, even though his face flushed dark red with anger.

Margo held Julia while Karen sat holding her hands to her face, sobbing silently, tears streaming down her sallow cheeks. Her child sat curiously silent, clutching Margo's neck, watching her father being taken into custody. I wondered if this wasn't the first time she had witnessed this particular scene.

I stood back, unable to help in either case. Kimo didn't need me, and Karen, just assaulted by a man, needed a woman's help more than mine. Margo was warning me with a look that told me to stay away.

Everyone reaching the same conclusion that I was useless at this kind of thing was not something I could challenge with any conviction.

"Call the police," Kimo ordered, once he had Billy confined.

"You want Dispatch?"

He nodded. "Get me a patrol car, not a motor."

I went below and made the call, telling them Lieutenant Kahanamoku had a felony suspect in custody and needed transportation. They asked if an officer needed assistance, and I told them no, just help in moving a prisoner downtown. They said there was a car near the *Arizona* memorial that would be there shortly.

I heard the siren before I returned topside, looked at the twin scenes of misery in my backyard and decided that someone needed to walk down to the marina parking lot to direct the officer.

The two policemen—well, maybe they might have preferred the term "police officers" because both were female—arrived as I came around the corner of the restaurant and I led them back to my slip where Billy Graham lay facedown on the concrete dock, the big Hawaiian detective standing over him like a lion protecting its kill. While the police took care of police business, injecting the young man into the state of Hawaii's criminal justice system, I went to see about Julia and Karen. Knowing nothing of young children's resilience, or this one's capacity to withstand the kind of violence visited upon her mother by her father, I felt uncomfortable approaching the two women and the child, thinking that maybe everyone's conclusions about my inadequacy in these situations might just be right.

And I realized that Margo and Karen shared a bond that I could never know. It went far deeper than the "sisterhood" perceptions I thought I understood. These two women from such disparate backgrounds had lived similar lives. I recalled that night when I met Margo Halliday, literally running for her life, and I remembered the ex-husband who treated her as if she were some kind of disposable property that he and only he could dominate or determine the fate of. Women weren't human beings to these men. They were less than chattel, mere objects to be owned, used, or disposed of at will.

It made me wonder where people get such ideas, where they get the right to treat others that way. I'd seen my share of sociopaths and bullies, and many had regretted that our paths had crossed, those who had lived. I looked at Billy Graham and wished now that I'd hurt him a little more when I'd had the chance, and then rejected that thought. That kind of viciousness would have reduced me to his level, and I wanted to believe I shared nothing with him. Nothing at all.

"Are you okay?" I asked, knowing it was a stupid question. I'd brought the husband to her as she had requested and he'd beaten her while I stood close by, giving him the opportunity because I wanted to believe her fantasy that everything would be all right now that they were together.

"I'm fine," she said through a split lip. One side of her face was puffy and would soon discolor. A fine bright line of split skin showed in the tight swelling flesh over her cheekbone. "This has happened before, Mr. Caine. Usually when he's been drinking."

More guilt flushed through me, adding to my normal load, my stomach grinding its contents. Hadn't thought that one all the way through, did you, old man? Didn't think that by allowing him to drink so you could handle him easier, he wouldn't be a mean son of a bitch once he got here, now did you? His behavior in the Monkey Bar didn't register?

I looked at his wife and at the solemn, silent face of his child, and wished I'd taken off last night, the way Margo had wanted, slipped *Olympia* from her bonds and taken her to sea. Margo's glance was the one you'd give something you might find on the bottom of your shoe after you walk across the lawn in the middle of the night.

When I didn't go away, she got up and went below.

The little guy in the back of my head, the one who had already burned the big red flag he used to wave because I ignored him no matter what he did, finally spoke up. "But you wanted to help," he said, his voice heavy with sarcasm, "so you took on a project for free because it sounded easy, a charity case, pro bono, for the good of everyone. You knew how it would end, right at the beginning. Yet you, the White Knight, come charging in, find the husband and bring him here knowing what he was going to do, and then you turned your back on him and let him do it. You thought you were helping, and you thought you were the only one who could, and the lady had no one else to turn to. You didn't think it through, did you? Anybody could have done what you did, and done it better. What hubris! Don't you ever learn? I give up! I quit!"

I couldn't blame him but I knew he'd be back, if only to torture me. It was his job.

"If you think you need medical attention I can drive you over to the hospital in Aiea," I said, offering anything I could think of to make amends.

"I don't think anything's broken, Mr. Caine, but thank you just the same. Mrs. Halliday got me some ice, and I know it'll hurt terribly for a day or so, but then it'll get better." She spoke with the assurance of a veteran who had been through it all before. Her prediction about the injuries were right on the money; clear indication she knew what she was talking about.

"If you change your mind, let me know."

"Mr. Caine? What are they going to do with Billy?"

"I don't know for sure. He's going to jail. He'll probably be there until tomorrow, and then they'll have a hearing and the judge will set bail, and he most likely can be out by tomorrow afternoon." What I didn't say was that Kimo was charging him with two felonies and the bail would be high, and even if he paid it he couldn't leave the Islands and go back to the Mainland while he out on bail. And then there was his Controlled Industrial Area card, his means of access to Ford Island, where he worked. Once they found out he had been arrested for a violent felony, the Navy would revoke it and he would lose his high-paying job.

And the guy over on Salt Lake Boulevard whose name I could not now recall would probably not get his transformer installed in the morning.

I shook my head. The agonies kept compounding. There was a lesson here, but I wasn't certain exactly where or what it was.

"So what will happen to us?" Her voice shook as the reality of her precarious position finally hit home. "How will we get along? We can't stay here. You're going someplace, Mrs. Halliday told me. And I can't stay here, anyway. I've got to get back home."

"Do you have family?"

"Dad's dead and Mom's in a home paid by the Social Security. There's nobody. I have a sister in Baltimore, but she's worse off than I am."

I wondered how that could be possible.

"One thing you aren't going to do," said the little man, back from his strike, "is let this woman down again."

"I'll see what I can do," I said.

The two officers escorted their still-dripping prisoner away and Kimo climbed aboard again. Squatting on the deck next to Karen, leaning close like a lover or a father confessor, he gently questioned her, letting her talk, allowing her to say what she wanted without leading her. She was less of a valuable witness than she would normally be in a case like this because the arresting officer had been there when the crime occurred and could provide all the testimony needed for a conviction.

When he had finished, Kimo thanked her and gently took my arm and we walked down the dock toward the parking lot.

"You and me, we still got some business, but I got to go downtown and make sure the paperwork is right. I don't want this guy getting away. And you"—he pointed a thick brown finger at my nose—"I don't want you going anywhere, either. You were planning on taking Mrs. Halliday to Kauai to hide her there. You might still do that, but not until I talk to both of you. Understand?"

"Karen and her child can stay here another night, but eventually we're going to have to do something about them."

"We?"

"Well, not you and me, but all of us. Everyone. Everybody."

"Like who? Like what?"

"I don't know."

He shook his head. "You have a lot to learn, but tell you what. I've got a spare bedroom or two at the house. I'll call Neolani and have her come get them."

"At your house?"

"Sure. Couple of the kids are at school on the Mainland. We've usually got a yardful of kids. Not sure whose they are, most of the time. One or two more won't matter, and Neolani will take good care of Mrs. Graham. Once she feels better we can all figure out what to do. All of us. Everyone. Everybody."

I nodded. It made more sense than anything I could think

of, but I was admittedly out of my element. "I could drive them," I offered.

"Thanks, but it's on the north shore, way out of your way. Neolani won't mind. And besides, I'm not sure I want you to know where I live."

10

Neolani brought along Kimo's grandmother Tutu Mae, a spry, wizened kapuna approaching her own century mark, a woman who took charge of everything and everybody the moment she set foot in new territory. I had never met her before, but I knew of her and knew her kind.

Kapunas are cherished elders, valued as precious assets. Tutu Mae was legendary. *Hawaii* magazine had recently done a cover story on her. One of the last repositories of Hawaiian history and culture, she had begun years ago to store her knowledge on computer, the system designed to her exact specifications so she could store text and graphics and multimedia. She had added scanning and now was engaged in videotaping and digitized storage of ancient hula rhythms and chants. The program was now so voluminous that the University of Hawaii had established a chair of anthropology in her name. Scholars, students, and writers made regular pilgrimages to her home, and at her age she still gave—free—hula and other lessons to Hawaii's children, regardless of their age or race.

She sized me up as useless in a glance and brushed by to get to Karen and the child, enfolding them in her arms, mothering them as if they had been her charges all of their lives.

Neolani, Kimo's wife, was a tall and gracious woman, the kind of pure pre-contact Polynesian beauty who would have made sailors jump ship two hundred years before. Her loveliness and her size were nearly overwhelming when you first confronted her, before you knew the woman herself.

"You must be John Caine," she said to me, extending her hand. "Kimo's said so much about you, I feel that I know you."

"I am very pleased to meet you," I said. "I hope some of it was good."

She laughed. "Most of it," she said. "He said you collected trouble and women, and you've collected a couple of women too many and you didn't know what to do with them."

"Karen and her daughter are stranded here. The husband—"

"I know the story, Mr. Caine," she said, lowering her voice and giving me a look I never wanted to see again. "Kimo told me he arrested the husband when you both caught him beating her. He told me the rest of it, too. They need help, and we're here to help."

The Hawaiians have a custom called hanai, which is adoption, but it really means much more than that. As a verb it also means to raise, to sustain, to nourish. It is common here to hanai people when they are homeless or destitute, to bring them into your home and nourish and sustain them until they can get on their feet again. It is specifically Hawaiian. Not all the Polynesians did it, but the Hawaiians perfected the practice of unofficially adopting people—usually children and infants, but sometimes even adults—when they had been abandoned, or got into trouble they couldn't handle. There were no orphans in pre-contact Hawaii. Kimo's cousin had hanaied me after Kate's death, when I'd lost my boat and all of my possessions, and I stayed at his home in the mountains of Kauai for four months, resting and recuperating from injuries that had been both physical and spiritual. And Ed Alapai had made it clear that I could return whenever I felt the need to do so.

From the little that Kimo had told me of his family I knew that he and Neolani had four children between them, and had somehow acquired another six, most likely by hanai.

In a way it was what I had done for Karen and Julia, and for Margo Halliday, although it was only small-scale and temporary. With Kimo and his family, it was impossible to tell how long they'd be there.

As long as they needed it, I supposed. Hanai isn't state-run, or state-regulated, and there are no limits on the amount of care and compassion a family can provide.

I helped carry Karen's meager possessions to Neolani's Cherokee, patted the still-silent Julia on the head and received a kiss and a thank-you from Karen. I tried to avoid her eyes, but she made it impossible to do so.

"Thank you, Mr. Caine, for what you tried to do."

I nodded. To "try" is to admit to the possibility of failure. I'd tried and succeeded in bringing her husband to her, and I'd tried and failed to bring her old life back, an impossible task. Perhaps it was time I stuck with things I knew how to do. It was a short list, but I could do them well. At my stage of life, when I ventured past the limitations of my expertise, I found that failure would more than likely be the result. Even little simple chores like this one tended to turn into disasters.

It was something to consider after my evening run, when the chilled glass of Chardonnay sat before me and the sun began to set way out on the Pacific, and, if the conditions were right all the way to the horizon, I could look for the green flash that I'd seen only once or twice in a lifetime of searching. Perhaps then I'd take out this new idea, polish it up, spin it around, look at it from all the angles and see if it was for me.

Kimo's grandmother ignored me and climbed into the shotgun seat, but his lovely wife shook my hand and asked if I'd care to know how Karen and Julia made out.

"Of course," I said, surprised at the question.

"I didn't know how long you would be gone. Kimo said you'd be leaving Oahu for a while. Check in with us when you return."

"I will," I said, grateful to be learning that Kimo had once more transferred me back to his list of trustworthies. "Thank you for what you're doing."

"For what?" She gave me a cool look, an acknowledgment that she did not wish to pursue the subject.

"For everything." It was a poor substitute for what I had been about to offer, but the lady's intentions were clear.

"We going or not?" The querulous voice of Tutu Mae shot from the window of the Cherokee. "I have to go to the bathroom."

"I'm coming," said Neolani. "You take care of yourself, Mr. Caine."

"I will," I said, wondering what she meant, and wondering what else Kimo had told her, and why he would care one way or the other what happened to me.

Neolani closed her door and drove away, and Karen waved shyly from the backseat. All I could see of Julia was the top of her little blond head, snuggled in the back seat beside her mother. It looked as if she stared straight ahead, not paying attention to anything except the road ahead and whatever else lay before her.

Keep it up, little girl, I thought, watching them drive away.

Never take your eyes off the road ahead.

That way you can see them coming a long way off.

11

Y ou son of a bitch!" Margo Halliday was not a happy client, if, in fact, she really was my client. She stood across the lounge, fitting her shoulders against the teak bulkhead, arms crossed, glaring at me, spitting out the invective like the opening scene from *Macbeth*.

But then again, she still thought she could use me. Otherwise she'd be gone. I had no use for her and, considering my recent track record, it was probably better for her if she sought advice and protection elsewhere.

"We've been told to stay here until Kimo talks to us," I said, tying double knots on my Nikes, preparing for my afternoon run. "That's what we're going to do."

"And you're going to leave me here alone. Again."

"Unless you can hold an eight-minute pace. If you can, then come along."

"And you don't care what happens to me!"

I considered my reply, thinking that honesty was most likely the best policy, at least on one side of this conversation. "You picked me, I didn't solicit your business. We don't have a professional relationship because we don't have an agreement. What I've done for you so far has simply been a favor to Chawlie. We don't have a personal relationship either. We met accidentally last year, and I stopped your ex-husband from putting holes in you with a gun. I have not seen you since. You took up with Chawlie, and now you're dumping him and seeking my help, or he dumped you and you're running from him—I really don't know which is the truth. You invade my boat without my permission, intrude upon my life, and now you're asking me if I care what happens to you?''

It was cruel, but accurate, and her reaction might put some light to the lies she'd told me. She didn't even blink.

''What about those men?''

''What men?''

''Out there!''

''You said you saw some men last night on the beach, but you don't know what they wanted. You're afraid of something that Chawlie can't fix. Is that what you're telling me?''

''They're out there. I saw them!'' She pointed through the porthole toward the open-air restaurant at the head of the dock. ''Those same men, sitting at the bar, watching this boat. They're waiting until you leave me alone.''

I looked, but saw only a few sailors and officers in summer whites sitting at the railing, mixed with some middle-aged couples in tourist uniform, but nothing that looked like a threat.

''When did you see them?''

''Just a few minutes ago when you were walking back from the parking lot. I recognized them. They looked right at me!''

''Look again.''

She did, shaking her head in frustration. ''They were there.'' She turned and faced me, either an actress who should be working steadily or a woman truly frightened. ''Chawlie told me about you, and after what you did that night I believe him. There are others I could call, but nobody can protect me like you can. And you've got this boat. I need to get out of here now!''

She turned and fled to her stateroom, and I thought she was making one of those dramatic exits that people make when their emotions got the better of them and they can't think of anything else to say, but I was wrong and she returned with a small cloth bag in her hand.

"Chawlie told me about the diamonds you recovered for him. I've managed to save some of my money and invest in emeralds." She reached into the bag and drew out a small folded paper envelope, opened it and spread out its contents on the lounge table. Three bright green emeralds lay on the paper. "Per carat, these are worth more than diamonds. This is just a sample of what I have. Would they buy your time for a month?"

It made me smile when she related Chawlie's version of the events that resulted in my recovering a briefcase full of diamonds and him and me sharing the profits. I had no idea what these gems were worth, and couldn't even tell if they were real. I would have to take her word for it, not a usually reliable source. Sometimes, however, it's best to go with what feels good.

"I know nothing of emeralds or diamonds. They're pretty. Some people pay good money for them, I've heard."

She held one of the stones to the light, catching a sunbeam from one of the starboard portholes. The pure green stone was not like a diamond and didn't breathe fire, but it seemed to capture the light, glowing from within. It was beautiful, but I had no use for it. I'm sure Chawlie would know what to do with it.

"Twelve carats," she said.

"So?"

"These three are yours if you'll help me. That's the best I can do. They're worth, oh, give or take, twenty thousand dollars each. Is that enough for a week of your time?"

"Where did you get them?" I knew that Chawlie's interests lay in many areas, and that he somehow knew instantly how to divest himself of the diamonds I'd given him, so it followed that trading in gemstones might have been one of his legal businesses.

"Not from Chawlie. I didn't steal from that man."

I raised my eyebrows. Her declaration excluded those from whom she may have stolen the emeralds. "Good decision. But you didn't answer my question."

"They were gifts. Can we leave it at that?"

"Certainly. And you can pack your suitcase and get off my boat."

"I can't do that. You've got to help me. Those men are out there, and when they see me leave, they'll come after me and kill me. Without your help I'm dead."

I glanced out the porthole again, seeing the same landscape with the same familiar people. No killers lurked there.

"Okay," I said, deciding this was just one more Margo tantrum. "I'm going for a run. It helps me get through my days. I'll look around while I'm running. If I see anything that looks weird I'll come right back. If I don't, I'll run my usual eight miles. That takes about an hour, because I have to warm down afterward and if I don't stretch and walk, I cramp up."

She looked stricken.

"Lock the boat behind me. Don't let anybody in except me. You told me you have a gun. Use it if you have to. Stay inside until I get back. If you have to use the gun the security police will come running. Navy SEALS are right across the water, and they might come running. If I hear shots, I'll definitely come running. You're safe. Believe it."

She looked doubtful.

Another thought hit me. "Kimo might come by while I'm gone—"

"That cop looked so happy to see me here. He wants me in jail for Glen's murder."

"He was happy because he thought I'd lied to him. It had nothing to do with you. Kimo told his wife that we were going to Kauai. He told me he knows we're going but he wants to talk with us first. That means he doesn't intend to stop us. He won't jail you unless you really did it. He's not that kind of cop."

"What's he want then?"

"I don't know. He was about to tell us when that idiot kid bashed his wife. He's downtown now doing the paperwork. He'll be back. If he gets here while I'm gone, let him in. With him around you have nothing to fear."

The doubtful look remained in place. I wanted to tell her that if she told either one of us the truth the whole situation might be a little easier, but I knew that would be just wasted energy.

"Just let him in. It's inevitable. Or you can leave. Right now. Take your emeralds and get out. I'm sure Chawlie would take you back, if only for the emeralds. He's first and foremost a businessman. If you make him a business offer—even if he's threatened to kill you—he'll consider it. Or you can stay. If you stay, you'll have to play the game by my rules, or by Kimo's rules."

"I'll stay," she said, her brave words not mirrored by the look on her face. "Go for your run. I'm sure I'll be safe here while it's still light. Nobody's going to try anything until after dark."

"And you'll let Kimo in?"

She nodded.

"I'll be back." I climbed the ladder to the deck and looked around. The sun was a fiery ball in the western sky, hanging above the Waianae Mountains, sending down rays with real weight and heft. The air was moist with humidity. It, too, had weight. Combined, the two did not make for running weather, but it was something I did when I needed to think through a problem and it helped put everything in perspective.

I ran the footpath along the northern shore of Pearl

Harbor, one of my favorite runs. About this time of day the trade winds usually blew in from the east, cooling breezes that moderated the summer temperatures. When the trades didn't blow, the weather changed. Sometimes it brought the kona winds, those subtropical breezes loaded with additional humidity, and with them came incessant rains and cloudy days. Sometimes the change brought hurricanes.

I truly wished the trades would come back.

No one skulked in the parking lot. I saw no swarthy types wearing Aloha shirts to conceal illicit firearms. No one bothered me, and nobody showed any untoward interest in my yacht. My run remained unremarkable from beginning to end, and when I walked to warm down, I took an intense interest in the crowd on the second deck of the marina and saw nothing at the railing that would indicate Margo had attracted the attention of those who would do her harm.

It seemed to be another of her constructs, some story she created either to gain attention or distract me from her real goals. The fact of the emeralds had been instructive. If she offered to pay me with three, I imagined she would have many more hidden away. That kind of money would be motive and opportunity enough for her to flee Hawaii and start a new life elsewhere. Always someone's mistress, always the hanger-on, the pretty party favor, she would have resented her role in a life she could not control, forgetting, of course, that we create our own destinies by the choices we make.

I decided to take the threat seriously. That kind of money could also attract the kind of violence she reported, and had she stolen the jewels from someone other than Chawlie, it would be wise for her to keep her head down and hide. That's what she was trying to do. That's why she came to me.

And by all reports her husband was very, very dead, so somebody out there seemed capable of extreme violence. No wonder the woman seemed shaky.

So, of course, I bring home a stray mother and daughter,

and then add the missing husband as a kind of tragic-comedic circus act, attracting just the kind of attention she desperately wanted to avoid.

Couldn't blame her if the woman considered other avenues. After the alley fight she had thought of John Caine as Rambo. What she found was closer to Bosco the Clown.

At the jogger's fountain I saw Kimo's blue Mustang muscle car in the parking lot. My legs had stopped wobbling, my heart rate recovered, and it was time to return to *Olympia* and face the music, whatever the tune.

I took two steps before a bullet shattered the windshield of a Mazda Miata next to me, accompanied by the unforgettable bark of a large-caliber rifle fired in one's direction. I ducked and rolled behind an official Navy sedan, frantically trying to find the source of the gunfire. Three more shots pounded the sedan and all the window glass exploded above my head. One heavy-caliber slug penetrated the sedan's side door inches above me, punching on through the Miata.

That gave me an approximate angle of travel for location of origin.

I pressed myself deeper into the asphalt and crawled around to the front of the Navy car and peered out from behind the tire but saw nothing. The bank on the hillside above the restaurant was thick with kiawe and ironwood trees. Nothing moved but for the dark green leaves, disturbed and fluttered by a slight breeze. Somebody could easily conceal himself in a shooting nest in that thicket and not be detected, waiting for as long as it took for the target to come into focus. I'd passed by that spot just a few minutes earlier, but I'd been paced by another man, a captain I knew from Ford Island, out for his afternoon jog. Perhaps the hitter had orders to make certain only one victim was hit, ancillary damage in this assignment not authorized.

No more shots came my way, and I guessed the excitement

was over, the shooter getting his gear together and bugging out.

That's what I would have done, had it been me up there. Failure this time would force a fallback and regrouping, and an examination of the planned contingency.

All the same, I squirmed beneath the sedan and waited, feeling vulnerable and naked, unarmed and unable to respond if the shooter decided on a final, suicidal attack.

None came, and I began to understand something of the person who wished me dead.

I heard shouting from the direction of the restaurant and sirens approaching. Kimo was on his way from *Olympia*, that much was certain, and so were the cops, both Honolulu PD and the base security people. The place would soon be swarming with armed, angry men and women, looking for the shooter and panting to put some lead in somebody's ten-ring. Getting up and running around now could lead to an unpleasant confrontation.

Content to let the assassin flee and others give chase, I pillowed my head on my arms and enjoyed the sunshine, letting the sun warm my back. Rescue was on its way. I didn't have to do anything but relax and wait.

As to the shooter, I didn't worry. This had been no accident. There was no misinterpreting the target or the intent. It hadn't been a civilian hitter. There had been a military precision about the task, up to the final moment when the shooter's craft failed him, the moist tropical air, or a wayward tree branch, or even karmic mysteries somehow spoiling the careful calculations of the shot.

Margo wasn't in danger here. This was an impersonal affair, an assignment of a dispassionate distant killer. Whoever it was would take me out as quickly as possible and get out of the Islands immediately after. He would not know why he killed me, nor would he care. We had never met before, and we would likely meet only one more time.

I could take Margo to Kauai. I could sail across the sea to the Mainland, fly off to China, climb Mount Everest, apply for the space program and land on the moon. I could go anywhere, do anything, change my name, my profession, shave off my beard, dye my hair, walk with a limp, speak with a lisp. But if this assassin truly wanted me dead, he would find me.

That being a given, there was only one thing for me to do.

T ree branch. You were right." Kimo Kahanamoku held up a cut limb from a kiawe tree, the seared scar of a bullet track across its gray bark. He drank another one of my Edelweiss beers while he interrogated me, a habit I was beginning to view as police brutality. I might never have another chance to buy more from Pa. "Wind came up just at the right time. Tumbled the bullet off aim. Otherwise they would have found you dead instead of asleep."

"Asleep?" Margo's eyes flashed disbelief.

Kimo glanced at her, a knowing smile on his brown moon face, his eyes merry. "One of our officers found him sleeping beneath one of the cars that got shot up, covered with broken glass, snoring away like Rip Van Winkle. Our guy thought he was dead, but fortunately, or unfortunately, depending, the bullet missed. Close, but still no cigar."

"You were asleep?"

"The sun felt good on my back. I had nowhere to go."

Kimo took another long draft of the Dunkel. "Mrs. Halliday," he said, "you must understand that Caine here is not showing off. He's probably telling the truth."

"Macho bullshit."

"Maybe, but it's what he is."

"Spoken in true male solidarity," she said, disgusted. "He gets shot at, saved by a freak breeze and a tree branch or something, and he just goes to sleep."

"They found a nest," continued Kimo. "Somebody's been there at least a couple of days. Left some trash—newspapers, food wrappers, and other junk that might be traced back to the Fast Stop on the other side of the highway. They cleared out pretty fast, leaving mostly junk. A little too fast. They left a piss tube."

That got my attention.

"What's a piss tube?" Margo's interest wasn't feigned. But then, she had more than one reason to pay attention.

"We used them in the jungle," I said. "It's a long funnel. Pound it into the soil and pee into it and take it with you when you leave, covering the hole. It doesn't leave a trace of your presence." The ammonia urine smell is unmistakable in the natural environment, lingering afterward, advertising your passing. It probably wasn't necessary in an urban setting, but in the heat a shooter and a spotter would drink a lot of water and they wouldn't sweat all of it out. A piss tube was the answer.

"What does that mean?"

"Could mean anything." What it meant was that the shooter had military experience and knew his way around the bush. His menace went beyond training. This guy had actual fieldwork behind him. My forearms went chicken-skin, my body finally understanding how close I'd come to joining my ancestors, but for a wayward breeze blowing off the surface of Pearl Harbor, gently pushing a small, soft branch into the path of the heavy-caliber slug. It had been a close thing. Too close for me to have fallen asleep immediately afterward. Was it macho bravado? Or mere denial, the mind shutting down, trying to avoid consideration of a brush with oblivion.

"We'll try to get fingerprints off the tube and the plastic food wrappers," Kimo continued. "Lab's taking the stuff, handling it carefully. Even Henry Lee would approve. They tell me they'll get prints. If the shooter's in the system, we'll nail him."

"Don't count on that."

"You know something?"

I nodded. "He wouldn't get that careless. This was not a thrill shooting, not some dumb son of a bitch going postal. It was a hit. The guy was a pro, if only a sloppy one. He's no loser. He won't be in the system. He failed this time. It happens. He took off. But he'll be back."

Margo went pale.

"It wasn't for you, Mrs. Halliday," Kimo said, his voice soothing. "The shooter had been there for at least two days, maybe three. That was before you and Mr. Caine got involved."

"We are not *involved*," she said, indignant, the emphasis heavy.

"I meant when he started working for you. Somebody's been watching this place, lying in wait in that jungle across the way, waiting to take a shot at Caine. Probably figured you'd come here, the same way I did. When they got a clear shot at Caine, they took it."

"What do you mean?" Sometimes Kimo's thought processes are as convoluted as Chawlie's. I liked that about him.

"With you out of the way, they'd have a better chance to take Mrs. Halliday. For whatever reason, somebody wants her dead, but they might want to find out what she knows before she's dead."

"What?" He had lost me.

"Who knows both of you? Where's your link?"

"Chawlie." Margo went pale, the blood rushing out of her face. "He wants me dead?"

"You've angered somebody, Mrs. Halliday. What have you done?"

She shook her head. "Nothing, really. But Chawlie?"

Kimo shrugged, drained the bottle and set it down. "I haven't reached any conclusions. I'm just a simple investigator, trying to find some truth amid the muck. Neither one of you is helping to clarify things." He looked over at me, the corners of his mouth rising into a smile. "Of course, with Caine, here, it could have been a hit just on him."

"Thanks. You're a big help."

"You've been a bad boy all your life, and it might be catching up with you. It might be a better question to ask who *doesn't* want to kill you."

"Most of the people who fit that category aren't around anymore."

"More bravado bullshit," Margo said, shaking her head.

"Watch your back, Caine." Kimo no longer smiled. "Just watch your back. It wouldn't hurt a lot of people's feelings to know you're a candidate for a chalk outline, but Neolani seems fond of you, and from time to time you do manage to do some good. You should have known Chawlie would have dragged you into this. You told me you weren't involved. But you don't know how unsurprised I was when I came to your boat and found Mrs. Halliday." When I started to protest he shook his head. "You always know more than you say. With you it's never the other way around. Just do us both a favor next time and give me the straight story from the beginning."

"And you," he said, looking directly at Margo, his dark eyes heavy and serious, "be careful. A fellow's been making the rounds offering a contract for your head. It isn't an immediate problem because most of the contract-for-hire killers are undercover cops, but you need to know somebody's serious about killing you." He shifted his attention back to me. "It might be the same thing as your problem, come to think about it. The little guy doing the asking is an untouchable, a diplomat for the Colombian government."

"What did you guys do?" I knew Kimo would do something, let the buyer know somehow. Honolulu police are some of the toughest in the world, and they don't take crap from anybody, diplomatic passport or not.

"We shook him down at his hotel suite. It was a rough arrest. We used SWAT, a lot of action, a lot of shouting. Knocked the door down, threw him to the floor, put guns to his head, letting him think whatever he wanted to think. We shook him up pretty good, too, before we threw him out of the islands. But the truth is that if he knew he blanked here he could go somewhere else and hire somebody. There's plenty of assholes in Los Angeles willing to take out the lady for twenty thousand dollars."

"That much?"

"He was willing to pay premium for a simple hit. He wanted to get it done. That kind of money makes him a serious player." Kimo gave me The Look. It meant we both had a problem, and it involved professional hitters. It might be related to my problem, or it might not. Somewhere down at the core of my being I shuddered. Just a little shudder, barely perceptible. I could not imagine facing two teams of hitters. Not at my age.

"She says she saw two guys up at the restaurant earlier, the same two guys who tried to take her off the beach last night. Two Latin types. You think they might be Colombian?"

Kimo shrugged. "What difference does it make? You should know that your client is a target. And you are obviously a target. Whether or not it's the same people doesn't matter. As long as you two are headed for Kauai, you might as well say hi to Ed Alapai for me."

"You knew."

"As you said, it's a small island, Caine. And where else would you go?"

I nodded. Kimo was right. As usual. Ed would provide the added security of a guy with combat experience. He was not only a warrior, he was a blooded warrior, a Vietnam vet and a man with little patience for idiots and bullies.

Ed keeps a well-oiled M-14 in his house. A few years ago, after Hurricane *Iniki* devastated Kauai, the then-mayor of Kauai, fearing an outbreak of leptospirosis and other water-borne diseases because the purification plant could not function, thought it best for the inhabitants of that island to turn off all the water to the north shore. Apparently this Stanford-educated politician thought the people better off dying from dehydration in the intense post-hurricane heat than getting sick from tainted water.

After a day of bouncing off stone-headed bureaucrats and politicians, Ed took his rifle and walked thirteen miles into the mountains to the purification plant and ordered the manager to turn on the water again. Immediately. Ed told the man that the people there knew how to boil water, they weren't all yet ruined by a Mainland liberal arts education. The manager looked at the huge Hawaiian with the big rifle, swallowed hard, and the water flowed.

But Ed wasn't done. Shouldering his rifle, he hiked the rest of the way over the mountains to Barking Sands, the Navy missile base on the southwest corner of the island and some-how arranged for the Navy to donate a generator for the purification plant. He returned in grand style, perched in the open door of the helicopter with the generator dangling below. Once they got it cranked up, he walked home, a good day for him, and for the north-shore residents who had suffered enough from nature and needed no further suffering at the hands of the idiots in charge of the place.

I'd taken refuge at Ed's home before. It was one of the safest places I knew.

Kimo told us he would be watching our backs. The police had put out an airport alert for known hitters, or those who fit the profile, but he warned us to be vigilant.

"You're better off on Kauai right now," he said to Margo. "And Caine here will protect you."

He didn't say who would protect old John Caine.

"We'll leave in the morning," I said. "Tell Ed we're on our way."

"Why not tonight?"

"We'll be okay. The Navy's probably embarrassed enough that they'll be attentive. At least for tonight."

"I'll leave a couple of cars around until you shove off."

"Thank you."

Kimo gave me a huge smile, as if something had just occurred to him. "You're going to see Chawlie," he said.

"Thought I might pay him a visit."

"You want backup?"

"From a cop?"

He nodded. "No," he said, his face unreadable, but I thought I saw a little hurt. "I don't suppose you do."

W e spent the remainder of the afternoon getting ready while trying not to attract attention. Earlier, if Margo could be believed, there had been two bad boys up at the marina watching us. If they saw us buying provisions, filling the tanks, or shaking out loose gear, they might get their own boat and follow. *Olympia* wasn't a speedboat, nor was she suitable for a high-seas chase.

With no place to hide out there on the ocean's tabletop, a faster boat could take us easily.

When *Duchess,* my previous boat, sank, all but one of my guns sank with her. When I bought *Olympia* in California, my client there gave me all of her late husband's firearms, including some fine long guns fitted with scopes, world-class handmade shotguns, and an English-made Gibbs fifty-caliber, double-barreled elephant rifle neither the husband nor its current owner had ever fired, both of us a little afraid of the kick. I wasn't sure of the reach of those big old slugs, but within their range they would arrive with devastating force. I thought of it as a personal artillery piece.

All I could hope for would be to use the long rifles to keep any would-be pirate from getting too close while Margo got on the radio to the Coast Guard. It wasn't much of a plan, but it was something.

When the sun went down, once again enveloping Pearl Harbor in shadows, I dressed in black Levi's and a dark blue long-sleeved denim shirt. In place of my sandals, I wore highly polished steel-toed Redwing boots. My Buck knife was secured in a leather sheath on my belt. I looked like a construction worker out on the town, ready for anything—pleasure or trouble, either one or both.

"You're going to see Chawlie?" Margo appeared at my stateroom door as I was tucking in my shirt. I turned around and zipped my jeans before answering.

"You know I've got to."

"When will you be back?" Her acceptance amazed me. She knew I was going to see Chawlie specifically to talk about her, to learn the things she wouldn't tell me. Yet she made no protestations. It didn't make a lot of sense, but then little did about this woman. I wondered if I could understand her better once I'd spoken with Chawlie. If he was willing to talk with me.

If he hadn't been the money behind the hit.

That would be the big question of the evening. He'd done that before. But somehow I didn't believe it. Things had changed between the two of us. I had reason to believe he liked me.

Of course I also had to assume that he liked his son, Garrick, before he arranged to have him killed.

"Two or three hours."

"There are policemen here?"

"Two cars. They know I'm going. They'll watch you closely."

"Oh." She said it with such disappointment it made me wonder if she had planned on taking *Olympia* out by herself after I had gone. That could explain her lack of curiosity.

"Stay below. Read something. I don't have a TV, but there

are plenty of CDs and tapes. Or you could try to get some sleep."

She just looked at me, her face inscrutably blank.

"Or don't."

I took my old black day pack and slung it over one shoulder. If I ran into trouble, the Colt .45 Gold Cup and the extra magazines inside would provide some small comfort. I didn't like carrying loaded firearms. But until this thing shook out, I wasn't going anywhere unarmed.

The patrol cops waved to me as I went past them in the Jeep, drinking the strong Blue Mountain I'd perked for them, not wanting them to fall asleep on the job. I waved back, my pack beside me.

The fastest route to Chinatown from Pearl Harbor is the Nimitz Highway and I steered my old Jeep to the upper deck, getting off at Dillingham and negotiating the remaining streets toward the Nu'uanu Stream and River Street, where Chawlie kept his place.

The restaurant was crowded as I walked through the double glass doors. The old criminal was missing from his usual haunt in front of the place, just inside the entry, perched on an old plastic chair like some impoverished king surveying his meager domain. Gilbert, his newest favorite nephew, saw me enter and rushed to assist me.

"Mr. Caine, how nice to see you!" Young Gilbert had recently returned from Switzerland, where he had studied hotel and restaurant management. The word was that Chawlie would send him to Hong Kong as soon as his new hotel was completed there. Chawlie had expanded his holdings in the former British colony since the Communists took over. When questioned about it he smiles sheepishly and says he's not sure why people had rushed big money back into Hong Kong, but most likely it is because things didn't turn out as bad as everyone had feared.

"Your uncle here?"

"Yes, Mr. Caine, but, ah, he's entertaining private guests. I can't interrupt him. You know how he gets."

I dug the three emeralds from my pocket and surreptitiously placed them in Gilbert's hand, the way you'd slip a twenty to a recalcitrant maître d'. "Why don't you show him these. See what he says."

The young man looked at the jewels and instantly closed his hand over them.

"I'll be at the bar," I said, heading for the ornate gold-leaf-and-red-lacquered bar at the end of Chawlie's restaurant. Victor, the bartender, knows me well and had the Chardonnay poured before I sat down and pulled off the pack, letting it sit gently on the floor between my feet.

I took a sip of the Kendall-Jackson. Chawlie originally imported the brand into the islands solely for my consumption, but now he sells a lot of it. California tourists like it, the ones who find their way into Chinatown at night.

I knew what Gilbert meant when he referred to "private guests." Chawlie may be an older gentleman, but his sexual appetites rival those of any nineteen-year-old adolescent. I didn't know how long Gilbert would take to get up the courage to interrupt the old fellow who might be his uncle or might be his father, and I settled down to watch the other patrons in the restaurant. Some looked out of place. All Asians, some of them looked too tough and too hard to be tourists. Sitting in well-placed booths along the wall facing the entry were three tables of young toughs. Bodyguards, I thought. Chawlie's army. The gym bags on the banquettes next to them looked too heavy to hold soccer balls.

They watched as I sipped my Chardonnay and I watched them watching me, while we all waited. It wasn't clear if they knew me, but I felt their scrutiny with an intensity that nearly made me uncomfortable. Untutored, they should have known me and watched the doors. After a few moments I dismissed them as mere muscle, nothing more than fodder. If the hard times came, these boys would be the first to go. Chawlie's real protection would be elsewhere. It took me a few moments to find the real shooters, older men, stationed strategically to counter an attack.

It wasn't a long wait. Probably the only thing that Chawlie likes better than sex is money, possibly because he equates the two. At his age, given his proclivities, he might not get one without the other. The emeralds were a powerful calling card. Gilbert touched me on the arm, surprising me.

"Chawlie says you should come to his private quarters now, Mr. Caine."

I took the wine and my pack and followed Gilbert into the back room through the gold-leafed-and-red-lacquered circular doors that meant something positive in fêng shui, but I didn't know what.

Gilbert abandoned me at the door and I went inside alone, groping in the darkness. While my eyes adjusted I saw Chawlie lounging in the corner, supported on pillows, with two young beautiful Asian girls, one on either side, clothed in heavy silks. Neither of them yet twenty, they looked of a type, as if they had been chosen not only for their beauty, but also for their similarities. They were recent imports and kept their faces averted from the big haole who had entered the sacred, private room of their patron.

"So. You find Mrs. Halliday? Or she find you?"

"Somebody took a shot at me today, Chawlie. You know anything about that?"

"You are doing it again, Caine. Don't answer one question with another question. These stones. They belong to some unhappy people. How you get them?"

"My fee," I said. "Are they yours?"

"No. But could have been."

I waited for an explanation. When none came, I asked, "Who owned them?"

"Colombian bigwigs. Have done business with them for

years. Much trust. They trust me, I trust them. Margo was courier, coming to Hawaii to make exchange with me. She courier for her husband, very trusted. They liked her, liked her style, her looks. She tough lady. Then they came to trust her. Big mistake. She stole shipment meant for me. They don't know that. Now no trust for Chawlie, either."

"How much did they lose?"

His eyes smiled. "Many stones. Don't know exactly, but can guess. Normal shipment. Probably five million dollars' worth, retail. All Colombian emeralds. All cut, polished, faceted. Few inclusions. All the finest kind."

"She took them? Why did she come back to Hawaii?"

"She proud of herself. Came to me, told me what she had done, wanted me to front the money for her to get rid of them. I told her she one very stupid girl. They kill her, kill me, too, if I help. Told her to get out of the Islands soonest time."

"She went home and then what?"

"Don't know. Think she called her husband to protect her. Next day, day after that, whatever, he dead, she in jail, charged with crime. Soon, too soon to help, she out and disappear. She come to you, eh?"

"Yes. She came to me."

"And you say somebody shoot at you today?"

"Yeah. They'd been lying in wait for a couple of days, waiting to take the shot, as if they knew she'd come to me."

"They miss."

"They missed. Don't look so sad. They took off, but they'll be back."

"What you want from me?"

"Just the truth, Chawlie. Was it you?"

He studied my face for a long moment, his eyes carefully watching for signs only he could understand.

"What do you think?"

"You'd do it if you had a good reason."

"Maybe not even then, eh?"

I nodded, remembering. "There was no reason. We both lost something that time. And the man who killed your son is dead."

"You killed him good," Chawlie said softly, his thoughts far away. "And so," he said, his eyes coming back into focus, "you think I do it? Or not?"

"Not when you think you can still use me."

He barked a harsh, short, nervous laugh. "Some surprise, seeing these emeralds. I tell her the story of you stealing Thompson's diamonds. She was impressed. She also liked the way you break her husband's arm. You protecting her?"

"Trying to."

"Here." Chawlie handed me back my emeralds. "You say they your fee, you keep them. You earn them this time, you bet."

"Thanks, Chawlie. I'll earn them, you bet."

"You need anything, you tell Chawlie. He help old friend John Caine. For a fee."

I handed him back two of the emeralds. It was a hell of a fee, but worth it if I needed his resources.

He smiled. "You know how to do business. Not like some silly girl. She will use you like she used me, like she used husband, like she use everybody. Let her go if you are smart. She will find her own way in the world. If she wins, she wins. But she will not win. The others, they're bad people, worst bad people I know if angry." He shrugged. "Maybe she learn this time. Come back wiser next life. Not so greedy."

"I do need something. You still have the Glock?"

"Sure. Thought you didn't like it."

"Thought the extra firepower might come in handy."

"Sure." Chawlie said something in Mandarin and one of his girls got up and left the room. She was gone for only a few heartbeats and returned with the pistol, holding it carefully with two hands, as if it were something poisonous. I tucked it away in the day pack.

"Reach Gilbert at the front desk if you need anything else. He can take a message. Just don't make it complicated. He have to write it down. That's what they teach them these expensive schools. Write everything down. Record it. Get ready for lawsuit." He shook his head. "All his life I teach him *never* write it down. Four years they fill his head with crazy notions. I always tell him never write when you can speak; never speak when you can nod; never nod when you can wink. Now he write everything down! Put it in the log!" He sighed, clearly upset, clearly unsure what to do. "That all you wanted?"

I nodded again. I'd never considered the problems of second-generation hoodlums trying to go straight. The upheaval of the cultural clashes must be tremendous.

"Then good night, John Caine."

He looked longingly at the young women at his side. Our business was over. He wanted to get back to them.

"Good night, Chawlie." As I left I saw him present an emerald to each of the young women, almost like a party favor.

Hell of a party favor.

I left the restaurant carrying the pack over my shoulder and the remaining emerald in the pocket of my jeans, mindful of the stares of the second-stringers lining the wall. What I'd learned had been expensive, but worth the time and the money.

Of course the jewels weren't real money. They were mere baubles, pretty, but useful only in a funny kind of way, the way Chawlie had used them: party favors. Had I had a woman who loved them, it might have been different, but no such woman existed in my life and probably never would.

Barbara liked rubies, her birthstone. She liked their blood-red color, the way they glowed when the light hit them just so. She also liked diamonds. She—

I shook her picture from my mind. Some days it pays to daydream. With a price on the head of your client, on the day when you had been a moving, but lucky, target, and after watching your old friend hiding behind his private army and exhibiting fear of reprisal for something his one-time girl-friend had done (the same woman who now resided aboard your sailboat), it doesn't.

I climbed into my Jeep and headed home, the day pack on the seat beside me, its top unzipped, both pistols cocked, locked, and within easy reach.

I returned to *Olympia* and joined Margo in waiting for the sunrise. I had a great deal to say to the woman but held it, not wanting to spook her. She knew where I'd been and probably guessed what I knew, but thankfully she remained silent. It was a long wait, even though it spanned only a few hours. The woman cocooned herself in silence, curled up in a corner of the lounge surrounded by throw pillows, reading one of the James W. Hall novels I kept on board. I left her alone. Now that I knew the answers, there was no reason to push it, or her, any further.

While I waited I cleaned and oiled my firearms. All of them, the long guns and the handguns. I emptied the magazines, oiled and checked the tension on the springs, reassembled and reloaded them, the smell of Hoppe's No. 9 and gun oil permeating the cabin. When I had finished with the guns, I sharpened my knives.

We lingered below until we had our morning coffee, hiding out, half expecting trouble to arrive before the sun. But it was as peaceful as it was unsettling. And once the morning traffic thinned we went up on deck, looked around for our shadows like some bewildered groundhogs, and prepared to get under way.

I turned on the bilge blowers to rid the engine compartment of any residual fumes and checked the gauges. It wouldn't do to blow us up before we left the dock. Satisfied, I turned the key switch and the diesels ignited, vibrating the deck with a sensuous growl that traveled up my body from the soles of my bare feet, a powerful sound, like the purr of a large, contented jungle cat.

As the engines idled I jumped down to the dock, unhooked the utilities, and slipped the dock lines and *Olympia* floated free.

A small breeze pushed her against the mauka dock bumpers. I boarded and stowed the lines and took my position behind the wheel. Margo brought me another cup of coffee and we pushed away from the dock into Pearl Harbor.

Leaving the marina always has a holiday feeling for me, but this time the perception was more intense. The sun reflected brightly off the water and the breeze was a welcome buffer against the mid-morning heat. Margo and I were off on a trip to another island with no particular timetable and no particular agenda. We were not really refugees.

A stranger, one of those federal workers at Ford Island or a tourist at the *Arizona* Memorial, watching the big suntanned man and the pretty woman taking the sailboat out for a morning cruise, would have thought us lucky. He wouldn't know about the murder of the woman's husband, the theft of millions of dollars' worth of emeralds, or the beckoning strangers with guns hidden beneath their Aloha shirts, and he would not know that the woman was fleeing, the target of assassins. Even if he had heard about the shooting the day before, he might not make the connection.

For all that, or maybe because of it, it felt good to be out on the water again.

Once we cleared the narrow entrance to Pearl Harbor, Margo helped with the sails. When they were deployed we turned off the engine and let the canvas do the job.

I cherish that moment when the engine shuts down and the wind fills the mainsail and the boat catches a little bit, shuddering with the change of momentum—from being pushed by the stern to being pulled by the sails—and the gentle snapping and sighing of the canvas cleanses the ugly sound of the machinery from your ears. It's an ancient relationship, a sailboat and the sea, and I feel fortunate every time I take a sailboat out past the breakwater and let her do what she was designed to do. There's a freedom out here, something that people shackled to internal combustion engines and a work schedule seldom experience.

I set a course for Barbers Point. We'd pass that corner of Oahu and then point *Olympia*'s bow northwest toward Lihue, the major port on the east coast of Kauai. Beyond the reef, the whitecaps told me what kind of passage to expect.

"How long until we get there?" Margo was not a sailor and seemed to have the misgivings normal people do watching the only solid earth in the neighborhood retreating into the distance. She still hadn't mentioned my visit with Chawlie, and didn't look as if she was going to trespass on that particular subject unless I forced it.

That was one thing I wasn't going to do.

Not yet.

"Ten, twelve hours, depending on the wind. It's a long sail. You'd better brace yourself. It might get rough."

"I don't get seasick."

"There are two kinds of people in this world: those who have been and those who will be. Everyone gets seasick under the right conditions."

"Even you?"

I nodded. "Even me. With diesels going and a following wind, I'd almost guarantee it. Before it happened the first time I was always in the 'will be' group and didn't know it, but eventually it caught up with me. Now I'm a little more sympathetic to those in the 'have been' category. It's miserable, especially since you can't get over it until you're on dry land."

She blanched and I quickly changed the topic.

"We're taking a course the ancients took, heading directly to Kapaa, on the eastern shore. We might be able to see both Oahu and Kauai at the same time if the weather's clear. It's not like the Maui roads, where you can see three islands at once, but it's something, and we shouldn't get lost."

Her eyes widened.

"I didn't mean we'll get lost. It's difficult to do in these islands. I've done this once or twice, sailing between them. I can even find my way most of the time."

Margo didn't look convinced. "I even managed to get here from the Mainland. This very boat. I've got my Boy Scout compass right here, and I know how to use it. Honest."

"What can I do?"

I hadn't thought of that. There were plenty of books aboard, but reading on a small moving sailboat is recommended only for the heartiest of constitutions. The inner ear tells the brain that you're moving in subtle ways it doesn't think you are supposed to and sooner or later the stomach decides that your eyes have been lying to you and everything you've recently eaten is suddenly and violently urged to get out of the body by whatever means necessary.

"Not much," I said. "You can play some music, the CD player is rigged to speakers out here. Or you can just enjoy the sunshine." Or she could go forward and watch for any strange boats out there on an intersecting course. I thought that, but I didn't say it.

"Okay," Margo said, "I'll see what I can find," and she vanished below. I didn't need the music, preferring the sound of the sea rushing across the hull, but sometimes it's a pleasant background. Of course that depends on your taste. If she was into rap or heavy metal or even the whiny sounds of country singers, complaining about one thing or another, it would not be so wonderful. But I didn't have anything like that aboard and didn't worry. When the mellow Celtic strains of the Chieftains flowed from the mast-mounted speakers, I smiled. Maybe the woman did know a thing or two about taste.

Margo appeared in a brilliant yellow tank suit that showcased her generous body. I'd expected the briefest of bikinis, but this one exposed nothing while highlighting everything, a nice compromise. She grasped a towel and carefully headed toward the bow, moving from handhold to handhold, making sure she had a firm grip before letting go of her previous anchor. I watched her until she disappeared in front of the cabin structure. There's a good place up there in the bow, flat and sunny, but unprotected from the wind. The day was warm and I thought she'd last, enjoying the sunshine and the breezes, and she did, remaining for over an hour.

Thankful for the peace, I connected the wind-vane steering, kind of an automatic pilot for sailboats, and relaxed against some cushions piled against the fantail railing. The trade winds propelled us at close to our top speed, and we rode the tops of the waves as if they were hardly a ripple. *Olympia* ran like a greyhound.

We would sail through the morning and the afternoon, reaching Nawiliwili Harbor just after sunset. If Ed had a telephone I'd call him, but his little camp below Anahola Mountain, the same jagged green spire you see in the opening fade-in of *Raiders of the Lost Ark,* had no telephone. As I told Margo, Ed and his family lived rough. We'd have to rent a car in Lihue and drive up to his place. I knew Kimo could contact Ed and I wondered if he had told him we were coming, and then decided it didn't matter. Ed and his family would take us in no matter what.

I needed to get to him early, before Margo had a chance to upend this arrangement and do whatever it was she planned on doing. Now that I knew there were more emeralds. A lot more. And now that I knew she had stolen these jewels from some South American gentlemen, and that they knew it and were most unhappy with her.

Somewhere in the back of my mind I recalled the fact that coffee, cocaine, and emeralds came from Colombia. Blue-green, not the deep, dark forest-green of the Asian emeralds, Colombia emeralds were among the world's purest. And those gentlemen who plied the other major export, and I didn't mean coffee, were also heavily involved in the emerald trade, sometimes loading shipments of cocaine with emeralds and vice versa.

What the hell had this woman gotten herself into? Her ex-husband, quite the entrepreneur, must have had to augment his income with imports. Do business with them and eventually they'll own you. Steal from those macho muchachos and you're guaranteeing yourself a place in the cemetery. After a long, long time of intense personal suffering.

I slipped the gears in my head and gazed out across the waves toward Oahu and, beyond, somewhere far over the horizon, the western shore of the United States.

I found myself missing Barbara more and more as the days passed and wondered about giving up my useless boat-bum existence here, trading it for the good life with the good woman along the coast of California.

I examined the idea all the way around, looking at it from every angle. I'd have to wear shoes most of the year. The ocean there was cold and murky. There were few rainbows. On my last visit a biting, unforgiving wind blew down from the North Pole the entire time. I knew few people in northern California except Barbara, and as much as I cherished her company I wasn't certain I knew her well enough. And there were things she didn't know about me. Things I could never tell her.

Thirsty, I went below for a beer. I grabbed two from the cold locker, took dinner out of the freezer to thaw, and climbed up to the deck through the forward hatch.

Margo was lying on her stomach, minus the yellow suit, stretched atop the flat surface of the cabin roof. Thick auburn hair nearly obscured her face. The one visible brown eye widened when she saw my head emerge.

"Oops," she said.

"I'm gone," I said, dropping back out of sight. "I brought you a beer."

"Who's driving the boat?"

"Nobody. Want a beer?"

A disembodied arm reached down into the gloom of the stateroom. I put an opened bottle in the hand and it disappeared outside. I stood there for two quick heartbeats and then returned to my position by the wheel.

I remained in my place until she came clambering back, wrapped in yellow Spandex once again, making slow but certain progress along the deck rail. I wondered why she didn't go through the interior of the boat.

"I didn't think you could leave the wheel," she said.

"Well, there's nobody to run into out here."

She smiled. "Thanks for the beer. I was getting thirsty."

"It was only a mission of mercy. Believe me."

"How long now?"

"Are we there yet, Papa Smurf?" I said, my face deadpan. She laughed. "I guess it's like that. I lay out in the sun until I pinked and now what do I do? Are we there yet, Papa Smurf?"

"You can prepare lunch. I'm thawing some shrimp in the sink for dinner later on. We can have scampi tonight because we'll arrive a little too late for the restaurants, I think, once we're settled. You know how to vein shrimp?"

"Uh-huh. I can cook and I can clean and I even do windows."

I wasn't certain if she was serious. "I didn't mean it like that. I usually prepare my own meals."

"I didn't mean it like that, either. I'm happy to help. It's something to do."

"There's shuffleboard at two; and then there's a bingo tournament at five, be sure to bring your own buttons; and this evening in the lounge we're featuring Lola Liver and Her Three Spots, Just in from the Coast."

Margo made a face at me and went below and busied herself in the galley.

I listened to her rattling pots and pans and kept myself busy watching the horizon, looking behind us every few minutes to watch the last of my island as it traveled away from us. The tou tai, those ancient Tongan navigators who explored most of the South Pacific in tiny dugout canoes, imagined themselves on a stationary platform while the world moved around them, sort of a tou tai–centrist worldview, I suppose. They didn't sail toward something, they made it come to them. They didn't sail away from an island, they made it go away. I watched Oahu go away, verdant island in an azure sea decked with leis of pale clouds, and then searched the opposite horizon for the telltale V-shaped cloud formation that denoted an island mass below. Another navigator trick Ed Alapai taught me during my time of recuperation from wounds and sorrow. He taught me land-finding techniques that had been used on the Pacific for over a thousand years.

Olympia had about every modern electronic navigational aid available, but I wanted to use the old ways. The basics are not really difficult, once someone explains *their* basics, but the subtleties make all the difference and take a lifetime to master. I had once sailed from Mexico to Hawaii using only those ancient navigational arts Ed Alapai taught me, and even though the land mass of Kauai isn't readily visible from Oahu waters, you could almost pick out its location simply by watching the clouds. Like the ancient paddlers, I set my course for Kapaa, dead-center on the eastern flank of Kauai, and hoped for the best.

Margo brought lunch on paper plates and we ate in silence, aware of the vast gulf between us. I knew she wanted to ask me about my conversation with Chawlie, but she kept her questions to herself.

I pointed out a lone Laysan albatross, the gooney bird of Midway Island, as it skimmed across the surface of the water, heading for Oahu. She shrugged. I wondered if all she saw was a big white bird, looking something like a giant seagull, or if she thought about it at all. The more I learned about this woman, the less complicated she became. A thief, a former party girl who wanted something for herself. But if it was as Chawlie had suggested, that her ex-husband—the guy I'd stopped that night from firing a gun at her—had been killed trying to protect her, had, if you follow the logic, been killed as a direct result of her actions, things got more complicated.

There are abusers and there are enablers. I wondered what Margo had done, what buttons had been pushed in the drunken ex-husband to make him lose his temper. And if it had been a conscious decision that went wrong.

I've never hit a woman in anger. No matter what buttons are pushed, it would not be possible to bring me to anger by mere words. But there are men who, especially when they've been drinking, do not have the center to reach for when they're tantalized by an enabling partner. I don't know much about spousal abuse, other than what I've seen, but I do know that after the first time it's a dance between two willing partners, both responsible, the woman responsible sometimes solely by her continued presence.

That brought Karen Graham to mind. She didn't look like a button pusher, but she wanted to keep the marriage together, and that could have been her responsibility for the abuse. Billy wasn't worth the effort. The moment he first hit her she should have been out the door, taking her child and never looking back. By her act of remaining with him, continuing to believe she could change him with her good heart, she enabled him to do it again.

I hoped Neolani and Tutu Mae could show her how a real family operated.

I pointed out the cloud formations floating over Kauai's peaks, dead ahead of *Olympia*'s bow. Margo went below and left me alone after that, unwilling to endure more nature lessons.

I was grateful for the peace and tranquillity.

Olympia sailed through a golden afternoon and when the sun began to sink toward the curving horizon, the seas calmed and the wind transformed into warm gentle breezes that filled the sails but didn't bite exposed flesh. No clouds littered a mango-colored sky. Conditions looked about right.

"Margo! Come on up. I want you to see something."

She stuck her head out of the cabin. "What?"

"Have you ever seen the green flash?"

"What is that?" She came up on deck and sat across from me on the cushions.

"Watch the sunset. Sometimes when it goes down out here, the very last microsecond, just before it disappears below the horizon, you might see a brilliant emerald-green flash. Just a small one, and only for a tiny moment, but it's worth it. Watch."

The ball of fire slid steadily into the ocean out beyond the edge of the world. It looked so close, you almost expected steam. Its descent seemed to increase after it was halfway down and in just a few heartbeats it nearly vanished. And then it was gone.

"What?" Margo demanded, blinking her eyes. The only color had been a blinding yellow-white. "I didn't see anything."

"Well, it doesn't always happen," I said, "but it was a fine sunset, anyway."

"Whatever. Dinner is almost ready." She went below,

clearly annoyed, leaving me with a pale yellow sky, an after-sunset fugue. I didn't move, remaining on the fantail, watching the last of the sunset until its glory was spent and night claimed another day.

They're rare, those green flashes. I was ten years old when I read about them for the first time in one of my father's *Reader's Digest*s. I spent the next thirty years looking for one. I've only seen three in my life. I don't know the conditions that create them, so I just watch and hope. As I do with so many other things.

It didn't matter. The sunset was a glorious one, although sunsets always make me sad. One more fine day gone. One day less to enjoy our allotment. If Margo was smart, she'd take notice, too, and appreciate every one that was given her. There were contract killers after her. That kind of thing tends to limit the time allowed us here.

I strained to see ahead and made out the dark gray coast of Kauai approaching through the gathering dusk. *Olympia* had made good time, but we still had a few miles to go to reach Nawiliwili Harbor.

I was about to announce our impending arrival when I happened to glance back at the fading sunset and saw the boat behind us. It wasn't a fishing boat, and it didn't look like a pleasure craft out for a day cruise. Although it was still too far away to see who was aboard, it bore down on us in a steadfast, intersecting course I found menacing.

It looked as if our pursuers might have caught up with us after all.

15

The boat ran without lights, a dangerous endeavor. With night rapidly approaching, the craft would be invisible to other vessels. There are reasons why some people leave their lights off, but none are legal. It could be a smuggler, its course mere coincidence. Hawaii suffers a plague of overloaded smuggler boats that attempt to bring their hopeful human cargo to the United States through these islands. Most are caught by the Coasties, but enough get through, especially the smaller craft, and this might be one of those, loaded with brave unfortunates from one war-torn Asian nation or another, bound for a better life on the Golden Mountain.

Because the boat acted strangely I kept my eye on it, tracking its movement across the water. It soon became apparent it wasn't a smuggler. It moved across the surface of the ocean in a vector toward *Olympia* as we neared the Kauai coast. A desperate smuggler would not sail toward another boat. He would avoid it and head for the closest landfall to dump his load, and then rocket back out to sea if he didn't join his passengers in a flight of his own.

I checked our relative positions and calculated that if we did not alter course, the darkened boat would intersect ours within the next fifteen to twenty minutes. This guy could have been an innocent, but because of the shot already fired across my bow in the parking lot of the marina, the ominous warning from Kimo, and the way the boat was acting, my already outsized case of paranoia had grown to the point where I had to take some action.

I turned the bow into the wind and the sails deflated, the canvas luffing and snapping, complaining of misuse.

"Margo!"

She appeared at the lounge hatch, dressed now in a baby-blue cable-knit sweater and stone-washed jeans.

"I'm going to need some help up here. We're dropping the sails."

Even though I didn't completely trust the woman, the one thing I did like about her was her not questioning everything I asked her to do. While I secured the wheel, she helped me lower the mainsail and tie it to the boom. We did the same with the mizzen. In less than five minutes we had them all down and gathered, not a record time, but for a green crew in the last hours of daylight, it wasn't bad, either.

"I'm going to act like a motorboat now," I told her, revving the big diesels and running straight toward shore.

"Okay."

"There's a boat way out there, you can barely see him. That way." I pointed while she squinted into the distance. "He's coming directly at us, running a course straight from Oahu."

I waited for a reaction, but she didn't say anything. I think she waited for me to tell her more.

"If they're looking for us, they'll be looking for a sailboat. We have our sails down, but we still look like a sailboat." I pointed up the main mast toward the two running lights atop the spreaders, the green one and the red one. They were sixty feet up. Somebody had to turn them off. "Can you hold the wheel while I go up there?"

She nodded, her eyes widening.

"Just point the bow at that big light over there." I consulted my chart. "It's a hotel, and there's a rocky beach below it. I'll be down before we hit the rocks, but there's deep water under our keel for at least twenty minutes. You understand what you're supposed to do?"

"Just keep the boat pointed that way, toward that white light."

"Great." I retrieved the bos'n's chair and a pair of electrician's pliers from the tool locker and rigged the chair to the main mast. It wasn't something I wanted to do, but I had no separate switches for the mast lights. I'd never thought of it before, but as I cinched myself into the bos'n's chair and started the long, swinging climb to the top of the main mast, the hull below getting smaller and smaller in the dark, putting them on a separate switch went right to the top of my list of things to do the next time I had the chance.

Simple physics usually doesn't bother me because I accept its laws without question. I understand the law of gravity. I can comprehend inertia. I once even took a long, hard look at relativity and have an insubstantial grasp of what that means. But the principle that affected me while atop that slender pole was the one that says the farther you are away from the fulcrum the more distance you travel in an arc. I forgot what they call it, but I sure had it explained to me in painful detail.

The ratios are hazy, but even a tiny motion at the level of the hull is amplified when it reaches the top of an eighty-foot mast. I wasn't at the top, but close enough to appreciate that a one-foot change at the bottom of the mast translated into an eight-foot swing in both directions, about sixteen feet, total. And climbing a mast aboard a small boat on the open ocean in the middle of the night can be a white-knuckler of monstrous proportions.

Grabbing the mast helped prevent me from dizzily swinging off into space, arcing out over the white-tipped waves and then ramming into the oak on my return, like inept horizontal bungee jumping. My hands were wet and I slipped once or twice, making the round trip more times than I wished. It took some serious concentration but I finally got it done, wrapping my legs around the mast, turning off the spreader lights while leaving the hull lights, and I gratefully slid down the mast to the relatively stable platform of the hull.

Now we were a motorboat.

"You sure took your time up there," Margo said.

"Turn the wheel that way," I said, pointing toward the east, away from Kauai and the other boat, toward the open ocean.

"They saw us."

"Okay. They saw us before. We don't know they're really looking for us. That was just in case."

"They're coming."

I looked. Sure enough, they were coming much faster, as if they had not been certain before, but now knew exactly what their goals were. Most likely my little inspired trick of turning us into a motorboat had confirmed their suspicions. First you have a mast, then you don't. What else would they be expected to do but check it out?

Brilliant. I'd been brilliant. All they had seen was a sailboat. They'd probably sighted dozens between Oahu and Kauai. I'd given them a reason to come looking.

"Keep the bow pointed that way," I said. "I'll be right back."

"What are you going to do?"

I went below to the gun safe and loaded the 7-mm magnum Remington ADL and the .505 Gibbs, the elephant rifle, took every box of ammunition I had for the two guns, and returned to the deck. Margo's eyes widened when the saw the weapons. I handed her a pair of noise-reducing earmuffs. A rifle makes a punishing noise. If I had to open fire with the elephant cannon, the noise would be deafening.

"Cover your ears," I told her, sticking my earplugs deep

into my own ears. Some people can shoot with muffs, but I'm not one of those. "We can still hear each other if we speak loudly enough, and it will save you some pain later on."

I set up on the deck over the main cabin, inside the dinghy, using its transom as a shooting rest. It's as stable there as any-place aboard, and my line of sight was better.

On our current course we rode the swells easily, and it wasn't difficult to get a good sight picture while we were on the crest.

Not knowing the effective range of the Gibbs, I slung the big rifle across my back, choosing the 7-mm Remington as my primary weapon because I knew its capabilities and limitations. The darkened boat was still out of range, but its speed was greater than ours and it was only a matter of time before I would be able to make out faces through the scope. Even in the dark, even without lights, I could track it by the green phosphorescence churned up by its bow wake.

It wasn't long before things started getting interesting.

Their running lights flashed and a spotlight flared, reaching out for *Olympia*, not illuminating us, but coming close, blanketing the tops of the waves with a field of white light. I moved the scope away from the glare of the spotlight and confirmed their intentions.

Lights came on in an interior cabin, revealing two men readying submachine guns, loading long, curved magazines into the bodies of short, black weapons that looked like Skorpions. Small, dark men with enormous mustaches, they worked on the guns with some difficulty, bracing themselves against a table, as if they weren't accustomed to a deck rolling beneath their feet. Two more men joined them in the preparations. They all looked ready to go to a party, not to commit murder, dressed as they were in bright, colorful shirts of wild fuchsias and greens and oranges in geometric patterns; not Aloha shirts, but tropical clothing from the Caribbean. Each man wore a heavy gold watch too big for his wrist.

Getting your first look at the enemy is always a memorable event. If they're not in the act of killing you, or just about to, and it's not your very last look at this world, too, it's instructive. Were these the guys who took the shot at me? They didn't meet the image I'd created for the shooter. They didn't look like ex-military sniper types. There was little discipline in view. They didn't have the look of men who would patiently sit in mosquito-and centipede-infested tropical vegetation for two to three days waiting for the perfect shot. Men like these wouldn't venture much past the paved road. They looked deadly, but only on their own turf.

"Come on, man!" The little fellow in my head, the one who is supposed to keep me out of trouble, begged me to listen to him. "Take the shot!"

It would have been easy. I centered the crosshairs on the chest of one of the men in the cabin and then crawled the sights across to the next man, squeezing a little on the trigger each time I acquired a target. Both men could have been dead before their next breath. I moved the sights to the bridge. It was black inside, except for the orange glow of a fat cigar, a steady beacon behind the glass, a real target. If there was shooting to be done, this would be my first target. The one on the bridge probably knew what he was doing. The others might be helpless out here on the ocean, floating around in the dark, and might forget about us, more intent on their own survival.

Maybe, maybe not, but if somebody else came up to the bridge and looked as if he knew what he was doing, I'd shoot him, too. I scoped the length of the boat again, finding armed men everywhere. I lost count at nine, but there could have been more. And that didn't count the cigar smoker on the bridge. When the shooting started he no longer counted because he was dead. He just didn't know it yet.

Everyone seemed to be armed with those Skorpions, a Czech submachine gun and a fine weapon that could produce a huge amount of firepower but used a pistol cartridge and had little range. I looked for long guns but didn't see any. That didn't mean they didn't have any, but so far it looked as if they had the speed and the maneuverability, but I had the range, and therefore the advantage.

They were on a course that would bring them alongside of us within the next five to ten minutes, and they looked as if they intended us harm, but that wasn't sufficient for me to take their lives. Maybe I'm getting soft and sentimental in my old age, but I wasn't about to start this thing without absolute provocation. Too many things can go wrong in a gunfight. If I could prevent one we'd all be better off.

The problem was I just didn't know how to get away with it.

"John!"

I took my eye from the rifle's scope and glanced down at Margo. She pointed at something ahead of us. I turned and saw a car barge dead ahead, one of those four-story inter-island barges towed by an oceangoing tug. It wasn't difficult to spot, about the size and shape of a mid-rise office building, lights burning over its vast frame, and it was headed directly at us. I wondered why I hadn't seen it before. I turned the rifle on the barge and found my answer. It had just emerged from a bank of fog. So intent had I been on the pursuing boatload of assassins, I hadn't looked ahead to see where we were going. That had been Margo's job and she had done it well. I realized I'd trusted her because there had been no one else, and she hadn't let either one of us down.

"Head toward the barge! Just behind it!" I motioned with the rifle barrel.

"Behind it?"

"Right there!" I pointed again, to a point twenty to thirty feet behind the mammoth barge.

She nodded grimly and turned the wheel.

I might get by without shooting anyone this night.

I looked back. The boatload of pirates—I had no reason to think of them as such, but I had no reason to think of them otherwise—had gained on us. Because of the oblique angle of our opposing courses, *Olympia* just might elude them by slipping into the fog just behind the barge if we put on a little more speed. The Colombians would have to go around the other side. By the time they reached the fog we'd be gone.

The tug blew a long warning blast, perhaps thinking we were on a collision course.

We were.

Olympia came off course a few degrees.

"Don't worry about the barge. Keep it tight!" If she didn't keep it close, they would be on us.

She looked at me, dark eyes shining, and nodded, turning the wheel slightly to keep our courses converging. The tug's warning sounded again.

The pirates came closer. Through my scope I could nearly count the hairs in their mustaches. It would have been so easy to kill two or three before slipping away, but now we had witnesses. That helped keep the dogs of war leashed, giving me mixed emotions. I didn't want to kill anyone, but if this didn't work we would have used up our only advantage, our superior range. Once they got close they'd have all the advantage. The tug wasn't really a help unless we used it correctly. Without it, without witnesses, I could have kept them at an adequate distance, the long reach of the 7-mm magnum an iron-clad guarantee they would not approach.

It was a mixed blessing, this barge. Waste this opportunity and we were dead. What I feared was that the barge would prevent me from taking action when I needed to and then disappear when the pirates were close enough to do damage with those deadly short-range guns.

The tugboat's mournful wail sounded again, but this time much closer. The tug's captain, maybe deciding we were trying to ram him in some suicidal charge, changed course, heading toward the motor vessel. It made sense. The motor yacht would have more time to change direction than the closer craft.

I looked back.

The pirate boat turned to avoid being run down by the tug and barge. It looked as if we might make it.

I dropped down into the cockpit, stowed the rifles in a dry corner, and took the wheel from Margo.

Her hands shook as she took them from the wooden spokes, her knuckles white, her face a pasty gray color. She wouldn't look at me, and said nothing when she relinquished her position. I lost sight of her for a moment and found her curled on the cushions, her back toward me.

And as we passed the huge floating city with only a few feet to spare, gliding into the dense fog beyond, I noticed that my hands shook, too.

16

The fog bank was dense but not deep, like a small stray cloud floating atop the ocean's surface. We were no sooner enveloped in the thick gray mist when we broke through the other side and the lights of Nawiliwili Harbor appeared again in the distance. More patches of fog lay ahead, huge amorphous ghosts, specters of the immense gray wall stretching across the horizon to the northeast. It looked as if we had passed through a finger of the encroaching fog.

I gunned *Olympia's* engines, hoping to put as much distance as possible between us and the pirates before they blundered out of the finger of fog behind us.

Lihue lay some eight to ten miles away. It was difficult to know exactly where we were in the dark, but some of the lights along the shore matched remembered landmarks. The charts would give me a general notion; GPS an exact one, but I didn't have the time to check either of them. Lihue's brilliant glow was a beacon ahead and confirmation enough. There's nothing else like that small city on any of Kauai's coasts.

"Margo."

Curled in a fetal position on the cushions, her head buried in her hands, she didn't respond.

"Margo!"

"I don't care what you want; I won't do it."

"If you don't help you might as well cut your own wrists and jump overboard. You're shark bait either way."

She rolled over and looked at me, her eyes resentful, as if I were the one who had caused the pirate ship to follow, as if I were the one who had stolen the Colombian emeralds. "What?"

"Take the wheel."

"What are you going to do, climb the mast again? Run us aground? Get us run over by a freighter this time?"

"Head for the fog bank. Take the boat just inside the fog. *Just* inside." I wanted to see the pirates and do what had to be done and still have a back door for escape. The fog bank provided us a chance to hit and run like a stealth bomber. We weren't fast, but we could be smart.

Margo looked ahead at the gray wall and then back at me, staring uncomprehendingly.

"They're still behind us. The boat will be out this side any moment. When they see us, they'll shoot." I tried to gauge the distance between the roiling gray wall behind us and the curtain ahead, but it was impossible. It looked to be no more than a hundred yards back. If their lights still burned, it was an easy shot for the rifle, but well within the range of their guns, too. They wouldn't be accurate but didn't have to be. Spray enough bullets around, they'd be bound to get lucky.

"You're going to kill them."

"I'm going to make certain we're going to live."

She looked behind us once more. Nothing existed but the wall of fog, no ghost ship emerged from the mist, no specter pursued us. Overhead, stars twinkled in the same brilliant canopy that had graced these waters for thousands of years, a peaceful, familiar collection of flashing jewels in the velvet sky. Night was full upon us, a warm benign tropical evening with cool trade winds, signifying a welcome turn in the weather.

I picked up the Remington and checked the load.

"You're going to kill them."

"I mean no harm," I said. "If there's shooting, they'll start it. Wait and see. They mean everybody harm. Cut hard to starboard, you're getting close to the fog." The lie came easily, probably because it wasn't really a lie.

She did as I asked, slipping *Olympia*'s black hull within the fog, but I could almost smell her fear as I passed her. I shut off our running lights and climbed onto the roof of the cabin, where I settled behind the improvised bench rest. I wished I had a Starlight scope, or whatever low-light image-enhancement equipment they're using these days, but the pirates didn't seem shy and had their lights burning as they came at us before. And then there was the captain with that fat cigar, my primary target.

I might be able to take out only one. If I managed to take out the captain, the risk would be worth it.

I checked and double-checked the sight picture in the scope and watched and waited.

It wasn't a long wait. The pirate craft slowly emerged from the fog, as if the captain had been feeling his way along just as we had done before him, afraid to find another one of those huge car barges in the cotton mist.

They came on ready for a fight. No lights burned, nothing moved on deck. They were dogged down and stripped for action. I sensed a purpose about the craft that hadn't been there before. I scoped the windows of the wheelhouse. Whoever was in the wheelhouse had doused the cigar. I saw nothing but flat black glass, a yawning maw against the white super-structure.

The brightest thing about the boat was its churning wake, a pale phosphorescent green at the bow defining its passage. The glowing microbes in the aggravated water looked angry, and I watched as the boat picked up speed.

Trying to recall the exact spot where the cigar had been,

cursing myself that I hadn't taken more careful notice earlier, I guessed, picking a spot about a foot above the sill, laying the crosshairs over what I imagined was the target. I took a breath and held it, gently squeezing the trigger, my whole hand closing on the walnut stock and the trigger mechanism as if I were the most gentle lover in the world, steadily increasing pressure slowly while devoting my full concentration to holding the sight picture absolutely steady.

The rifle fired.

The barrel kicked and my hands worked automatically in perfect synchronism to eject the spent cartridge case and feed the second round into the chamber. Controlling the weapon again, I found the target and sent another boat-tailed bullet into the wheelhouse, punching a hole a couple of inches lower than the first. Reloading a third time, I fired once more, and the entire sheet of tempered safety glass imploded.

"Turn starboard! Right! That way!" I shouted at Margo, directing her deeper into the fog, pointing with my arm to make certain she understood.

She spun the wheel and *Olympia* disappeared into the mist.

I slid down into the cockpit and shoved her toward the hatch. "Get below and get down, as low as possible," I ordered, taking the wheel, spinning it, changing course again, trying to disappear. "Get below the waterline if you can!"

The response, I knew, was only moments away.

I changed course again, zigzagging through fog.

Margo disappeared into the cabin as the first return fire arced through the air. I goosed the throttle.

Olympia gave me all the power her diesel engine could provide. Stern-to, we presented a smaller target, but she's a big boat with a lot of freeboard. Another volley of gunfire scattered through the air around us, splashing close to *Olympia*'s hull. A third passed harmlessly overhead, zinging through the rigging.

I altered course and motored us right into the fourth burst, bullets chewing into the cabin superstructure, shattering a porthole and bouncing around inside the galley, caroming off stainless steel. I hoped Margo had had sense enough to keep her head down. I huddled as low as I could, stuffed inside the cockpit's footwell, trying to keep my head down and still be able to see something and keep my hands on the wheel, a losing compromise.

Most of the final assault splashed harmlessly into the water behind us, but one lucky round, perhaps loaded a little hotter than the others, splintered a spoke in the wheel near my hand, stinging me. At first I thought I'd been hit directly, then saw the long slender oak dagger lodged in my left hand, protruding through the fleshy web between the thumb and the forefinger.

I yanked it out and thick blood welled. I took a rag from the cockpit toolbox and wrapped it around the wound, gently moving my fingers and thumb as I did, marveling that the tendons, blood vessels and bones had all escaped injury. Both lucky and unlucky, the wound would swell my hand and cause me some pain, but would do no permanent damage. It would limit my activities for a few days, but I'd suffered wounds before and knew how to deal with them. Once the initial shock of the injury is over, you take care of it as best you can and get on with your life. This one had carved a hole through my hand I could almost see through, but the wound would close and I would have only another scar as a souvenir.

"Margo!" I shouted. "You okay?" I kept low, mindful of the boatload of angry assassins, or whatever, behind us.

"You bastard!"

"Stay down. It's not over."

"You're goddamned right it's not over!" She appeared at the hatchway, crouching low, as if she'd gone through a course in combat survival. I smiled. In a way, she had.

"What are you laughing at? I nearly got shot!"

I chuckled, which was the wrong thing to do. She came

scrambling out of the cabin like a scalded cat, slamming into me with her shoulder, pummeling me with fists and elbows, knees and feet.

She bit my ear, pulled my hair, scratched me with her nails, struck with her fists and kicked with her feet. I have fought men and women before, in singles and multiples—even fought one-handed—but this was an entirely new experience. I didn't want to hurt her and was doing my best just to keep her fended off so she wouldn't beat the living daylights out of me.

"Prick . . . bastard . . . jerk . . ." She panted an obscene mantra while she attacked me.

She kicked me on the point of the chin so hard the world went black for a few moments. Before I recovered, she boxed my ears, tore a flap of skin from my cheekbone and viciously punched me across the face, altering the alignment of my nose.

—"Fucking man!"

Off-balance, with her full weight on my chest, I couldn't use any of the esoteric martial arts I knew so well without really hurting her. Unwilling to cause her pain, I relented, allowing her to vent her wrath.

"Think you're so smart!"

There was more to this assault than simple anger at John Caine for starting a minor shooting war. I had become a symbol. And I couldn't do anything about it while she was beating on me. And short of killing her or knocking her unconscious, the only way to end the fight was to surrender, as a symbol or as a single example of what she fought.

"Uncle!" I said, extending my arms out from my side, palms up. She hit me twice before she realized what I'd done.

She stopped and drew back, panting, leaning against the cabin bulkhead, her chest heaving. We spent a long minute staring at each other. It was an intensely sexual moment. I felt the heat rise from her and was astonished to discover I was hard, my penis twisting painfully inside the bunched folds of my shorts. And this for a woman for whom I had no feelings other than distrust.

Sometimes it's difficult being a man.

"You're bleeding," she said, her heat vanishing like a soap bubble in a rosebush.

"Not surprising," I said, wiping the blood from my nose and feeling a couple of loose teeth. It would take a while for me to forget that moment, even though I'd already started to go soft, my body coming back to reality.

"Were you shot?"

"Just a splinter." I told her where to find the hydrogen peroxide and the bandages to replace the dirty, bloody rag on my hand, a raging systemic infection something I could ill afford, what with having just shot up the neighborhood.

"Macho asshole," she said, easing back into the cabin. "You're just trying to regain some dignity. You're acting tough because I beat you up."

"Yeah," I admitted, "that's probably right." It could have been a humbling experience had I only understood what had happened. At the moment, however, I was still trying to put everything together.

She snorted and disappeared below, leaving me pierced and pummeled and bleeding, looking over my shoulder and wondering what the hell was going to happen next.

L et me see your hand." Margo extended her own, a peace offering.

"You won't hit me again?" I said, trying to hide the grin. This woman had more grit than I thought. She'd have to, robbing the people she'd robbed, knowing the penalties if caught.

"No," she said. "I won't."

After wrapping my damaged hand in clean bandages and caring for the ripped skin over my cheekbone, Margo spent the rest of the night below, abandoning herself to fate and the questionable abilities of one John Caine, a fellow she had so recently and soundly trounced in hand-to-hand combat.

We were both lucky. I spent the night keeping *Olympia* inside the fog bank, away from other craft, friendly or unfriendly. Running without lights, we weren't run over or fired upon, and we didn't run aground or sink. And we saw nothing more of the pirates. When the sun came up and the fog burned off we found ourselves dead on target, about two miles off Kapaa, some six miles north of Lihue, *Olympia* running on a heading away from the big city, up toward the north shore.

The morning sea was a glassy lake. Hardly a swell disturbed its mirrored surface. The peak of Mount Waialeale was visible, a rare occurrence. Emerald slopes of grassy foothills rose away from the blue Pacific like carefully arranged folds of velvet. Along the rocky coastline tiny cars and trucks rolled along with self-appointed purpose. The Garden Isle, a place I'd come to know as sanctuary, looked peaceful in the clean clear morning light. I prayed I had not come here this time bringing the world's chaos and Margo's demons along with me.

"Let me see your hand. I promise I won't hurt you."

I held it out to her. Overnight the offended flesh had swollen to half the size of a catcher's mitt. There was some pain, but not enough to complain about, the throbbing getting worse when I raised my arm above my head, better when I kept it lower than my waist.

"That looks bad. A doctor should take a look at it."

"Maybe. When you're safe."

"Oh, it's just a scratch, huh? Are you being macho again? That arrow through your shoulder? Pour whiskey on it from a broken bottle and keep on fighting off the Indians one-handed? I saw that movie. I thought it stunk."

"It doesn't hurt much. I'm all right."

"My god, Caine, you're serious." She looked at me, her eyes squinting into the bright sunlight. It was the first time I'd ever seen her in real concentration. "I thought about it all last night when I was alone. Things have changed. I have changed. You scared me. They scared me. Those men, they're after me, they want to kill me, but I don't care. Not anymore. I was afraid of them. Hell, I used to be frightened of everything. But after last night, after we were shot at and nearly run down by that, whatever it was, that huge *thing* out there, I just don't think anything could scare me again."

"Now who's being macho?"

"You know better." She unwrapped the bandages and poked at the lacerations. The teak splinter had carved a narrow channel through the web between my thumb and forefinger, swollen flesh pulling the skin so tightly it looked polished. Margo poured more disinfectant into the V-shaped cut and watched it bubble.

"You know what I'm talking about. I don't think you are ever frightened. You seem like you're always having a grand time, like it's all some cosmic joke, even when you're about to be crushed by some floating island bearing down on you from out of nowhere. Even when you've been shot. You were so—I don't know—so intense last night. So *fixed*. You had death in your eyes. You should have seen your face. I would hate to have been those men in that boat. They never would have survived."

"Don't admire."

"Oh, I don't. I couldn't. I've never killed anyone. I don't think I could . . . take the life of another human being. Even at the final moment, if it was them or me, if it came down to that, I still don't think I could do it." She looked at me, studying my face. "But you could. Without a second thought. I saw it last night. For all I know you did kill someone with that rifle. I don't know. I don't want to know. You scared me more than they did."

"Then why?"

"Why did I steal those emeralds?"

I nodded.

She sighed, letting her emotions subside with her breath, her shoulders slouching in resignation. "I knew this might happen. They, the ones I took the marbles from, they demand and expect total obedience. Always. It was unthinkable, what I did. Somehow, I thought I could avoid it."

She brushed the hair from her eyes. "But I was so tired of always being some *thing*, somebody's wife, or somebody's girl-friend or somebody's mistress. I had fun, but I was always dependent. I hated that, always looking to the man for all of my needs. I have dreams of my own. I'm not just some blow-up doll that a man can use and then deflate and put away until the next time." She finished disinfecting the wound and wrapped my hand again. There was little pain.

"That's the way I felt. No matter what gifts I was given, no matter what money I had, it was never enough. My lifestyle, the things I had, were expensive to keep up. Then, suddenly, I had enough right in my hands. It was enough for forever."

"Forever isn't very long if they send out a boatload of people to kill you."

"It's long enough. You'll get me out of this." She said it with such conviction I wanted to tell her she'd put her faith in someone with feet of clay. I was not a basket any woman could put all her eggs in.

"And another thing, Mr. Caine. You've seen me naked twice and you've never laid a hand on me. I want to thank you for that."

"My pleasure."

She smiled. "A woman wants to know she's desirable. It's important for her ego. But you seem to have some sixth sense. You treat me well, I have no complaints, but you keep me at arm's length. I don't know how you feel about me, except I know I'm not desirable to you."

When I started to speak she said, "Hush. That's not a bad thing. Not for this old party girl. I'm retired now. I don't want a man pawing at me. I'll be the one to decide when and where from now on, and I really needed the breather. And it makes me feel safer when you're around."

"What about Chawlie?"

"I won't talk about Chawlie with you. You're too good of a friend to him. The man loves you like a son, you know. He's very proud of you."

"Me?"

"Of course. He sees a lot of himself in you. And he trusts you as he trusts no one else."

"He wanted to kill me once."

"He told me all about it. He knew he was wrong at the

time, but the way he explained it, it was a cultural thing. He said you talked him out of it."

I laughed, remembering that golden afternoon, sitting in his restaurant with my back to the door waiting to see if he would send someone to kill me. "Yeah, in a way I did."

"And he was grateful for it. For everything you did."

"Not everything."

"He said that, too, but he knew what he was doing."

Chawlie had apparently unburdened himself on this woman. It was uncharacteristic, but it's the kind of thing you would only do with someone you trust, with someone who also has the intelligence to understand the demons you are trying to exorcise. I'd never thought of Margo as that kind of woman, but I had not looked closely. I almost apologized for underestimating her.

"It's nice, you know," she said.

"What?"

"Being with a man who doesn't want to bed me. I feel as if you even think of me as a person, not just a woman."

"*Just* a woman?"

"You know what I mean."

I nodded, feeling slightly guilty. I'd thought of her as a ditz, and a crooked one at that. I didn't trust her. Not even a little. She had used Chawlie, used her husband, even now was trying to use me.

"You have someone?"

"I do. She's in San Francisco. She won't live here and I won't live there, so she flies over here when she can get away, or I fly over there and stay until I get tired of all the people and the chill and the winds, or she gets tired of me and sends me home."

"It sounds ideal. Bring the man to me, then banish him when he bores me."

"She wants me to move there. I'm thinking about it."

"But you won't."

"Now we all know that."

"You're afraid you'll lose her."

"It's crossed my mind."

"Depends on what she wants." Margo watched a big white-and-black Laysan albatross wing toward the island, returning from a long-range expedition hunting for food far out at sea. "That's another big seagull."

"Albatross. There are no seagulls in Hawaii."

"Really? An albatross? Like 'The Rime of the Ancient Mariner'? Water, water all around, and all that?"

"I'm the ancient mariner."

"Hardly." She eyed me. "Pretty good shape for an old man. Makes me wonder about you. If I wasn't retired, and if you weren't otherwise occupied." She let her eyes wander, and I got a reminder of the same sexual pull I'd experienced the night before, only this time she didn't have to hit me to get my reptile brain breathing heavy. "Hey, where are we going?"

"Hanalei Bay. I've changed my mind since those pirates showed up last night."

"Pirates?"

"That's the way I think of them. All they needed was a Jolly Roger and a couple of cutlasses and they'd have been all set. The original plan was to dock at Nawiliwili, but that's compromised now. Most likely they will be there. We're better off in a smaller harbor or a bay. It can be rough on the north shore this time of year, but *Olympia* will do just fine there. I can get you ashore."

"You know what you're doing."

"Wish I did."

She smiled. "How's the hand?"

"Fine. Swelling will go down in a few days. I heal good."

"You've done that before."

"Yeah."

"Still the macho bastard."

"I prefer stoical."

My cellular telephone rang. I'd put a call in to Penny earlier, leaving my number on her answering machine. She lived in a Kauai pole house down by the banks of the Anahola River. She would deliver my message to Ed Alapai, if I could reach her. She was one of the island's fine bodyworkers and teachers, and usually spent her days on the road or in session. One of her sessions lasted two hours.

"Caine."

"How was the voyage?"

"Good morning, Lieutenant Kahanamoku. Where are you?"

"Sitting by the pool, enjoying the Kauai sunshine, sipping an orange juice with a little paper umbrella in it and watching the tourist girls in little tiny bikinis getting sunburned in places I guess they don't expose much in Indiana or Illinois."

"You're here?"

"Got the young lady settled, checked in at the shop and found it had been a quiet day in Honolulu. When you're gone, crime rates go way down. Figured I'd fly over. Thought you'd need some help."

"Can always use some help. Got some dishes to do here, some window washing. Maybe you could do some painting?"

"Where are you?"

"Sailing toward Hanalei. How about you?"

"That big hotel in Lihue, the one near the airport. Cocktail napkin here says Marriott. Nice place."

"You alone?"

"Waiting for a rental. I'll stop by Ed's place on the way. I know Hanalei. Drop anchor in the bay. Scoot to shore in your Avon and we'll meet you there. How long?"

"About an hour, hour and a half."

"Great. I'll finish breakfast and round up my gear. See you there." He coughed into the phone, "Oh, Caine. You run into trouble last night?"

"How's that?"

"A boat pulled into Nawiliwili this morning, superstructure full of pukas. Looked like the work of a high-powered rifle. They had some blood in the wheelhouse, too, but they said one of their guys cut himself on a fillet knife. They didn't look like fishermen, and it must have been one hell of a cut, but we couldn't do anything about it."

"Why not? Couldn't you search the boat?"

"Nope. They all had Colombian passports, the diplomatic kind. Couldn't touch them even if we found a dead body."

"The same as—"

"The same as the fellow who was out shopping for a hitter on Mrs. Halliday. Get the picture yet?"

"Yes."

"Thought you might. I'm working with the local authorities. But I don't think it's a good idea to bring that lady to my cousin's house. He has eight kids and a pregnant wife and I don't think that would mix well."

"What do you suggest?"

"We'll see you at Hanalei. I'm meeting the local police in a few minutes. They can watch out for these desperadoes."

"See you in about an hour."

"Keep your eyes open. I'm watching their boat right now, but they're spreading out around the town. They've contacted a couple of locals, too. I think they're looking for you. This is a very small island. There are only so many places you can hide. Watch yourself."

"I didn't think you cared."

"You're not as bad as you seem to think you are, and Neolani likes you. That's enough for me."

"Thanks, man."

"No problem, brudda. Just watch your back."

18

We wouldn't have made Hanalei Bay had we tried it a month later. Winter surf on the north shore of any of Hawaii's islands is dangerous, but in Kauai, the most northerly of the archipelago, it's especially lethal. North shore Oahu is famous for its winter waves, luring world-class surfers from every corner of the planet to try its curls and tubes. Kauai's winter surf is equally renowned, but as the locus of a seafarer's graveyard. More ships have gone down along Kauai's northern coastline than anywhere else in the Islands. The thirty-foot combers that are so popular at Waimea Bay are hull-crushers here against rocks and reefs.

But that was in another month. Winter surf is dangerous. Autumn surf can be tricky, but not always deadly.

On the way up the coast I told Margo about the arrangements.

"He's here to help me?"

"He said he was here to help me, but you're the reason he made the flight over."

"I don't understand. I thought he was still investigating me."

"It's standard for Kimo. You know how he took Karen and Julia in without any hesitation, just moved them into his own house? You met Neolani? And they accused me of collecting people. They've got ten kids, six of them adopted. Kimo may still be investigating you—he's a cop, that's what they do until they are satisfied that they know all about the case they're investigating—but unless you actually shot your husband in cold blood you won't find yourself standing in front of a judge and jury. He's a fair man." I didn't say, because I thought she would argue with me, that he was one of those who looked for the truth, not merely the facts. It defined him.

"So why is he here?"

"I don't know, to be honest. He knows about the shooting last night. The pirates hit landfall at Nawiliwili Harbor this morning. There was blood on the boat. The authorities could do nothing because the men aboard carried diplomatic Colombian passports. They told them one of them cut himself fishing."

She opened her mouth, closed it, and opened it again, like a fish thrown onto the dock trying for the oxygen in the suddenly thin environment.

"He's got people watching them. Local cops, I think. He called from the Marriott in Lihue. Only reason he'd be there is because he's watching them."

"So what's going to happen?"

"Who knows?"

"When you get flippant, it just pisses me off. I'm scared, John. That doesn't help. The shooting in Pearl Harbor, then everything that happened last night. Now you tell me they're already here." She looked toward the coastline of Kauai, peacefully sleeping under the morning sun five miles away. "I thought I could be safe here. It's a scary place, now," she said.

"Kimo's here. His cousin, Ed, is here. The local cops are here. I'm here. These guys, whoever they are, are out of their territory and way out of their league."

She smirked. "Big words. They mean nothing."

"These are actions, Margo. You've got an army between you and the Colombians. We'll protect you. The cops will arrest them and deport them. That will give you a little time to get your gear together so you can figure out where to go."

"What?"

"You're looking to get out of here. You told me so yourself. Okay, I understand that, and I'll help you. These clowns are minor league. They're dangerous, but they're on our turf now. They might have the ability to set up a shooting nest and wait two or three days for just the right spot, but they missed, and that makes them bush league. Or unlucky. Whatever, Kimo will get them. And I won't let them get you.

"Now, where do you want to go?"

She shook her head.

"Come on, *Olympia* will go anywhere in the world there's water deep enough for her keel. It might be a rough trip, but she'll get you there."

"I'll . . . think about it."

"You do that."

I pointed out the old Kilauea lighthouse as we passed and she nodded curtly, deep into her own thoughts and prayers, annoyed by my intrusion. I vowed to keep such things to myself.

From Kilauea it wasn't far to Hanalei. The middle of Hanalei Bay is deep and full of fast currents, but it has a decent anchorage. We brought *Olympia* through the reef easily enough and Margo helped me toss out the four bow anchors that would ensure our stability and still let her swing with the current. The bay was calm, with the exception of one rogue swell that came out of nowhere as we sailed through the channel and lifted the hull, twisting the bow around, pushing *Olympia* a little too close to some nasty coral heads, giving us a thrill ride for a few seconds before it subsided.

It didn't take long to set the anchors and bring down the sails and get the Avon dinghy over the side. For all her protestations about not having done this before, Margo was becoming something of a seasoned sailor, never protesting, never complaining, leaping to any task assigned. But for her mood swings, brought about by the continual collision of her dreams with her fears, she would have been easy to have around.

Of course, I'd never had trouble enduring the company of pretty women, even if, as she'd taken pains to explain to me, there was no sexual tension between us. And that, too, felt comfortable. Despite the mutual heat that her pummeling had driven to the surface—and that was something I wanted to explore in my own mind sometime later on, when the dust had settled—the fact of our relationship was strictly business, and I liked it that way. I didn't trust her, most likely the main source of my inhibition, and I had my commitment with Barbara, but even in a vacuum there would have been no attraction. I recalled my reaction when I first saw her running down that Chinatown alley. It was an appreciation of the form without the lust, the way I'd admire a beautiful statue or a painting by a master.

My Avon brought us to shore without difficulty, and I steered the little inflatable toward a familiar ancient green pickup I saw parked along the sand at the public beach. Kimo and Ed Alapai stood beside the truck, two warriors big as mountains, men with whom I had shared some of the deepest emotions and experiences of my life, here because they had decided it was necessary. Of course, with them, there was the sound of musketry, and men like these had always run toward the sound of guns.

I jumped out of the Avon and Ed helped me drag the dinghy up onto the sand. As he helped Margo onto dry land he smiled and introduced himself to her, shaking her hand gently. "You the woman everybody want to kill? Can't see that. You made for huggin', not killin'." Then he hugged her and she almost disappeared beneath his mammoth arms.

Ed is not like a normal man. Aside from the fact that he is huge and has waist-length gray hair that falls in matted tangles down his back, he is tattooed from the top of his head to the soles of his feet. The markings are not just your standard tattoos, either, done in some sterile shop along Ala Moana. They're ancient, hand-applied decorations that reflect the history of his people, done over a period of decades. His face and chest are lined with zigzag lines and circles. He has a star map on his back, tracing the route from Tahiti to Hawaii. Even his tongue is branded. Every pattern is authentic. Each illustration is significant. Ed is one of the few pure Hawaiians left. He has made his home on a heiau, an old temple site that he discovered and cleared the land himself. He grows taro there, and lives in a small house he and I built together several years before. Like Kimo's grandmother, Ed has made the preservation of his people's culture his passion.

Standing six feet six, weighing some three hundred pounds, his face covered in tattoos and hair hanging down to his waist, Ed is a scary fellow. But he can be exceedingly gentle, as he was with Margo, and she didn't flinch when he enveloped her with those big arms of his.

When he released her, he came at me, giving me the same treatment.

"How have you been, brudda? Kimo tell me you got your hands full, what with dis and dat. He say he makin' house for some tita and her keiki you try to help, but her cockroach husband's a real bummah, so he go to jail. Den some buggah take a shot at you, so you run to Kauai to get away. Dat true?"

"About sums it up," I said, smiling, watching Ed try on his tourist pidgin, knowing it was for Margo's benefit.

"Ho!" he said. "We beef this humbug and get back to da kine. Cool head main t'ing. Everyt'ing be mo bettah soon." He turned his attention back to Margo, and put one meaty hand on her shoulder. "Little lady, you came to the right place. You're safe now. Not'in' can harm you. Not with Ed around, and this help I got."

Kimo rolled his eyes. Ed had a wife and eight children and, from what Kimo had just said, another one on the way, but he liked his females in all shapes and sizes, and he had never been too particular about keeping his marriage vows. Margo had suddenly become a target. I wondered how she would handle it, coming from this human picture map about the size of an Indian elephant.

"Oh, Mr. Ed," she said, smiling sweetly. "I feel so much better already."

"Hey, lady, Mr. Ed's a horse."

"I know," she said, turning away, toward Kimo. "Detective, thank you for coming."

"Doing my job, Mrs. Halliday."

She nodded. "I understand. How are Karen and Julia getting along?"

"The little one's having a bad time of it. Neolani said she cried most of the night, but this morning she's eating. Some neighbor kids are coming over. They'll be fine."

Margo smiled. "I know they will. Thank you."

"You're welcome to come visit. They hardly know anybody here."

She considered that, then shook her head. "Thank you, Lieutenant, but that probably won't happen. I seem to bring trouble along wherever I go these days. I'd just as soon keep it away from your family."

"I understand. Just thought you might like to. If you want to. If you're here afterward."

She nodded, her dark eyes far away, thinking, I knew, about afterward.

"How did you make out with the locals, Kimo?"

"They're watching them now. They don't have much in the way of undercover here, it's mostly uniform constable work. Anything they need for that kind of work they borrow from my department anyway, so I told them to watch with what they had and we'd get back to them. They know about the shooting the other day. I told them it's related, which we don't really know, but then nothing else follows the logic. Unless there's somebody gunning for you, too, Caine, which would make this entire exercise kind of futile. I'd hate to think I brought all of us together and then find you're the target and not Mrs. Halliday."

I thought about it. Most of the people who wanted me dead were pushing up daisies themselves. I had a dearth of warm personal enemies, knew of no current threat, and said so.

"Then there's these guys from South America. Hitters, pure and simple, with an emphasis on the simple. It shouldn't take more than a couple of hours to draw them in, overpower them, take their guns away, and arrest them. If we do this right, if we do this my way, there will be no *more* shooting." He looked at me when he said it, putting heavy emphasis on the word "more." "I took a look at your boat out there through the field glasses, Caine. You've got some interesting pukas in your boat, too, and then there's that bandaged hand. You shoot it out with those guys last night?"

Margo started to say something, and then caught herself. I jumped in.

"We were followed from Pearl Harbor. I scoped the boat and saw a bunch of little hairy guys in party shirts loading Skorpions. You know what I mean? Those Czech submachine guns the terrorists love so much?"

"I know them."

"We escaped by hiding in the fog. There was some shooting. Not much. Just enough to know what they are about."

"You shoot back?"

Margo watched me while I answered, but gave nothing

away. I shot first. She knew that, but she'd protect me. At least until she could find some advantage to feed me to the wolves.

"Of course."

"That explains the blood. You hit somebody. Maybe fatally. There was that much blood. Most likely whoever you shot is feeding the fishes right this moment." Kimo looked at me with his cop look again. "Course there's no complaint. And it could have been fish blood for all we know. There's just your word. And you, too, Mrs. Halliday. It happen the way he said?"

She nodded, watching me. "Yes, Lieutenant. Exactly."

"Then there's no problem yet. The minute they're in custody they're gonna start screaming, and they will most likely mention being attacked by some black sailboat like yours. You may have to hire a lawyer, but I don't think the Coast Guard is going to give you too much of a hard time. Way I see it, it was self-defense. Even if you did shoot first."

"You think I shot first?"

"You're still alive, Caine. So is Mrs. Halliday. If they had automatic weapons and a powerboat, there's only one way you could keep them away from you. You think I'm stupid? It's what I'd do, I was in your shoes last night."

"For the record—"

"There is no record, Caine. Let's just keep it that way. I'm just telling you I know what happened and you don't have to say anything. You know I hate it when you lie to me. That's insulting."

"You made your point."

"Hope so." He turned back to Margo. "We put a plan together. You're a part of it. You want to hear it?"

"Yes."

"You've got two choices. One, we can hide you until this blows over. Two, we use you for bait. The advantage to that is that we'll take them quicker, and have a better case, if we catch them in the act. The disadvantage to you is obvious. We can arrest them without an attempt on you, depend on the court system to see it our way, or we can get a sure thing, something not even the best defense counsel from the Mainland can beat. But it's strictly up to you. I can't make you to do it. I feel bad just asking you."

"Asking me what?"

"I'm asking you to sit out in the open and wait for them to come to you. Caine will be with you." Kimo looked at me, challenging me to disabuse him. I didn't, wanting to hear from Margo. These were the people who had tried to kidnap her, who had frightened her into running in the first place, the people who wanted her dead.

"They won't stop until they find me, will they?"

"No. The way we see things, there won't be any shooting. I can't guarantee it, but we'll try to overwhelm them when they show up. Caine will protect you. It's one of the few things he's good at."

"You're comfortable being shahk bait, little lady?" asked Ed Alapai.

"I'm not comfortable as it is. I can't see how it could be worse."

"It gets worse, Mrs. Halliday," said Kimo. "Much, much worse."

"I'm probably dead either way. At least this way I'm doing something about it."

Kimo and Ed left to bring their sons back to watch *Olympia* in our absence. There wasn't much to fear for her, riding at anchor a quarter mile out in Hanalei Bay, but she'd been spotted before, in Pearl Harbor, and tracked to this island, and if anyone came calling, the two boys could alert us. Kimo's boy was on vacation with his cousins, a regular event. He assured me they were both nimble enough to get out of harm's way if trouble came calling, and they were both smart enough to know when it was time to get out. I detected some deep-seated pride in his voice and didn't challenge him.

While Ed and Kimo were gone, Margo and I rode the Avon out to my boat to finish our preparations.

Kimo's plan was to use us as bait. As the Colombians came for us, law enforcement would surround and arrest them, overwhelming them with armed men. I was allowed only one gun, my .45 Colt in my belly bag. Margo and I would be dressed as tourists. There was no way to conceal anything other than pistols, I was told by those in authority. They would handle everything. We had no reason to worry.

Having long ago stopped trusting anyone in authority—I'd done that back in the seventies, and they'd sent me to Vietnam—I listened to the little man this time and made a reluctant decision.

"Improvise," said the little man inside my head after listening to Kimo explain our rights and our duties. "And hide what you can't improvise."

We reached *Olympia* and I held the boarding ladder while Margo went topside with the painter. When she had secured the dinghy I climbed aboard.

"Dress in something comfortable," I told her, "but something you can run in. No high heels, no slip-ons. If you've got tennis shoes, wear them. They're better than jogging shoes for this kind of work."

"Yes, sir."

"Trying to keep us alive."

"You don't like the plan?"

"I don't enjoy being bait. I'm not as brave as you are. If the shooting starts, I want to be able to shoot back."

"I saw that last night."

"You saw nothing last night. It didn't happen."

She nodded. "I'll just change my shoes," she said, going below.

I pulled out the .505 Gibbs and broke it down into two parts, wrapped each of them in oily rags and stuffed them into a ballistic nylon duffel bag that usually stored my dive gear. A private gunsmith in the Manoa Valley made the cartridges for me, laughing at my order. Forty rounds for an elephant gun? On Oahu? What the heck was big enough to shoot with an elephant gun? I told him I'd seen a cockroach. The smith laughed, throwing back his head, and wiped his eyes. Crazy haole. Crazy John Caine.

I placed the two boxes of elephant-killing ammunition into the duffel, along with four boxes of double-aught shotgun shells.

Last year I had recovered most of a stolen fortune for a

California widow, saving her and her company from bank-ruptcy and ruin. During the process I'd borrowed her late hus-band's gun collection, replacing my own that had been lost during a hurricane. When I left San Diego the widow gifted me with the guns. To her, they represented something she didn't need to revisit, and she thought I might need them. That's where I got the old elephant rifle as well as the 7-mm Remington. And that's how I came to acquire the matched pair of Purdy over-and-under shotguns in 20-gauge. Other than the fact that they would cost some thirty thousand dol-lars to replace, they meant nothing to me.

Easy come, easy go.

I rummaged around in my tool chest until I came up with my hacksaw and three new blades, found some honing oil and laid everything out on the deck over an old rag. It looked as if I were getting ready for an operation. Satisfied, I went below to my gun safe and took out one of the Purdys and examined it. Stocks of burled walnut, barrels of Damascus steel, the Purdys were handmade and world-class, possibly the finest shotguns made. It seemed an obscenity what I planned to do but this one had cost me nothing and it could save my life, given the circumstances.

I brought it up on deck.

I set up the vise and clamped the barrel in its jaws, making certain it was tight, protecting the Damascus steel with the rag. Why I bothered with that I didn't know, but it seemed the right thing to do. Insulting the gun further by scratching the barrels with the vise just wouldn't be right.

I visited the toolbox again and came up with the fine-toothed Japanese saw I use for hardwoods. Choosing my line, I cut off the burled walnut stock at the pistol grip. When I'd finished the decapitation of the stock, I sanded the hardwood smooth, rounding the cut edge enough to prevent splinters. Satisfied, I took the hacksaw and broke two blades on the tough steel barrels before I was able to cut through the last rim. Milling with a file took only a moment and I had a compact, powerful argument for the last word.

I taped a piece of white nylon line around the pistol grip and trigger guard so the gun would point at the ground when it hung from my neck.

In times when I had to go into harm's way, my ace in the hole was usually a 12-gauge double-barrel shotgun, the muzzle cut down to the foregrip, slung from a lanyard around my neck. Regardless of whatever else I carried, the shotgun came in handy a time or two, a lesson learned. If everything worked out right, there would be no shooting. Or, as Kimo had pointed out, no *more* shooting. I believed in the Easter Bunny. I believed in Santa Claus. I'd buy a bridge from some Fast Eddy type in Brooklyn, but I didn't believe there would be no shooting. Not after last night. Those boys were angry, and I'd made it worse. They were two down and would play catch-up as hard as they could.

"What do you have there?" Margo appeared at the hatch, watching me tape the final winds onto the pistol grip.

"An old and trusted friend."

"You really like shooting people, don't you?"

"I don't like to be the only one in a rainstorm without an umbrella."

"Macho," she said.

"Think that when the storm hits."

"You seem so sure they won't protect us."

"Kimo means well. They all mean well. But their job is to bring those shooters to justice. We're bait. We'll be in a lonely place if it all turns sour. I would love to believe it will happen just the way Kimo wants it to. Except for Ed, whom I trust, and myself, everyone's attention will be on the bad guys. Nobody's there to protect you but me. And nobody's there to protect me but me. Get the picture?"

"If we get shot it will be just too bad."

I nodded. "Not a tragedy. Just too bad. You said it yourself. You're already dead."

"I know. I guess I didn't know what I was talking about."

"Few people do."

"But you do."

I nodded and dragged my black day pack over, the one with my Colt and the Glock. I slipped the Purdy into the cargo bag, barrel first. It fit perfectly. I should be able to reach it over my shoulder if the fertilizer hit the fan. "Sometimes. About some things. Maybe I'm getting older, but I sincerely hope that Kimo's plan will work and we won't have to shoot anybody. But I'm not so old I'm not certain he's right."

"I'm scared to death, Caine."

"Me too."

"Don't say that."

"No. It's true. These things scare the hell out of me. That's why we survive. If you're scared, you'll be alert enough to keep your head down." A sudden thought hit me. "You have a gun."

"No."

"You told me you had a gun."

"I lied. You have the guns. You'll protect me."

"But if I can't, you'll want one. Be too late, then."

She considered it and nodded. "I think, maybe, yes."

I took the Glock from my pack and handed it to her. "Recognize this?"

"Is this the one?"

"Belonged to your ex-husband."

She hefted it.

"Careful now. It's loaded. Cocked and locked. See this lever here?" I pointed to a little black nub near her thumb. "That's the safety. It is on now. You can't fire it. If you want to fire it, push it up and point and pull the trigger. Try to point it at what you're going to shoot."

She practiced it. Guns aren't that difficult to operate. "What about kick?" she asked.

"It's a nine-millimeter. Nothing heavy. Don't worry about it."

"She nodded. "Thanks, John."

"Now put the safety back on and put that thing away. You won't have to use it, but it's better having one if you need it. Better than the other way around."

She tried to smile and failed, stuffed the Glock into her purse, stood up and kissed me on the cheek. "Sure. We'll be fine."

"When I was a young man, hardly more than a boy, I got sent to Vietnam with one of the first SEAL teams. We had a saying back then. I don't know who started it, but it caught on. You ought to know it."

"Okay."

"Yea, though I walk through the valley of the shadow of death I shall fear no evil—"

"The Twenty-Third Psalm."

"—For I am the meanest son of a bitch in the valley."

She laughed, and then stopped. "You really mean that, don't you?"

"Stick close to me. Do exactly what I tell you. Every time. Without question. I am the meanest son of a bitch in any particular valley you could name. If it starts to go south on us, if Kimo can't contain it, I'll protect you. And if I can't protect you, you'll have to do it. You can do it, Margo. I saw you last night. You were scared, but you came through. You have nothing to be afraid of. You're hell on wheels. It's the other guys. They should be scared of you."

"You don't mean that," she said. "But it's nice hearing it."

"I mean it. Every word."

"Okay, Butch. Let's go get those Colombians."

"That from *Sundance Kid?*"

"God, I hope not. You remember how that ended?"

"That was Peru, and they took a lot of them with them."

"But that, my friend, doesn't count. Promise me we'll be standing when this is over."

"And I'll buy you a drink at Duke's."

"No." She put her face close to mine and looked directly into my eyes. "You offered to take me someplace where I can hide. As soon as this is done I'll take you up on that offer. And you must promise to tell no one where we went. We'll just vanish, right now, today, right after this is over. No waiting for morning, no more collecting women with little kids and support problems. We go back to the boat, pull up the anchor and get going. When we're at sea I'll tell you where I want to go. Agreed?"

"Agreed."

"I'll pay you with three more emeralds. Will that get me what I want?"

"I don't know what you want, but it will get my attention."

She nodded. "That's good enough." She stood up, brushed herself off and gazed across the water to the beach. "Your friends seem to be back," she said. "Let's go."

"You up for this?"

"No. Can you ever be ready for something like this? I'm so scared I've got goose bumps everywhere. I want to trust you, and I feel as if I can. I remember that night when you saved me from Glen. But this is different."

"Yeah."

"Say something profound. Say something that will make me feel better."

"Well, I already told you I'm the meanest son of a bitch in the valley."

"Good enough," she said, and climbed over the railing into the Avon floating next to *Olympia*'s black hull.

I slung my pack, handed down my duffel, said good-bye to my home, and followed her.

T his is Charles." Kimo gently pushed a gangly teenager toward me, a boy who was a distant echo of his father—a
slimmer, younger one. "Say hello to Mr. Caine."

The youth took my hand, a limp grasp, wishing, no doubt,
he were somewhere else. He didn't look me in the eye, staring
somewhere at the sand near my feet.

"Pleased to meet you, Charles."

"Yes, sir."

"And you know Filipe. Everybody just calls him Junior."

"Hello again, Junior," I said to the second young man.
Filipe had changed since I'd last seen him, the way young men
change from children to proto-adults. He looked nothing like
his father when I had first met him. Now he was robust, like
his dad without the tattoos and long hair, and with the deep
chest of an ocean swimmer. The slender reed had grown into
a young but sturdy tree.

"They'll watch your boat, Caine. She'll be fine here. And
they got the cell phone and my number to call if there's trouble. But there won't be any trouble, will there?" Kimo looked
at the boys. They each mumbled something and, as if by prior
agreement, or by nonverbal communication that was as peculiar as that of birds and fish, they both took off toward the

Avon beached upon the shore. I noted their spines quickly straightened once they were free of the adults' presence.

"Good kids," I said.

"Huh! They better be. Junior, he's one good athlete, but he's no scholar. Charles, he's smart as a whip, tops in his class at Kamehameha School. Also an artist. Could be an architect. Wants to be a doctor. But he swims like a fish, and he knows computers and stuff I'll never understand. They're cousins, and best friends."

I wondered what it would be like, having those options again, having the choices of a lifetime ahead with few constraints. I'd gone so far down the road that I was stuck with the decisions I'd made. "Ed's okay with this?"

"Yeah. Said Junior would be good to keep watch. He's steady. They're both good swimmers. Nothing can harm them on the water." He looked at me with that steady look of his that meant he knew more than he would ever tell me. "You ready?"

I'd dressed the part of the tourist, with a black tank top and faded olive-green boat shorts and my old Tevas. My cut-down shotgun lay safe inside my day pack. I had the Colt in a belly bag strapped to my waist. My duffel sat on the sand.

"Don't touch anything you don't know what it is," Kimo told the two boys, who were about to shove off from shore. "That's is a nice boat. I wanna see it that way when we come back."

"And if we see anybody coming?" Charles's voice morphed from tenor to baritone.

"If you see anybody coming, call me and get off the boat. Take the Avon or swim to shore. Get out of there as soon as you call."

"That's all?"

"I think they'd prefer to repel boarders," I said to Kimo sotto voce.

"I think so, too." He looked at the two young men and

smiled. "No heroic stuff out there. Just do as you are told. Call and quit. We'll handle the other stuff."

Charles nodded, but I could tell that if there was trouble, he'd try to get involved. Kimo saw it, too. I walked into the surf until it brushed my calves and put my hand on the gunwale of the dinghy.

"You want to impress your father?" I asked.

"What?"

"You want to impress your father?"

"I dunno."

"The best way to do that is to do what he says. Don't get involved any more than you already are. If somebody shows up, make the call and get out. Go to college. Be a doctor. Heal people. That's what'll make him proud. Not fighting."

"But—"

"Listen to me. It's what I do, this fighting. I don't like it. I hate it, in fact, but I do it well. I'm a hard case; been that way all my life. Never had a permanent woman, never had a permanent home. It's what I am. Your father, he understands that. He knows what it's like. But you, you have a future. Don't do anything but cut and run. These people, they're bad news. Nothing we can't handle, but bad enough for you two. Cut and run. Understand me?"

"Yeah."

Kimo joined us and hugged his boy, squeezing him like ripe fruit. "You do what the man says. I don't want you growing up like him."

"But you said he was a good man."

Kimo looked embarrassed. "I never said that. He's a bad man, but he's not evil. You know the difference?"

The boy shook his head.

"There's a difference. We'll talk about it later. When this is over. Meanwhile, you see anything, you call me and bug out. That's an order."

The boy nodded, more emphatically than before.

"You sure?"

"Yes, sir."

I helped Kimo shove them off and waded back to shore to retrieve Margo, finding her at a picnic table beneath a palm tree playing solitaire. She didn't seem to be winning.

"You ready for this?"

She looked up from her cards, her eyes bright. "I'm scared to death."

"You're good. You'll get through it. Just stay close to me."

She nodded and gathered the cards and put them in her purse. "We already went through this. I'll . . . I'll be fine. Let's get it behind us." She looked up into my eyes again. "You remember your promise?"

"Of course."

"You won't let me down?"

"Never."

She nodded. "I know."

The Avon reached *Olympia*. Charles turned the dinghy smartly, so it just kissed the hull of my sailboat. Filipe scrambled up the boarding ladder, the painter in his mouth, and secured it while Charles secured the motor. Young watermen, they seemed to know their way around boats.

I wondered about Kimo's boy. He clearly loved his father and wanted to do the right thing, but there was some hero-worship there, too. I didn't doubt he'd do exactly as he'd been instructed, but I could see a tendency to rebel.

I looked at Margo. Had I not been there for her she could have turned to Chawlie. He would have protected her—maybe—for a price. A substantial one. Or maybe he would have turned her over to the Colombians to settle his account. Wouldn't put it past him. I hadn't been exaggerating when I told her he was a businessman first. To get those goons off his back, he would sell her down the river, especially once she'd broken his trust. If John Caine were not around she might be dead now, the victim of her own greed and stupidity.

Is that what I did? Did I make a living saving people from themselves?

The only way out for Margo was to stick her head into the lion's mouth, something that few people ever have to do. A party girl who'd grabbed the gaudy baubles from the devil himself, looking for a way out of the trap her life had become; I did not expect her to take any action other than to run. But she wanted to stick it out and make a stand. She'd either hit bottom or hit her peak, either way willing to hit back.

I wondered if I could help her. I'd promised, given my solemn vow to take her and her jewels far away from here and give her the chance she'd wanted. Leave it to the government and she'd get screwed, one way or the other. We all knew that. Even Kimo, with his big heart, would go the official route because he was a policeman, given to obeying the laws of the land. He would turn her over to someone or somebody, and soon Margo would become just another cog in the machinery of justice, and processed accordingly, forever lost.

I kept my thoughts to myself. What had Kimo called me? A bad man, just not an evil one. That's about as good as it gets, I guess, considering the human condition. But then he'd told his son I was a good man. Hard to maintain distance like that for an adult, harder still for a young man. Must have been confusing to him. I knew it was to me.

A white Kauai police car parked next to Ed's green pickup. A big local in a dark blue uniform squeezed out of the car and approached, watching us steadily through mirrored sunglasses. He filled every inch of the uniform, straining the buttons, and his belly was expansive. Were it not for his Polynesian features, he would have resembled one of those redneck Southern sheriffs harassing the front-of-the-bus riders a few decades back.

Kimo greeted the policeman with the easy manner of a man who knew both sides of the street and had the run of it. I hung back with Margo. This was cop business.

"Who are you?" demanded the cop, motioning toward Margo and me. "What have you got in your fag bag?"

"It is a gun, and he's licensed to carry it. He's a PI from Honolulu, here to protect this lady." Kimo showed his identification to the local cop and the tension dropped a notch or two.

"Hi," I said, extending my hand. "My name's Frank James. This is my sister, Jesse."

Kimo gaped at me.

"That the yacht that was in a gunfight last night?"

"We're not certain," said Kimo. "I've been investigating. Could you step over here for a moment and let me speak with you privately?" He led the big cop behind Ed's truck and spoke quietly with him.

Ed shrugged and looked sheepish. "I could tell him I was hunting, but he wouldn't believe me." He nodded toward his M-14 hanging in the rear-window gun rack, double-taped magazines loaded into the breech; faded web gear suspended from the rack, bulging with ammunition. Whatever he was hunting would take four hundred rounds minimum to bring it down.

Kimo and the cop finished their conversation and joined us, the cop still looking unhappy. He planted himself in front of me and looked me right in the eye, his thumbs hooked in his gun belt.

"Frank James, huh? You are a smart-ass. I don't like smart-asses. I don't like you, John Caine." He wiped his hands on his pants and addressed Margo. "And you, young lady, have brought violence to my island, and I don't like that. But I understand your problem, and we'll handle it." He glanced at Kimo, then turned back to the two of us. "You, Caine, Kimo, and Alapai here, are running along the edge of the law. You cross over and I'll nail you. All of you. This is my island. I don't like trouble. It's bad for business. Disrupts the quiet.

And from the sound of things you already brought more trouble than the last hurricane."

"We have a plan," Kimo reminded the big cop. "I cleared it with your chief in Lihue. You're here to help. Bring your people in at the right time, use overpowering force, and there will be no shooting."

The big cop looked dubious. I would be too, in his place.

"All right," he said, deciding. "You know how much I like this? This is cop business, not for guys like this Caine and Alapai. What do they know?"

"We've been to a doughnut shop a time or two."

"What's that supposed to mean?"

"We'll get by," I said. "Worry about yourself, and worry about your men. I specialize in protection. It's what I do best. This lady needs protection, and she's gutsy enough to volunteer to be the bait to take down some would-be assassins. And you get the arrest. You think of that? Your boss bought into it. The lady's willing, and you'd better get used to it."

"I still don't like it."

"You don't have to. But you'll have to live with it."

"Now wait a minute—"

"Caine, that's enough!" Kimo shoved himself between me and the cop, establishing himself as a buffer. One about the size of a koa tree. "This is Tyler. Tyler, John Caine. You're going to work together this afternoon. Our focus is to protect Mrs. Halliday and arrest the men who came here to kill her. Anything else can be settled later."

I nodded. There was nothing to settle. I wasn't the one who was steamed. Tyler, the big cop, scratched his jaw and shook his head. "Nobody talks to me that way, Caine. We'll work it out later, like he said."

"Fine with me."

"If you boys are through with your schoolyard games, I need to use the ladies' room. And can't we get this over with?

Does anybody know where these people are?" Margo went into the concrete-block public rest room.

"You were going to Lihue?" The big cop asked Kimo when Margo had gone.

"Yeah. Thought that would be the place to start."

"Don't bother. I've got my people watching them. Just before I got here they were in Haena, drinking beer at Peg Leg's, watching the traffic."

I knew Haena, a small town not far from where we stood, near the end of the Kohio highway. It nearly got flattened by Hurricane *Iniki,* but like most of Kauai it had been rebuilt. The last time I was there they had two bars with sidewalk lanais where you could sit and drink your beer and watch the sparse traffic going back and forth. Peg Leg's was one of them. Nothing much else to do in Haena, most of the time.

"Then why don't we go there?" I said.

"You sure your friend will be all right?"

"Oh, I wouldn't worry about Margo. I'll take care of her."

"Maybe that's what gets me worried the most."

"I was in your shoes, Tyler, it might worry me, too."

21

Haena town is a tiny tropical settlement with sports rentals and tourist gift shops, a wooden post office, a little stone church and two slat-sided bars. Surrounded by palm and banana trees, Haena is almost as far as you can go on the north shore before you have to get out of your car and walk. Or paddle. The Na Pali Coast begins just after Haena, with cliffs plunging from the spine of Kauai directly down to the surf. Haena is the end of the road.

It being the height of the tourist season, Peg Leg's, one of the town's two bars, was standing room only, so we parked across the street and tried Hoolihan's, finding a table with a good view of the men who pursued us. They hadn't yet tumbled to our presence, so we watched them watching the road.

Hoolihan's had three tables taken by a collection of healthy, buoyant Aussies. They looked like a sports team on holiday, except that they had a harder edge than most athletes, even professional athletes, ever get. But it was their haircuts and postures that branded them as military. I recognized a special ops attitude, too, something that you just *felt*, you didn't see, but it was just as real. I bet myself they were on leave from Pearl Harbor or Fort Shafter after combined war games with their U.S. counterparts. Six men. All fit. If shooting started here, I wondered what they'd do.

"G'day, sport!" One of the Aussies gave us a white-toothed grin as Margo and I took our table and ordered coffees. I nodded and smiled. Gregarious, and a little drunk, the Aussies whistled their appreciation of Margo's shorts and halter top.

"Good morning," Margo said, smiling.

"Going kayaking, sport?" asked their apparent spokesman.

"Too rough for me," I replied. In summer, Haena was the jumping-off spot for kayak tours of the Na Pali. This time of year it was an iffy proposition. Most of the tours closed by September.

"Getting soft, are we? Is he soft, lady?"

"He's a brick," said Margo, smiling, fluttering her eyes at me.

"Yeah, well, that's all well and good, but he's a little too old, don't you think?"

This was starting to become something more than we needed. The other Australians were looking at me, watching for me to pick up the bait. I spit the hook, signaling the waitress, and bought the young men another round of beer. Grinning at them, I nodded, raising my coffee mug to toast them and turned to watch the men across the street.

"Most definitely soft," said the young man to my back.

The boys were having their fun. Probably a little too early in the day for beer, but you can never tell with those Aussies. I once saw a training film where Australian soldiers had volunteered to be exposed to mustard gas for a government study. The men wore gas masks and little else. Mustard gas is a blister agent, designed to attack the mucous membranes. That's what kills, when your throat and lungs swell tight. It also causes major burns on the skin, and its worst effects collect on the neck, under the arms, and between the legs. They did it in exchange for additional beer rations. It was an ugly film to watch, and must have been extremely painful to experience, but they all came through it, most of them with brave grins on their faces. All for topping off a pint, as they call it. These guys probably had an extra dose or two of testosterone, too, but that didn't hurt. Not in their profession.

The Colombians, on the other hand, looked bewildered. Despite their garish party shirts, they didn't exhibit the festive picture I had seen the night before through the scope of my rifle. With no firearms in sight, they looked almost pathetic.

I guessed they kept their real firepower in their rentals. They wouldn't do anything in public. Not here. Not with the number of witnesses around. Their style would be to find us, follow until the road cleared, and then do a drive-by with submachine guns. Simple and effective. With no witnesses, and if they were lucky, if nobody found the shot-up car for ten or fifteen minutes, they could get away safely.

How these guys got to Haena I didn't know. When *Olympia* didn't show up at Nawiliwili Harbor, and without their sea captain to guide them, they may have decided to quit the sea and drive around the island. Like many islands, you can't drive all the way around Kauai. There's usually something that defeats the road builders. Here it was the Na Pali, those graceful green cliffs that tower above the surf line, starting due west of Haena and marching along the entire western coast of the island all the way to Barking Sands. It was difficult enough hiking the Na Pali Coast. Aside from being a sacrilege, a road would have been impossible.

The Colombians looked lost, one of them consulting a map. Hard thing to do on an island with only one road.

Ed and Kimo came in and sat at a table in the far corner of the lanai, ignoring us. Local enough not to have any connection with Margo and me, they appeared intent on their own conversation.

The cops were not here. The plan was to dangle us as bait in front of them and see what they did. After we were certain they had seen us, we'd get into the rental car provided for us and drive blissfully away. Kimo had picked the spot down the road, a likely ambush site, and law enforcement waited there. He would follow them as they followed us, radio ahead and have the posse make the intercept before any shooting started. It was a good plan, well-crafted, but it had too many moving parts to suit me. I am a proponent of Ockham's Razor: that which is simplest is best. Too many moving parts meant too many things could go wrong.

Margo and I were in it now, and there was nothing we could do except go through with it. It was like labor. Once started, we couldn't stop.

I saw Tyler's car cruise slowly up and down the street several times, giving both bars the hard stare before he disappeared around the corner toward the beach. Watching him, I was thankful for Kimo and Ed.

"There they are, Margo," I said. "Are they so scary in the light?"

"Scary enough, if you weren't here. And the . . . others."

I put my finger to my lips. "Don't give anything away. I think these clowns just got lost. They'll be back on the road soon. They're just taking a break. This is a golden opportunity. We've got to get their attention so they'll know who you are. Are you ready for that?"

She made a face. "I'm so nervous. I wish I wasn't, but I am. I'm scared."

"They're not going to harm you here. And besides, I told you, it's right being scared. Those guys are a threat. They've got guns. They want to kill you. Fortunately, there are those of us here with your interests at heart. And we're better than they are."

She looked at me, her brown eyes big and round. "Are you sure?"

"Yeah. I'll keep you safe. Depend on it."

She shook her head slowly, closing her eyes. "I wish I could believe you."

"Come on, Margo." I stood up and threw some bills on the table. "Take my hand. Let's go for a little walk. There's a place where you can buy tapa cloth. You ever see them make tapa?"

"John—"

I took her arm. "Let's go, honey."

"Oh, all right." She picked up her purse, slinging it over her shoulder.

"Looks like the lady don't want to go," observed one of the Australians, his voice laconic, his posture alert.

"Mind your own business," Margo snarled, whirling on the man, looming over him in the posture I'd seen before, when she'd beaten me aboard *Olympia*.

"Sorry, miss." The Aussie put his hands in front of him and smiled, warding off further offense.

"She's tougher than Xena, bud," I said. "You're lucky she didn't attack."

"That where you get that hand? She bite you?"

"If I'd have bit him, he wouldn't have it any longer!" Margo leaned closer, nearly nose to nose with the young man, her teeth close enough to take a bite of his own anatomy.

All his friends laughed and the man backed away, still smiling. "Thanks for the beer, mate," he said to me. "You must be okay to handle a woman like this." His friends laughed again.

"Danny." He extended his hand.

"John," I said, taking it. His grip was powerful, and he used it to grind my knuckles. I smiled and ground back. We stood there, smiling and shaking hands, not meaning either gesture, and grinding away at each other, wondering who was going to say Uncle first. I saw a glint of hatred in his eyes, and wondered briefly what I'd done to upset this young man. "Nice to meet you," I said, and tried pulling my hand away.

"Yeah, well," he said, still holding on to my hand.

"John Caine," I said.

"Danny Fenn."

I looked down at our hands, gripping each other so tightly our knuckles were white from loss of blood. Then I looked directly into his eyes and said, loud enough so his friends could hear me, "You know, Fenn, I just wanted to shake your hand. I didn't want to marry you."

The men roared.

Fenn's face blanched as white as his knuckles and he let me go. He said something I didn't catch because of the laughter swelling around us, but I understood his meaning without needing the words.

I turned my back on him and escorted Margo from the bar.

Kimo and Ed watched our departure. They weren't alone. I noted that the Colombians had come alive, recognizing their quarry directly under their collective noses. One of the men, as if unable to believe the gift, pointed before his hand was quickly slapped down by another, an older character who averted his face while we looked their way. I'd wanted a diversion and I got one, courtesy of the special ops Aussies, their strange sense of humor, and Fenn's weird hatred.

We crossed the street and strolled in front of Peg Leg's, less than three feet from the pirates. I felt Margo tense slightly as we passed, but she held her head high and had a smile on her face as she said, "Show me that tapa store, John. I've always wanted to see how it's made." And there wasn't a tremble in her voice when she said it. Not much of one.

Two doors down, the little wood-framed tapa shop was open, and we swept aside the rough cloth over the door and went inside.

An ample haole woman with short iron-gray hair and a long hippie dress ran the place, greeting us loudly, insisting we watch how her people manufactured the Hawaiian cloth in the traditional method. I watched the sidewalk while Margo indulged the woman. The shop also sold soap, candles, herbs, and oils. The accumulated cloying scents nearly drove me from the store before Margo joined me at the front window.

"Did you find what you were looking for?" I asked.

"Not this time." She kissed me on the cheek again. A sisterly kiss, it transmitted her fear.

"The car's out front. We're going to go for it now. If you're ready."

She nodded, closing her eyes, holding her belly. "Let's get this over with."

I grasped her hand and we walked out into the bright sunshine directly to the car. The Colombians no longer occupied their tables. Across the street, the Aussies had also vacated their spot at Hoolihan's. Ed and Kimo were nowhere in sight. Haena town felt deserted.

We had discussed with Kimo and Tyler how we were going to do this, but now that events were in motion, the movements felt wooden, a sham those possessed of even the lowest of intelligence could see through. But it was a plan everyone had agreed would work, and since I had no other bright ideas, I went along.

We got into the convertible rental provided by Tyler and I put the top down. The pack lay between Margo and me on the center console, easy enough to reach if the need arose. I would be forced to use the Colt and the contents of my backpack if things went wrong. It was a bright, beautiful day. Any tourist would put the top down. And it gave me better visibility when things went wrong.

I opened the trunk and retrieved the duffel bag with the rifle and ammunition. I felt a little foolish bringing an elephant rifle to a cockfight, but, as well planned as this operation was supposed to be, I had my doubts. I closed the trunk and tossed the duffel into the backseat.

I knew things would go wrong. Everything just felt right for everything going wrong.

22

They picked us up as we crossed the one-lane bridge over the Hanalei River. They weren't back there as we drove through the valley, but as we turned the corner and doubled back over the hairpin turn by the water tank I could see two white rental cars racing after us. I slowed on the rise to get a better look. A dark-colored pickup truck followed the Colombians at a distance.

I retrieved the microradio from my day pack and powered it up. When I tried raising Kimo, only the hiss of static answered my call. Line of sight and state of the art, these radios were good, but they had their limitations.

"Can you reach over the seat and get my gear bag?"

"Why?" Margo's lips parted, unasked questions forming, then fleeing like whispers in the wind.

I called Kimo again, and again received no response. Disgusted, I set the radio aside.

"I don't know why, but it looks like we're on our own." Our agreement with local law enforcement was that they would block the Colombians at the water tank. The hairpin turn, the large amount of cover, the paucity of people at the site made it perfect for an ambush. We had a fallback set up, but it was on the other side of the island. This would have been prime, quick and close. Somebody, somewhere, had screwed up.

It happens. That's why there's always a Plan B. Or C. Or even D. Once or twice it got all the way to Plan R before everything worked.

Margo paled, but reached over the seat and hauled my black duffel bag into the front seat. It was heavy and awkward. It didn't help when I took the corner a little too fast and the rear tires broke loose, nearly sending us into the oncoming lane.

"Watch it!"

"I'm all right," I said, gripping the wheel with both hands, ignoring the pain in my left. "I've got it."

"Most men suffer from the delusion that they're good drivers, too," she said, lowering the pack to the floor.

I looked in the rearview mirror. Nothing showed around the corner yet, but they were coming. Princeville flashed by on our left, a matched collection of shops and golf courses and L.A.-style stucco condominiums.

"What do you mean, 'too.' "

"I don't know who said it, but I heard it one time and it stuck with me because it is so true. Most men are handicapped by two delusions: that they're both good drivers and good lovers."

"Oh."

"I never forgot it."

"Okay."

"You think I'm criticizing your driving?"

"I wouldn't care about that."

"If it's any consolation, you don't drive a car any worse than you drive a boat."

"You weren't too happy with me," I said.

"I remember it clearly, John."

I shrugged. We survived. Sometimes that's all you're going

to get. And it's vastly better than the alternative. "You're not going to hit me again, are you?"

She shook her head and looked over her shoulder. "I'm scared. I trust you, but I'm still scared. I'll either grind on you like this or start screaming or end up in some kind of whimpering ball like I did last night. That isn't me. It isn't what I am. I hated that." She unzipped the main compartment of the duffel bag and peered inside. What do you want in here?"

"Look in the side pockets, the Velcro ones on the ends. You'll find a couple of small blue plastic containers. Shooter's earplugs. Open them and stick one in each ear. Give me the other two."

She nodded, found what I'd described, and complied. Before she stuck the plugs into her ears she looked at me and said, "You're going to shoot them again, aren't you?"

"Not if I can help it."

"You said that last night."

"I couldn't help it."

The road took another turn over another river after we passed the Princeville Airport. As we climbed the opposite bank I caught sight of the two white Pontiac Sunbird convertibles racing down the other side. When we crested the rise and found the straight road in front of us I floored the gas pedal. The little engine coughed, hesitated, and then caught, roaring like an angry sewing machine.

"I think I can, I think I can," I said.

"This is just like last night."

"Not the same. They can't really take us in public unless they're suicidal. They may be bad guys, but let's not assume they're stupid. They'll have to wait until they catch us on some lonesome road."

Margo looked around at the green jungles and verdant fields that stretched all the way to emerald mountain slopes on the mauka (mountain) side, and the deserted rocky shoreline on the makai (ocean) side. "Does it get more lonesome than this?"

"Oh, yes," I said. "Much more."

"Where are your friends?"

I shook my head. The two white rentals loomed large behind us, close enough for me to see the driver's face of the lead car, and that of his passenger. Both men scowled behind dark sunglasses, the aviator kind, perched above their noses, covering half their faces. Intimidators. Bullies. Bastards. Cowards. The words bunched up in my brain, trying to find a way out. I hated bullies. I wondered if these guys would live down to that reputation.

"You know guns?"

"My husband taught me. He'd make me clean them, too."

"Can you assemble a rifle?"

"I've never done it. Is it too complicated?"

"No." The road took another winding turn around a low lava hill and deposited us at the approach to another single-lane bridge. A pickup truck and two cars were lined up to cross, waiting for a cane truck to take its turn in the opposite direction. Another line waited patiently on the other side of the bridge.

"Never mind." I loosened the zipper on my waist pack, making it easy to quick-draw the big Colt nestled inside. I slowed and stopped behind a red Chevrolet four-door sedan filled with tourists. A woman in the backseat wore a huge white straw hat that blocked the rear window.

"John."

"No."

The two Sunbirds pulled along both sides of our convertible, blocking us. Eight pairs of sunglasses appraised our situation, our reflections mocking us in almost comic repose. The man in the shotgun seat, the one to my left, so close I could reach out and break his neck, smiled at me.

"Good afternoon," he said. "What happened to your hand?"

"And to you, señor."

"Hey, lady. You wanna fuck?" The driver of the other rental shouted to Margo, much to the amusement of his companions. They hooted and whistled. The woman in the car ahead turned and gaped.

"John."

"Not now!" Her hand, which had crept toward her purse, stopped as if I'd slapped her. "Leave it."

"You don't need him, lady. I'll show you what a man is." He demonstrated his prowess by licking his tongue all the way around his mouth, lingering in the hairs of his mustache, his member looking like a moist pink slug.

"You guys all good drivers, too?" I asked the guy across from me. The cane truck cleared the bridge and slowly lumbered toward the Sunbird. The car in front of us nudged forward, the woman still staring back at us.

"What?"

The driver of the cane truck leaned on his horn.

"Truck's coming," I said, pointing.

"Oh, shit."

The rental backed away from the oncoming cane truck, reversing down the highway until he disappeared around the last car in the line, around the corner. I didn't know where the sudden traffic jam had come from, but I was grateful to all of them, tourists and locals alike.

I moved forward experimentally to see what would happen. The Sunbird to our right moved with us, the driver smiling hugely, motioning to Margo with his fingers and tongue, his compatriots keeping up with his wit. Or trying to.

The red car with the woman in the hat crossed the bridge and I hit the gas and followed, riding their rear bumper. We moved as one vehicle, like two giant beetles mating. Horns blared on the opposite bank. What I was doing was sacrilege, unheard of. Up here on the northern coast of Kauai everybody, even the tourists, followed the rules without being reminded. And I was being reminded. Vigorously.

The rental on the shoulder tried to follow but got cut off by a local behind us in a three-quarter-ton pickup truck with gigantic mud tires, the driver unsure which of us to hate more, the one who jumped the line or the one trying to crowd him out. He yelled and pounded the horn on his steering wheel, finally settling for shooting both of us the finger and blocking the Colombians, crowding them with his tires, keeping them off the pavement until they couldn't go any farther, halted by the concrete bridge abutment. All they could do was watch as I followed the red car across the bridge amid a chorus of car horns and curses, the woman in the backseat watching our every move, until I got an opening in the next straight section of the road and passed them, leaving the bridge crossing and the Colombians behind us.

It wouldn't keep them off our backs. This is an island. There are few options. But it would slow them enough to let me put some distance between us and try to determine what had gone wrong back there with Kimo and Ed, why the local law enforcement had disappeared, and how I could turn this into some kind of advantage.

It wasn't easy. It never is, thinking on my feet. It's getting harder every year. And in the end there was only one thing I was trained to do.

"You doing okay?"

In spite of her fear, the woman smiled tiredly. "If I wasn't so scared, this could be fun."

"You did fine back there. Great, in fact. I thought you were going to shoot them full of holes."

"I remembered the gun."

"That's what I mean. You were great. Keep that up. Remember the clarity of that moment. What you felt. What you thought. They're the ones that'll get harmed, not you. Don't ever forget what you felt back there, what you learned about yourself."

"I was terrified."

"Not so scared you wouldn't fight back. I saw it. That's where you survive. That's where you'll get the chance to live another day."

"I've been hard on you. Now I understand."

"Only a little, but maybe enough."

She nodded and brushed her long auburn hair from her eyes. It was a simple, feminine gesture, devoid of guile, something that reminded me where she came from, and how she got into this mess. And it made up my mind.

"Hang on," I told her. "We're going for a ride."

23

It took them about an hour to catch up with us. The hour gave me time to put some real estate between us and them and to think about what to do next. I drove like Mr. Toad through Anahola, Kapaa and Lihue, trying to avoid radar speed traps and keeping a weather eye out for cops on the prowl. I wondered when the two white rentals would show up again in my rearview mirror. And I wondered if Kimo and Ed and the rest of the troops would ever catch up. I didn't know what had happened, and I wondered if they had decided to go directly to the secondary ambush site. Or why.

We had just passed the old sugarcane rendering plant in the heart of Lihue when they showed up again, wildly passing sparkling tourist rentals and dusty local trucks, winding in and out of traffic, doing everything they could to attract the attention of the local cops and failing miserably. They must have lived under some kind of guardian angel that day, because they broke almost every traffic law in the book with impunity, with nothing to fear from Kauai law. Or even the laws of physics. I watched them nearly clip the rear bumper of another car as the lead driver made a quick in-and-out in an attempt to get one car length closer to us.

"Our friends are back," I told Margo.

She turned. "So close."

"And yet so far away. Are you still frightened?"

"You mean, does getting shot scare me more than your driving? Don't take this as a compliment, but yes. It does."

"You're better than that. Don't worry about them."

She shook her head, looked back at the pirates following us, and then looked me straight in the eye. It was hard to keep eye contact with her and watch the road flashing by, but somehow I managed. "I worry if you're as good as you think you are," she said.

"So do I. It's something I worry about constantly." The road took an unexpected turn to the left, descending in a reverse bank that nearly turned us. I fought the wheel, braked hard to avoid an oncoming van, and brought us back to the right lane. Margo's knuckles turned white, but she held on and said nothing until I had the convertible under control.

"You have reason," she said, after a while, when she got her breath back. "Is there an answer?"

"We're never as good as we think we are. It's one of those immutable laws of nature. The good news is that it applies to those guys, too."

"You're sure?"

"Yeah. Of course, we don't know how good they think they are, now do we?"

"So it's relative?"

"Oh, yes."

"But you've got an ego, too. A big one. I heard what you said about how you're going to handle these guys without help, about being the meanest son of a bitch in the valley. You really believe all that, don't you?"

"I'd like to think so."

"Don't cop out. You know you can do it."

"There's eight of them."

"But you've got a plan."

"It isn't much of one. All I've really got is hope and an

idea. The plan may come later. The hope is that Kimo and the boys are ahead of us, although I don't know how they'd get there from Haena." I watched the Colombians maneuver to within four car lengths, taking improbable chances to get closer to us. There was a crazy intensity to their driving, something that apparently kept them alive. If I had tried the stunts they were performing I would have killed Margo and myself in the first mile. But like fools and drunks, these Colombians seemed to burn with a fierce kind of fire, something that protected them and drove them to take every advantage that they could, while they could. I'd seen their kind before. While the magic lasted, they were almost invincible. I'd been there, myself, a time or two.

The only good part was that when the magic deserted them, it left them without any floor. They would fall hard and they would fall fast, and they would fall certainly. No magic lasts that long. Not for anyone. Even beautiful princesses can die young.

A slow-moving trash truck blocked the road ahead, and I smoothly passed it just before a long line of cars coming the other way made it impossible for the Colombians to follow, magic or no magic. By the time they cleared the obstacle we'd gained a mile. One mile down and about thirty to go.

Our destination was Kokee, at the other end of the road. It's in the clouds most of the time. The road there is steep and narrow and winding. Kokee is very close as a crow flies to Haena, but to get there by car we had to drive all the way around to the other side of the island. It's high in the mountains, three thousand feet above the beach, up nearly impassable, or nonexistent, trails from Haena, up sheer green cliffs. The road to Kokee was our secondary site to take them down. Isolated, far away from the tourists and the locals, it filled the bill perfectly. All I had to do was get us there and draw them with us.

The next large population center below Lihue was the

Poipu resort. We flashed through the town, our red convertible followed by two white ones, the three of us running like a crazed caravan. They'd managed to make up the distance since Lihue, and now crowded our rear bumper, the lead driver and his crony grinning and making obscene gestures.

I slowed to the legal limits, daring them to try us in the open. They demurred, still all but grinding bumpers, but making no move to harm us.

We tried variations. I sped up, they sped up. I slowed to a crawl, they did likewise. During one of the slow times I asked Margo to open the pack and the duffel.

"What do you want?"

"The rifle and the shotgun. Load the shotgun and hang the lanyard around my neck."

"You want buckshot?"

"Yes."

She opened the box of red Winchester-Western shells and dropped two of them into the breech, probably the first time anything but lovingly hand-loaded skeet shells had violated those precious barrels. Well, it wasn't a skeet gun anymore. Margo snapped the barrels closed and passed the lanyard over my head. The gun lay across my lap and when I stood up would hang in front of me. To get to it, all I had to do was raise my hands to waist level.

"You think you'll have any problems with the rifle?"

She examined the stock and breech, and then the barrel. Working fast, she found the release pin and pulled it, married the two pieces together, pushed the pin in place and closed the rifle. "I don't think so," she said, examining the firearm. "What is this?"

"Heavy artillery. It's an elephant rifle."

"Should I load it?"

"They're—"

"I can find them. Should I load it?"

I glanced in the rearview mirror. Pancho and the pirates

grinned back at me, still riding our bumper. Ahead, the sign for the Kokee cutoff promised the intersection within the next ten miles.

"Sure. Keep the barrels down. I don't want our friends back there to know what we've got."

She opened the white box of handloads I'd ordered from the Manoa gunsmith. The .505 Gibbs was not something you could just walk into any gun shop to find ammunition for. You had to have the shells made. And these were a little different from the normal loads. Instead of the soft-nosed bullet to bring down the African giants, these held the green Teflon-coated steel-composite armor-piercing rounds that were normally fired from a fifty-caliber Browning machine gun. They were pricey, and illegal to possess. I'd never kill an elephant. I hunt nothing that doesn't swim the pelagic currents or walk on two legs. But I could foresee someday having to destroy a truck or a boat from long range, and I had planned accordingly. It looked as if that day had arrived.

Margo loaded and safed the gun and wedged it between the seats, the barrels pointing back toward our pursuers.

"What now?"

The land had leveled into a flat alluvial plain, and the road straightened out, a narrow arrow between farmers' fields and a rocky shore. I kicked up the speed again, this time meaning it, watching to see if the little GM engine had the guts to do what I'd ask of it. Traffic had thinned now, and they might be tempted to try us on the open road.

"Hold on," I told her, watching the speedometer and the rearview mirror almost at the same time. "We're going to give those boys a run for their money now."

"Are the cops up there?"

"Hope so." I'd tried the microradio a couple of more times, and was rewarded solely by static. I shoved the radio over to Margo. "You try them. See if they're still with us, or if they all went fishing."

She tried raising Kimo, and she tried reaching Tyler. No one answered her calls and she gave up.

"Where are we going?"

"Up there." I pointed toward the dark-green mountains ahead, their tops shrouded in fog. "Way up there on the other side is the rainiest spot on earth. Five hundred inches a year. Sometimes it rains for months at a time. There's only one road close to it. It's close by. If the cops are waiting, we'll have to see what we can do when we get there. Keep trying to get them on that thing."

"That's your plan?"

"I told you it wasn't much."

She looked back into the duffel bag, rooted around and came up with two boxes of rifle ammunition. "This all you have?"

"Why?"

"We're going alone?"

"Don't know. Could be."

She looked at the mountains, and then back at the Colombians chasing us. Then she turned toward me. "If it's all the same to you, could you let me out?"

"Say the word."

"You'd do that." It was a statement, not a question.

"You're the boss. You bought my time with those emeralds. You want me to leave you to the tender mercies of those boys behind us, I'll let you out."

"Sure you would."

I stepped on the brake Slightly. Just a nudge. But it was enough for her to shake her head and put her hands on my shoulder. "No! I didn't mean it. Speed up. I'll stay close to you. I trust you, John."

We came to the crossroads and we turned and drove across the gently sloping alluvial plains between rows of pineapples until we got to the edge of the mountains and the road began a series of twisting, turning, stomach-churning bends and corners and swoops and steep grades that took everything the little car had and everything that I had, and everything that Margo had to remain on the road and in the car. We went up and up, winding our way around the sheer face of the lush mountains until the jungle took over both sides of the road and we could no longer see the ocean in the distance. Then we ran into the clouds and we could see nothing but the two-lane asphalt ribbon running ahead of us through the foliage.

Our friends followed as best they could, but they were handicapped by two additional passengers for each car and they fell steadily behind.

All things being equal, it was more than I could have hoped for.

24

Try the radio again."

I nodded, risking a glance at the rearview mirror. Margo's suggestion seemed reasonable, seeing how I was getting us deeper and deeper into trouble as we drove toward the dead end of this serpentine mountain road.

We had climbed nearly three thousand feet since turning off the main highway. On this road, no straight passage, but an unbroken series of switchbacks and sharp corners and curves that took all of my attention, we had slowly outpaced the Colombians. We had half the weight and nearly identical engines, and little by little our rental car had pulled ahead of our pursuers. The clouds hampered visibility, making the already daunting job of staying on the road that much more difficult.

Margo took the plugs from her ears and put on the headset and fiddled with the buttons and dials on the little radio Kimo had given me. I kept my attention glued to the road ahead, trying to figure out where we were.

It had been years since I'd traveled up this canyon, but as I remembered it, the ambush site should be close. The winding road twisting through the cloud-covered rain forest held no sign of our pursuers, as if they had been swallowed by the fog.

I knew they were back there, somewhere behind us, coming on with a determination that was frightening. For all their comic-opera-pirate persona, it wasn't difficult to recall their primary purpose: killing Margo Halliday.

They'd tried to kill John Caine, too, their failure merely a matter of luck and a stray breeze. I'd told Margo that I was about the fiercest warrior around, but that was just to assuage her fears. It was no longer true. I've gotten along in years, and am no longer the young stud I once was, a man who could hump a rifle and a seventy-pound combat-loaded ruck up and down the hills and through the bush, living off L-rats and swamp water for weeks at a time. Maybe I never was that good. Now my knees hurt from running on the pavement, I sometimes drank flavored coffee, and I'd brought along a couple of bottles of Evian in the day pack.

"I've got them . . . somebody. Hello?" She handed the headset to me.

"Should have kept you on it earlier," I said, taking the headset. "You seem to have the touch. Caine here."

"Where are you?" Kimo's voice was scratchy and fuzzed with static. He faded and came back again, the signal interrupted by the terrain.

"Coming up the road toward Kokee. Are you near?"

"I can hear your tires, man. Slow down. Where are the Colombians?"

"Right behind us."

"Can you see them?"

"No, but they're there."

"You'll get to the hunting cabin. You know the one? It's on the right as you're coming up."

"I know it." A corrugated tin-roofed structure built by the state of Hawaii to shelter boar hunters, it lay ten yards off the pavement, just before the road forked.

"We're there. All of us."

"What happened?"

"Later, bruddah. You're here."

Coming out of a sharp turn, going slow but still nearly losing it, I saw the cabin flash by. I touched the brake again, but saw nothing. "I don't see you."

"That's the way it's supposed to be, Caine. Keep moving."

"What?"

"Keep moving. We'll take it from here."

Fifty yards down the highway we came to a lonely intersection of two rural roads, and I turned and pulled over to the red earth berm. "Can you drive?"

"What?"

"Get in the driver's seat and get out of here." I pointed to the rough pavement ahead. "You've done your part. You don't have to do any more. This road takes you all the way back down to the highway. It's safe. Take it back to Hanalei Bay and wait for me at the boat."

"No way, John. I'm staying with you."

"I told you to follow my instructions."

"You told me to stick with you. That's what I'm doing."

"But—"

"You're the meanest son of a bitch in the valley. That's what you said. I'm not sure about those cops. What are you doing?"

I retrieved the duffel bag and dug around for the elephant ammunition and stuffed them into the cargo compartment of my day pack along with the shotgun shells. I broke open and checked the loads in the Gibbs, closed it again, and got out of the car.

"I'm going to back-up the cops. You stay here."

She shook her head. "I'm sticking with you."

"Come on," I said, opening her door. "You'll probably get dirty, but that's the price you're going to pay for coming along."

"But—"

"And keep it down. You want this thing over?"

She started to say something again, but stopped herself, visibly thinking it over, and then nodded her head. Smart girl.

"Good. Stay close. Stay quiet. And when I say down, get down. Get all the way down. Make yourself a part of the earth. You understand?"

She nodded, her eyes locked on mine.

"And bring your purse."

She held it up for me, a prize pupil.

"Come on."

We crept along the top of the slope, above the cut made by the road builders, just enough inside the jungle to be hidden, yet still able to see the pavement. Despite the time lost I felt no urgency. I didn't want to get involved in this ambush. If the plan I'd heard came to fruition there were enough law enforcement types up ahead to detain each member of the Mormon Tabernacle Choir. Kimo had asked for an army up there. My job was done. Or would be as soon as I saw the Colombians in cuffs.

"Come on," I said quietly to Margo. "We're close."

She nodded, apparently committed to silence.

But she heard the sound of tires on the pavement when I did, and touched the back of my neck with her hand. They were coming.

"Down."

She complied immediately. I couldn't have asked more from a front-line soldier.

"Stay there." Using my best bushcraft, I moved through the dense green growth until I had a clear picture of the road. Twenty yards away, just about on the edge of visibility in the dense fog, the site unfolded like a tableau. I saw movement in the jungle ten yards to my right and three men crept forward. Wearing full camouflage, including green-mesh face masks, they carried automatic weapons at the ready. They were alert and poised, and very dangerous.

I eased the big rifle to the ready position.

Twenty yards on the downhill side of the hunting camp, the road comes out of a hairpin turn, much like the one on the north shore in Hanalei Valley, but even more treacherous because the road here has a reverse bank. The wet surface of the road makes it worse. Even when a driver is unusually cautious, this turn demands all of one's attention and skill. Too fast, and it's all over.

In the distance my ears picked up the sound of tires hissing on wet pavement. They were close, just around the corner.

Radios crackled in the bush around me. Men began moving toward the road, their attention focused on the task at hand.

I removed the safety and set the first trigger and sighted the heavy barrel where I expected the lead car to appear. I had never fired the rifle and I hated not knowing the full potential of the firearm in my hands. The barrels looked good, not keyholed or pitted. The ammunition, I knew, was first-class. But I did not know the limitations of the rifle. The shot would be an easy one, even for a pistol, and the target I had in mind was rather large. The gun would have to be totally out of alignment to miss.

I braced myself against an ohia tree trunk, trying to ignore my surroundings, concentrating on the site picture over the open iron sights.

The hissing sound drew nearer, amazing, since the normal sounds of birds and wind rustling the trees were silenced by the fog, and the sounds of the pavement seemed magnified. I centered my aim on the corner of the hairpin turn where I expected to see the lead car.

They came, close together and very fast. Too fast for the turn. The lead car came around the corner sliding out of control, the driver trying to keep the car on the rapidly diminishing band of asphalt before he slid off into the trees. He was either very skilled or very lucky. At the final moment he got it under control. Just. The car stopped dead on the side of the road, the front two wheels on the sandy berm.

The second convertible skidded past the disabled one, gathering speed coming out of the turn, and ran over a long, low strip of sparkling metal spikes lying across the road. All four tires exploded. The car slowed, rolling along on rubberless rims, cutting four grooves into the asphalt before it nosed into the cut bank and stopped.

Uniformed officers swarmed around both rentals, guns extended, yelling like Confederate rebels at Shiloh. They surrounded the car below me and were rewarded by an instant and unanimous show of hands by the stunned occupants. The driver of the second car, however, was not yet ready to surrender. He spun his wheels in the soft sand of the shoulder and reversed away into the highway, sending those behind his rear bumper diving for cover.

I took careful aim, considerate of the oblique angle of the target and the presence of those officers swarming around it. The car shimmied backward along the edge of the road, moving too quickly for those on the ground to do anything but make a frantic effort to get out of the way. One of the Colombians in the rear seat thrust his Skorpion from the car, aiming it at a running man dressed in jungle fatigues.

The convertible was free of the men around it and nearly out of sight at the bend of the road.

I fired.

The rifle sounded like a thunderclap, the power of the charge sending the huge bullet on its way as impressively as a force of nature. Even wearing earplugs, the noise nearly overwhelmed me.

The Sunbird slowed.

I set the second trigger, aimed, and fired the remaining barrel.

The convertible stopped dead in its tracks. Smoke and flames shot from under the hood.

A stunning silence, present only for a heartbeat, but lasting long enough to be pronounced, fell over the scene, broken only by the soulful expression of fright and surprise from an unseen someone hidden in the jungle a few feet to my right.

"Holy shit!"

The police recovered first, surrounding the Colombians and pulling them from the car. With dozens of guns in their faces, they meekly surrendered, submitting to the urgent demands of their captors.

A man dressed from head to toe in jungle camouflage, the one who'd uttered the oath, approached me with a 9-mm pointed toward the ground, both hands on the grip, his eyes bulging. He did not aim the pistol at me, but he was ready to use it.

"Who the fuck are you?"

"A friend." I held the empty rifle at port arms.

"You that guy in the red rental?"

"That's me."

His tension eased a fraction. "You're Caine, right?"

"What's left of him."

"The woman handy?"

"She's back there."

"Bring her out. Looks like the job's done."

"Yeah," I said. "Margo. Come on up here. It's over."

"That a shotgun?"

"Elephant rifle."

He nearly smiled. "My ears are still ringing. Think I'll be deaf for a week." He chuckled. "Fucking elephant rifle. Hot damn. Now I've seen everything . . . heard everything."

"Sorry. Didn't know you were there."

"That's the idea, all this camo gear. I didn't know you were there either. When that thing went off I nearly crapped my pants."

Margo approached, holding her purse in front of her as a shield.

"The shooting's over," I said. "They're in custody."

"It's over?"

"Yeah."

"We can go now?"

"I think the police will want to talk with us. Then we can go."

"You promised."

"As soon as it's done. I promise."

She nodded, disbelief written large on her face.

"We'll need to speak with Kimo and the Kauai cops about what happened. We'll give our statements. Then we'll leave."

"Sure."

"Don't lose that abiding faith in humanity, Margo. It becomes you."

"Did you kill anybody?"

"Just a car." I didn't tell her that the head of the driver appeared in my sights for an instant, the thought that this would quickly bring the event to a close lingering, before I put the first round into the engine compartment. The only thing that stopped me was the surrounding horde of cops with their rules and their limitations and their authority. Their presence saved the man's life. Saved all of their lives. Had it been only Margo and me against them, every one of the Colombians would have died.

"Let's get this over with," I said, slinging the rifle. "The sooner we do that, the sooner we're off this island."

25

The fellow in the natty jungle camouflage outfit kept a close watch as we worked our way out of the bush and walked toward the crowd of uniformed and camouflage-clad cops.

Carrying the elephant rifle over my shoulder, a sawed-off shotgun hanging from a lanyard around my neck, and supporting a heavy leather pistol bag around my waist, I didn't exactly look like an advertisement for Green Peace. Or any kind of peace. Except maybe *Pax Cainus*.

While two men put the fire out with extinguishers, the Colombians lay spread-eagled facedown on the pavement, hands stretched to the side about as far as they could stretch them. Law enforcement types, dressed in camo and jungle fatigues with body armor, and armed to the teeth with a variety of exotic black weapons, pointed those firearms at their captives and screamed like trailer trash auditioning for Jerry Springer. The ratio seemed to be five lawmen to one pirate, and nobody seemed to want to get close to the men on the ground until the assassins clearly understood that they had about as much chance of fighting their way out of this mess as they did flying to the moon. Everybody seemed to know his job, and yet there were many excited tenor and baritone voices shouting improbable and unfathomable orders at the men on the ground.

Finally, when the Colombians managed to communicate that they had no interest in further resistance, a few of the lawmen holstered their weapons, cuffed the suspects, frisked them for additional weapons, and then hoisted the unfortunates to their feet.

When all eight were up and restrained, the cops lined them up and shackled their legs. A chain was passed through each leg shackle and they were locked together. When that task was accomplished, the cops began to relax.

Margo and I waited until the police had finished confining the Colombians. Watching them now, they looked pathetic—scrawny, hairy men, chained to each other by steel and their hopelessness. From what I knew of their patrons, failure would be met with a fury that might have made it humane to have killed them outright. I remembered the soccer player who had died after he flubbed a shot on goal in the World Cup a few years back. If these men had families, they would suffer in their place if their patrons could not reach the men.

I strolled over to the rental I had shot with the Gibbs. The sheet metal had a neat, round hole where the slug had punched through, down near the wheel well. The real damage had been done under the hood. To save weight for fuel efficiency, most modern cars are constructed of plastic, ceramics, and resin compounds. The massive steel bullet had shattered the fuel pump and rocketed right on through the manifold, destroying the engine.

"Pretty impressive."

I turned. Kimo stood behind me. His eyes were bright, adrenaline still flowing in his veins.

"Hell of a gun," he said. "For a moment I was back in the jungles, thinking somebody had called in air support."

"First shot from this thing. Never had the guts to fire it

before." I took the rifle from my shoulder and broke the barrels and handed it to the big cop. "Wasn't difficult. Decent-sized target and range for a side arm."

"They want you to give a statement. Tyler wants to impound this gun. For evidence."

"Tell him to come over here and take it."

Kimo smiled grimly, hefting the rifle. "Thought you'd say something like that. 'Pry it from your cold dead fingers?' "

"Just tell him to grow a pair and ask me himself."

"He's kind of busy."

"Then it will have to wait until he's not so busy. What's he need it for? Evidence?"

"That's what he said."

"You think it's necessary?"

"Can't see why he'd need it; but why don't you let me hold onto it? These guys are all going to get bailed out and shipped back to Colombia within a day or two. We've got firearms charges, maybe illegal immigration. Already got felony cocaine charges. Can probably get federal charges, too. They've got a regular pharmacy in the other rental. About half a gallon of coke. I'll hang onto your cannon. You can trust me."

"I trust you, Kimo."

He rubbed his jaw, looked at Margo, then back at me. I wished I could crawl inside that head of his and try to imagine what he was thinking. "If the lady wishes to file a complaint about terroristic threats, we could hold them for a few more days. It would give us somebody other than the state of Hawaii for a victim. Judges listen to that kind of stuff." He shook his head. "Doesn't matter. They'd still make bail and split."

"How about attempted murder. Remember me?"

"So far there's no rifle."

"So no charges."

He nodded. "You'll just have to get over it."

A dark blue enclosed van slowly pulled up and parked near

the line of Colombians, followed by a tow truck. Two uniformed officers got out and opened the back. I watched the prisoners shuffle to the van and awkwardly climb inside the back. Now that they were in chains and disarmed, no one pointed weapons at them any longer. But they still had an escort of six or seven armed men watching their every move.

"I'll find a way." Margo caught my eye and shook her head. "We want to get out of here. Any way we could give you a statement later? Everybody here seems fairly busy."

"You want to meet us at the police station in Lihue?"

"We could meet you tomorrow."

"No way. Things have to be done a certain way. I can bend the rules a little, but then there's negligence and dereliction of duty." Kimo used his cop voice to go with his cop look.

"Like falling back to your secondary position without telling the bait?"

"That was Tyler's call. He said the primary wouldn't work. We choppered up over the mountain." Kimo shook his head. "Tyler said he'd contact you."

"So I'll see you later."

"Later?"

"Later this afternoon? Trust me?"

He considered it. "Let me speak with Tyler. And there's a lieutenant that came up from Lihue to command this operation. It almost went very bad there for a moment. Thank you for your help."

"I would have put the spike mat at the corner, just as they came out of the curve."

"They would have crashed."

"Yep."

Kimo shook his head. "I can't do that. You would. I know you would. It would make things simple. But I can't. Not that way. We just wanted to stop them."

"Men armed with automatic weapons? Give them a fighting chance? You really wanted the lead to fly?"

"We see things differently."

"Whatever. Fuck Tyler, ask that lieutenant. Margo and I want to get back to the boat and out of these mountains." I didn't like being in the fog. I wanted to get to the other side of the island where the sun shone. Something irritated me. "Frightened" was a more honest way of putting it. Something itched way up inside the back of my skull, in a place I couldn't scratch. The cops had found no rifle. I didn't like that.

"I want to speak to the Colombians."

"No way. You know you can't do that."

"You can't. I can. And you already said they're never going to get to trial. So who cares if I talk to them?"

"What about?"

"Ask them about the rifle."

"Why?"

"Somebody took a shot at me with a high-powered rifle in Honolulu. I'd like to see the weapon."

"We don't have one."

"That's the point."

He shook his head. "They probably ditched it after the shooting. It was a screwed-up shot, so they went for a different tack. Decided they'd better get in close with those chatter guns."

"I'd like to know if they ever had one."

"What do you mean?"

"Those boys, they're mean little shits, and they like the hot and fast little Skorpions, but do they look like the kind that would sit around in a shooter's nest for two to three days just waiting for a shot?"

"And then blow it?"

"That's not the point. That could have happened to any-one. Even the best. Even world-class. I'd like to know which of these clowns was the one who took the shot. If any of them did."

"You're an obnoxious son of a bitch, Caine, but I doubt

there's more than one group running around these islands wanting to kill you. Except for Tyler. And maybe me."

"You ever hear of Vincent Forrestal?"

"No. And I don't have time for it now."

"Used to be Secretary of the Navy under Truman. Thought people were following him. The doctors confined him to Bethesda Naval Hospital. In the psychiatric unit. Kept him there and treated him for paranoia. He committed suicide. Jumped off the roof and hit the parking lot."

"What's the point?"

"Turns out he did have people following him. A nation, brand new after the war, and friendly, wanted to know about their new best friend. They had assigned agents to shadow him. He might have been crazy, but he was right."

"So you're paranoid. So what?"

"Even paranoids can get it right. Probably most of the time. Ask them."

Kimo nodded. "Okay. You two stay put until I get some orders to the contrary. In the meantime I'll hang on to this . . . elephant rifle." He lumbered back toward the cluster of brass gathered at the hunting lodge.

"Well?"

"Well what?"

"Are we going?"

"You heard him. We'll wait. We'll make our statements, tell them what they want to hear, and then they'll let us go. They have to. We didn't do anything wrong. It was a good arrest. And a good shooting. Everybody's happy. They'll let us go."

"And then you'll keep your promise?"

"We make our statements and we're off this island as soon as we can get back to *Olympia*."

Margo crossed her arms and leaned against the car. An evidence technician shooed us away. We walked up the hill, toward the hunting lodge and the group of police commanders. I tried to peer into the surrounding mist, feeling very vulnerable. And not liking the feeling at all.

"All that stuff about the rifle. What's it mean?" Margo asked.

"It's not over."

"What?"

"Somebody else is out there."

26

They finally let us go, but it took them a long time to get around to us. We were their witnesses, after all. Our time was their time. By the time they got to us, the suspects had been transported down the mountain and enough time had transpired for them to have been processed into jail, taken a nice long shower, been fed a good hot meal, and then snuggled down in some comfortable cells in Lihue. Most of the Rambo cops had gone. Other than one or two detectives, no one was needed any longer. Even the forensic people had packed their black bags and gone home to supper.

When Kimo came for us, I told him I wished he'd have arrested us. It would have been easier.

Giving our statements didn't take long, but after we finished, a couple of the local police detectives wanted to toss me in jail and throw away the key. Tyler was behind it. He demanded that I be jailed for a variety of reasons, and he wanted to disarm me of every weapon I carried, including my old Buck Folding Hunter. Kimo quietly argued that without my intervention, ad hoc though it might have been, law enforcement officers would have been killed or injured, and that I was working with him as a special deputy for the city and county of Honolulu, and that Tyler had been informed about my participation before it all started.

Whatever he said—and I was not privy to everything he said because he collared the lieutenant and walked him off into the bush for a private meeting between the two senior administrators—it worked.

"You two can go now," said Kimo, walking back from his summit, ignoring the glare he received from Tyler. "And the county of Kauai thanks you."

"My—"

"I'll keep the gun. For a while."

I nodded. Sometimes you just can't push any further.

The day had darkened while the paperwork got sorted out. An event of mischief and mayhem that took less than two seconds to complete took five hours, and hundreds of man-hours, to memorialize. It was difficult to tell the time of day in the fog, but the sun seemed to be setting. Diffused light penetrating the clouds seemed dimmer, as if some giant had turned down the rheostat. I still felt uncomfortable about the rifle not turning up. I rejected Kimo's argument that they had ditched it. They'd kept everything else. Why not the rifle?

Hubris? Maybe. It was as good an explanation as any. It fit my rule about everybody not being as good as they thought they were.

But that little man inside my skull had his red flag flying again, and he waved it vigorously, as if his life depended on it.

"Looks like we're the last dogs at this party," I said, watching one of the last official sedans head down the mountain, the red taillights disappearing into the mist. "Thank you for helping us get out of here. We're heading back to the boat. Probably spend the night there and set sail in the morning."

Margo shot me a glance. I ignored it.

"You sailing back to Oahu?"

"Uh-huh." I hated lying to this cop, but a promise is a promise. "You got a ride?"

"Uh-huh. First one in, last one out. That's what I get for being an ex-marine. See you there. Ed went back to Hanalei to watch the boys. He can drive them home when you get there."

"Thanks, Kimo." I put out my hand.

"You're welcome, Caine. See you around."

He walked away, leaving me with my hand in the air, feeling stupid. It's difficult to tell how he feels about me. I think I create more problems than I solve for him. Were it not for our paths crossing while he was on the job he would not have anything to do with me. We're not friends. He had already made that clear. But he's a fair man, and I think a good one.

"You ready?"

Margo nodded. "I've been ready for the past four hours."

We strolled back to the rental. I would have liked to have the feeling of a good day's work done well, but that nagging question about the missing sniper's rifle would not let me rest on my laurels.

When we reached the rental I watched it from cover until Margo began complaining, and I approached quietly until she laughed at my caution.

"And I thought I was the scaredy-cat," she told me.

"I've just got a bad feeling, that's all. It means nothing. Indulge me."

"I've indulged enough men in my life. From here on in, you men are indulging me."

"Touché," I said, chuckling. "I think it's clear. With all the cops that were up here all day, this is probably the safest place on the island."

I unloaded and stored the Purdy in my gear bag. I'd sacrificed a fifteen-thousand-dollar shotgun to the cause and had not even fired it. Not something to complain about. I'd probably end up giving it to Chawlie. It seemed more his style. I'd have to get rid of it now that Kimo knew of it. Sooner or later he'd be around with his hand out, arguing confiscation for the sake of the public good.

With Kimo, it's just as in the military: Don't ask, don't tell.

A small herd of black-and-white cattle approached the road in front of us, appearing out of the fog like a spectral collection from Ben and Jerry's. I thought them lost, then decided they knew where they were going, the dense fog probably one of the things they contended with every day up here. Higher in the mountain, at the end of the road, was Kokee. Beyond that was the Akaki Swamp, the wettest spot on the planet, impassable, unexplored, a quagmire of mud, grass, and stunted vegetation. Signs forbid access. People have been known to disappear there.

Seeing the cows made me hungry. "You want to stop someplace for dinner? There's a good little steak place near Poipu."

"You have food on the boat."

"You need to buy anything?"

"I've got everything I could possibly need."

"How long of a trip are we going to take?"

"Long enough."

"You want to get out of these islands tonight?"

Margo sighed. "Stop this, Caine. Are you going to do what you said, or are you going to drive me nuts with your questions?"

"I'm making conversation." The herd had reached the road. They walked slowly, in no particular hurry, but their destination seemed certain. The leader stopped at the sight of our rental and gave us the once-over from the edge of the pavement, her huge bovine eyes appraising this unfamiliar apparition. The others stopped, too, waiting patiently.

"Well, stop. The subject is closed. We get to Hanalei, you get those kids off the boat, and we pull up anchor and get out of here. Tonight."

"Have to wait until the cattle drive is over, Margo."

The lead cow, having studied us and deciding in her cow brain that we were not a threat, started walking across the road again.

I sat behind the wheel, waiting for the herd to cross, debating whether to turn the car around and descend the way we had come, or to head down the rougher asphalt surface that was the northern route. The cows decided the issue for me, blocking the road ahead. All I had to do was turn around and go back the way we had come.

I started the engine.

The lead cow stopped and stared.

"Move."

The cow stood there, watching us watch her. I had the feeling she had the patience to stand there longer than I wanted to play the game.

"What's that word?" I couldn't back up because the rear bumper was against a rock. I had to pull forward for a few feet before I could turn the car around. The cows blocked us from going forward.

"What word?"

"That word. From *Out of Africa*."

"Have you lost your mind?"

"I can't back up and I can't go forward. I need to remember what that word was."

"I have no idea what you are talking about."

"With the cape buffalo. Robert Redford and Meryl Streep are in the middle of nowhere in a touring car and they're faced with an angry cape buffalo. It snorts, looks like it's going to charge. They're dangerous animals, those cape buffalo. Anyway, Streep says . . . she leans out of the car and says, 'Shoo!' That's it. Shoo." I leaned out my side of the car and said it to the cow in front of us. "Shoo!"

The lead cow stood there, watching me, unsure of what I was going to do.

I sat back down in the seat. That made two of us.

" 'Shoo' worked in the movies."

"Honk your horn!"

"You think that would work?"

She leaned over and leaned on the horn, giving it a long blast.

The cow jumped backward as if we'd struck her. Then she started forward at a trot, jogging toward some destination that only the cow knew about. Or cared. The herd followed.

"You can go now."

"Yeah. It worked."

Margo smiled at me, wearing a look of smug satisfaction. "Shoo?"

"I—"

That's when the cow exploded.

27

The cow saved us from the blast. The windshield saved us from the cow. In an instant, the cow's broad black-and-white body opened like a scarlet flower and rained down on top of us.

I had just opened my mouth to reply to Margo's remark when I heard something that made me react. The next thing I knew, the cow disintegrated. Body parts and fluids splashed against the windshield. A long, thick strand of intestine coiled over a side mirror. Slivers of hot metal zinged around us, fracturing the windshield, cutting divots through the sheet-metal body of the rental, and winging off into the jungle. Most of the animal's neck and torso landed on the hood, collapsing the front suspension, while remaining blood leaked from the carcass across the hood.

The explosion sounded a lot like a grenade, not big enough for a mortar. Although we were too far away to have actually heard the sound, somehow, in the deep recesses of my memories, I had recalled the vaguely familiar, soft, gaseous *pop* of a grenade launcher firing from a distance—an old friend we used to call a blooker—in time for me to react just before the world turned bright.

I reached across the seat and drove Margo down into the

footwell in front of the passenger seat, covering her with my body, knowing what would come next.

Before we had time to think about the grenade, a sub-machine gun chattered from the opposite tree line. Bullets raked across the rental, churning the grillwork and blowing out the remaining glass. Another weapon joined in, a heavier AK-47 or an M-16. The two guns worked together in harmony to pick our little rental convertible to pieces.

We were safe behind the engine block and what was left of the cow, but safety was a relative term, and wouldn't last.

I felt around between the seats, looking for my gear bag, cursing when I remembered that I had tossed it into the trunk.

"Stay down!" I whispered to Margo, my hands searching desperately for my fanny pack, the one with the Colt. Another submachine gun opened up, a steady, deadly torrent aimed at keeping us down inside the car.

The blooker launched another grenade, landing in thick jungle just off the road, showering us with dirt and small rocks.

Whoever was on the grenade launcher now had us bracketed. If he was any good at all, he should be able to put the next one right into the passenger compartment.

Rifle fire joined in. Accurate, high-powered rifle fire, picking off pieces of the car with an almost artistic bent. The heavy, authoritative bark sounded familiar. I had heard that bark somewhere before, and I knew that the bite was worse than even its bark. My old friend, the sniper, was back.

They would be coming soon. If they didn't get lucky with the next grenade, and if they didn't cap us with the distance shooting, they'd come at us and finish us off where we lay.

And we would be dead.

That's not the way I intended to die.

There was only one way out.

"Stay down there until I tell you. I'm going to get out of the car so I can hit back. When I yell for you to go, crawl out the driver's side of the door as fast as you can. Every second counts. Crawl on your hands and knees when you're out of the car until you're in the weeds. Disregard everything else. Don't think. Just crawl. Understand?"

She nodded, hands grasping her purse to her body. Margo had not forgotten her previous night's experience under fire.

"Good."

I had to get to the trunk. But I first had to get out of the car. Before I got out of the car I had to find my pistol.

I found the leather strap under the seat and pulled the heavy pistol bag toward me. Whoever was out there did not empty whole magazines at us. They fired four or five rounds at a time in short, controlled bursts, real suppressive fire that worked, keeping us down while they—whoever they were— approached at their leisure. No rookies, they knew what they were doing. The sniper had us in his scope. One mistake, one error of judgment, and he owned us.

The third grenade arced over the road and landed short, but close, rocking the rental, scattering steel shards and fragments through the air and into the convertible's body.

Margo cried out.

"Are you hit bad?"

"I don't know!"

"Wiggle your toes!"

"I can do that!"

"Worry about it later!"

I unholstered the big Colt and charged it. The bag held five more magazines and some loose change. Listening for a rhythm in the suppressive fire was useless. There wasn't one. Another sign that these guys were pros, and not just some street clowns forced into a killing pack.

I tried the door. It was stuck.

More rifle fire slammed into the car and the bovine corpse on the hood. I leaned back and kicked the door with everything I had, but the door would not move, jammed into immobility by the concussions.

This was taking way too long.

"Shit." I held my breath, gathered all of my strength, centered my thoughts, and kicked the door, visualizing my feet *through* the door. The impact jarred me from the soles of my feet all the way to the top of my skull.

The door flew open.

"Follow me." I took her hand and pulled her from the footwell and together we rolled out the side of the convertible and into the bloody road. She stopped when she hit the ground, and became entangled by the intestines, but I kept her rolling until we came up against the foliage at the edge of the jungle.

"Come on!" I took her hand and pulled her away from the road and we crawled into the undergrowth.

Once inside the tree line we changed directions and crawled parallel to the pavement, putting as much distance between us and the convertible as possible, trying to get out of the line of fire. If the grenadier shot long again he would have put one right on top of us. I dragged Margo along until we were fifty yards away, inside a clump of dark green ohia trees hidden by climbing vines. Experienced trackers could find us, and I had no doubt that whoever it was who seemed intent on killing us included an expert tracker or two, but the approaching darkness would slow them down a little, and I knew a few tricks that might slow them down a little more.

I hoped the armaments in the trunk survived, but I doubted they would. I could really use them now. Going up against a team of hotshots armed only with a pistol was the same as being unarmed. Or worse. Having a pistol gave one an undeserved sense of potential.

"Where are you hit?" Margo lay facedown on the moist ground beside me. She reached back with her left hand and felt the top of her left thigh, her other hand tightly clutching her purse. I crawled back until I saw the back of her leg. Thick blood welled from a filthy open wound just below the hem of her shorts. I could see the glint of bright metal in the shallow tissues, just beneath the swell of blood.

Another grenade went off near the car, followed by an increase in the volume of gunfire. Time was just about up.

"Don't scream. This is going to hurt."

She nodded, her mouth a tight line.

I dug my fingers deeply into the wound and twisted, popping out the metal shard. Margo tensed and then exploded breath as she fought the pain, but she made no sound.

"Is that all?"

She nodded again.

"You'll be fine."

She nodded. I was proud of her.

"Stay here. I want to see what's happening." The one thing I knew about this kind of warfare was that remaining in one place had its pros and cons. If they couldn't find you, and that usually meant they didn't know you were there, you were better off staying put. If they knew you existed, and knew your approximate location, you were always better off getting the hell out of Dodge and hoofing it to higher ground. Lying under a bush in the middle of the killing zone was not an option. Not for long.

But before we moved, I wanted to see what they were doing.

"I'll be right back. If I don't get back in a few minutes, you move quietly down the hill and keep going until you run into traffic."

"Who are they?" Margo raised her face from the ground. She was filthy, streaked with mud and blood and beginning to bruise from a blow to her left cheekbone. "Are they Colombians?"

"These are first-stringers. If the second string missed you, these must be the guys who come in to clean up."

"There's your sniper."

"Yep. Good to know I was right."

"You mean that?"

"Nope. If I knew I was right, we wouldn't be here. Not alone, anyway."

She squeezed my hand. "You'll get us out of here."

"I wish I could believe that."

"You're the meanest son of a bitch in the valley."

I shook my head. "This, my friend, is no valley. These must be the other guys, the ones who specialize in mountains."

"Get going. And hurry back."

The firing and explosions increased to a crescendo and then dwindled to a few pops, and then faded away to nothing.

"Stay down and stay quiet. I think our friends just got to the car and they're going to be pissed when it comes up empty."

28

I watched from the edge of the trees as the men approached the rental. If they weren't pissed, I would have hated to meet them when they were. They were impressive. Two teams of three men, each team covering the other, each man watching those in his own team, leapfrogging from cover to cover, positioning themselves in a small unit version of the classic infantry charge. I couldn't determine their race or country of origin, not that it mattered. Dead is dead. It doesn't matter who kills you. They wore balaclavas and black jump-suits, but fog and the increasing darkness would have made it difficult to make out their features, anyway. From the way they moved I could tell they were young, athletic and highly trained, world-class commandos, the best of the best, easily on par with Spetznatz, SBS, or my old unit.

My guess was that they had been held in reserve, waiting to see if the clowns succeeded. It wouldn't do to expose the varsity if the second-string could get the job done. Those first guys were expendables, low-overhead. These men were su-perb, much too good to waste on the simple hit of a jewel thief. But that didn't work out. When it didn't, the masters sent in the A-Team. Somebody really wanted Margo dead. And they weren't messing around.

The commandos no longer fired their weapons, but kept them trained on the rental while they advanced. The first of each team tossed grenades into the convertible, dropped to the pavement just before the twin explosions crumpled the car, immediately jumped back to their feet and rushed their target, guns extended, ready to execute survivors.

They signaled when they found nothing and dropped back to the asphalt, behind the cover of the wrecked convertible, alert to their peril.

The drag man on each team faded into the trees across the road, the reserve teams spreading out, covering the point men.

Now it would get dangerous.

Well, crap.

There was no purpose in trying to fight these men with a pistol. Even if I had the rifle and the shotgun it would be pointless. It might prolong the process. I might even take a few with me. But that wouldn't change the outcome. These guys were as good as any I'd ever seen. I'd have to be Superman to get through them. And Superman I was not.

I watched the two scouts work their way around the rental, exposing one man on each side, not knowing where the threat lay, the team willing to sacrifice one man to find out, and I knew that I was a dead man. And Margo was a dead woman. She'd put her hand in the fishbowl and had stolen the man's emeralds, and let him find out about it, and then put her trust in an old fart who thought he knew enough to keep her alive. Three mistakes in a row. Three strikes and you're out. Meanest son of a bitch in the valley, my ass. These guys could eat me for breakfast, then go out and jog ten miles and still not be out of breath.

Next life, Caine, when a lady comes to you in trouble with some Colombians, smile kindly as you offer your regrets, up anchor, and sail the hell out of there as fast as you can.

They'd pick up the trail soon enough. I edged through the

trees and crawled back to where Margo waited. I found her exactly as I'd left her, blanketed with cow's blood and red mud, lying absolutely still beneath the stunted ohia tree. She looked at me when I approached. Her face seemed totally devoid of fear.

"We have problems," I said, whispering in her ear, my lips barely passing breath. "Be very quiet."

She nodded calmly.

"We're crossing the road. Heading uphill. Uphill. Understand?"

She nodded again. I couldn't have asked for a better trench mate.

"This is going to get nasty. Nastier. Stick with me." I began crawling toward the road, using all the bushcraft I knew, trying to move silently, but quickly. Once they located our trail these guys would pounce on us without hesitation.

We crawled about a hundred yards parallel to the road before I angled over toward the asphalt. I tried not to think of what was behind us. They would be here soon enough. No point in sending signals. The sun had set and the clouds had settled in for the night, making the jungle feel like a large dark room where sounds were magnified or absorbed, depending on their point of origin. I liked the darkness. It might be our only ally.

We found an empty road and ran across to the other side and plunged into the brush. Fifty yards in we encountered a pig trail and followed it uphill, away from the highway. When it intersected a creek, we abandoned the trail and waded downstream until another trail came out of the jungle and we resumed our trek toward the heights. It was a poor attempt, but I dug out every trick and device I knew to throw off our pursuers. I had no illusions of losing them. Not these guys. But if I could slow them down we might be able to reach the relative safety of a populated area.

To do that we had to cross the mountains ahead and descend the face of the Pali along knife-edge ridges so narrow that two boots could not be placed on the trail at the same time, the trail balancing over cliffs so steep that one foot in either direction led to a hundred-foot drop. It wasn't a place I'd ever want to be, and before we got there we had to navigate the dreaded Akaki Swamp, the wettest, foulest, most desolate place on planet Earth. It was something only a crazy, foolish, or desperate person would consider.

And then the trail looped back toward the road, the way we had come, and I realized that the second pig trail had not been a different route, but the same one that meandered up through the forest and then back again. The stream bubbled merrily along in front of us. A few dozen yards beyond that lay the road. And the hunter-killer team. We'd outsmarted ourselves.

"Down," I whispered.

Margo immediately complied.

I saw or heard nothing. That meant nothing, given the circumstances. Deciding, I turned and went back the way we had come. Margo followed, demanding neither an explanation nor an order. She knew what I'd done.

And yet she followed.

I waved her toward me, and like a lover I cupped her head in my hands and whispered in her ear.

"Stay behind me at least five yards. No closer. Keep me in sight, if you can. But don't crowd me."

She didn't ask why. I was grateful. If they took me out with the first shots, there was the chance she could get away. Not much, but a chance.

We crossed the stream again and waded into the water until it covered our knees, silently and in tandem, and followed the flow of the water as it fell along the gentle mountain slope. We waded down the creek until it met the road. Margo followed me under the concrete bridge, where we paused to reflect on the good fortune that suddenly had come our way.

Two rental Jeeps were parked just off the road on the opposite side. When I saw them I nearly hit myself for not thinking of it sooner. Our pursuers had not walked up here. Like everyone else, they had to drive. The team had parked their transportation about a mile down the road from their ambush site. That would have been sufficient if they had killed us at the intersection. But they'd missed, and we were loose and we'd stumbled on their cars before they had found us.

A lone man stood guard, watching the roadway and halfway watching the stream. I'd caught a glimpse of him as we approached the bridge, froze where I stood until he strolled to the other side of the bridge. I then had moved silently and cautiously until we were concealed by the concrete span above our heads.

If this wasn't a trap, the commandos had unwittingly provided us with the means of escape.

The means were there. All we had to do was take them.

Maybe they weren't as good as they thought they were. I hoped at least that they weren't as good as I thought they were.

I grasped Margo's hair and pulled her ear close to my lips.

"Come with me to the far side of the bridge. Silently. You're good. You're great, as a matter of fact. Stay here until I call you. When I do, climb up there as fast as you can. Can you do that?"

She nodded.

"We're driving out of here," I told her, pulling her gently along, feeling better than I had a right to feel, and thanking whatever gods there were that everyone was human, and that it wasn't only old John Caine who made mistakes. Theirs was a whopper, although easily understood.

Underestimating the meanest son of a bitch in the valley can always be problematic.

We weren't out of the woods yet, but there was a glimmer of hope. If they had not set this up as a trap—something I had to consider, given their level of observed competency—we had found their one weakness. If it was a trap, there was nothing to do but to find out.

29

Kauai is famous for its red volcanic earth, which, when wet, becomes slick, slippery red volcanic mud. The bank beside the bridge was so steep, wet, and slick that I doubted I could have climbed it with a ladder. A few exploratory touches was all it took to convince me. Unaided, nobody was climbing up there this night.

Looking for a Plan B would involve splashing around in the dark below an armed and unfriendly opponent whose mission in life—at least for the moment—was to kill me and my client. One innocent splash would be enough. Knowing we were out here in the dark, he would be alert to anything out of the ordinary. One small sound would kill us both.

Under the bridge was stygian dark. I had to feel my way along. The concrete retaining wall must have been poured in place between loose form boards. Built in a time long passed, when contracts were awarded to those close to the power structure, not to the lowest bonded bids, the bridge might have been slapped together by unskilled labor. A slapdash job, it created opportunities. I felt enough excess concrete at the joints to support my weight by toes and fingertips. Farther up there were voids and cavities in the wall, more evidence of an inexpert concrete pour, but a regular harvest of hand-and toeholds. The climb looked to be no more than ten feet. Child's play. I'd seen worse. I'd done better.

I tucked the Colt away in the belly bag, loosened the Buck knife in its little belt sheath, slipped off my sandals and stuck them down the back of my shorts. Flexing my fingers, I wished I had some surgical tape. The concrete was granular-rough and would wear the skin from my toes and fingers before I reached the top. My left hand, swollen to nearly twice the size of its twin, would give me pain, but nothing I couldn't handle. Not with two lives depending on it.

I nearly fell the first time I applied all my weight to the tips of my fingers and toes. Somehow I held on, remaining aloft by the power of my fear. I hung there on the wall like a befuddled spider, my tendons and muscles getting accustomed to the strain, and then began climbing, one slow movement at a time.

Climbing by fingers and toes is extremely difficult. It's hard enough holding on with four points. The act of climbing makes it necessary to shift most of the weight onto the toes, using one hand to search for the next hold, the other hanging on for balance. Doing this barefoot was painful. With sandals it would have been impossible.

Slowly, hand over hand, I climbed until I reached the steel I-beam girders that supported the concrete roadbed. None too soon I grasped the bottom web of the steel beam, shifting my weight from my toes to my arms. Sweet success. My legs had begun shaking so badly I nearly lost control.

From there it got easier. It took no time to swing from one girder to another until I reached the edge. When I reached the edge, I crawled along like a tree sloth, slowly moving with my arms and legs until I got to where I thought was the middle of the bridge. With my feet braced against the beam, I swung around the side, hoping I would not find myself looking up some guy's nostrils.

Empty air above the guardrail was my reward.

I swung back in.

I swung out one more time, just enough to check once more before I committed.

No one there again.

Time to go.

Swinging back under the bridge to gain momentum, I braced myself and launched, determined to reach the railing. If I could grab on to the railing I'd continue over the side of the bridge and fling myself onto the guard, wherever he was.

The swing was good. I grasped the metal edge of a guardrail with my left hand, held on, and managed to get my right hand onto the railing, too, before I fell. I hung in space for only an instant, transfixed by the pain in my left palm, before I hauled myself up over the railing and onto the bridge.

My heart nearly burst from the exertion. No ninja warrior was I. Old John Caine might be forced to wheeze them to death, if nothing else.

Even a highly trained soldier will fail when faced with an unexpected surprise. The guard was more surprised than I and he showed it. Never expecting the threat to appear from the center of the bridge, he stood there looking at me for a long second, less than six feet away, his mouth open, his hand halfway to the sling on his shoulder.

I ran at him, head down, my right hand already holding the knife, the blade coming up, locking in place.

He backpeddled, trying to buy some space so he could take the rifle from his shoulder, sliding the sling down his right arm.

I plunged the blade into his diaphragm, just under the sternum, up under the hard bone. The blade only went in about an inch, all it needed, and he collapsed, dropping the gun.

It went off, bounced, went off again, bounced over the railing, and disappeared into the river below.

I ran to the opposite side of the bridge.

"Margo!"

Her mud-streaked face appeared at the foot of the slippery wall. She wore no expression, as though she waited for a taxi, as if her facial muscles had frozen. I'd seen that before, on some of the strongest warriors. Shock. Pre-shock. The mind's unwillingness to accept that the events it experienced were really happening.

"Come up!"

I lay down on my belly and reached down as far as I could. She scrambled up the wall, reaching for my hand, slipped, and fell back into the water.

"Shit!"

"Try again!" I said, trying not to think about the others out there. Hearing two shots, they would converge here. And soon.

She climbed to her feet and tried to scale the wall of slick mud again. Our fingers brushed and then she fell, sliding down the ramp into the river.

"Try again!"

It wouldn't be long before the guard's companions arrived. If they had been close, we were in trouble.

She slung her sodden purse over her shoulder, backed off to the middle of the stream, got up a good head of steam and ran partly up the wall, grabbing my wounded hand in a death grip. I held on to the guardrail and pulled her up while she propelled herself up the slick muddy slope, her legs pumping. It must have looked ridiculous, but it worked.

As Margo crouched on the top, exhausted by the effort, her gaze fell on the body of the guard lying in the middle of the road. "You shoot him?"

"Come on, get up." I looked for the keys. They were not in the ignition, or any place else I looked. The second Jeep did not have keys either. The guard had nothing in his pockets. He had been sanitized. But where were the keys?

"John?"

"I'm looking for the keys."

"Where are they?"

"If I knew . . . I don't know. Probably with the others."

"Can't you hot-wire it?"

"No."

"I can, but I'll need a light."

The soldiers would be closing in on us, drawn by the gunfire. A light would be a beacon.

"Too late for that."

I again searched the body of the dead commando, conscious of the time eroding away. I dumped the body into the back of the nearest Jeep. He had three mini-grenades attached to his web gear. I took the pistol and all three grenades, primed one, and wedged it under the clutch pedal of one of the Jeeps. If no one noticed it would sit there, inert, until somebody engaged the clutch. Then it would roll down under the seat and arm itself, hopefully unnoticed. Two point five seconds later, it should give the driver a nasty driving experience.

"Come on," I said, pulling Margo to the side of the bridge. We're going back into the river."

She looked back, as if the Jeep would explode at any moment. It could, depending. I'd wedged the grenade in loosely between the fire wall and the upper arm of the pedal, balancing it on a nub of a pin, held in by the spring-loaded arming mechanism. It was possible that getting into the Jeep would cause it to come loose. But then it might have the same effect.

If I had to fight them, it would be hit-and-run, a guerrilla war. They'd prefer to hit. We would run. If I could keep a step or two ahead of them, I could keep Margo and me alive.

There was only one place where we had a chance to survive—the Akaki Swamp. Uphill those few miles, and then over the small hills into the swamp. Only there could we lose them. And ourselves.

"Come on." I took her arm again, gently guiding her toward the brink. She hesitated, then swung over the side, using my injured hand as a lifeline, her strong legs pumping against the mud.

"Okay," she called.

I let her go and she disappeared down the muddy slope. A small splash was my reward.

"Hey, mate!"

I turned. Danny Fenn stood behind me, holding some kind of automatic weapon I'd never seen before, aimed right at me. I knew it was aimed at me because a thin red light reached out through the fog and rested on my chest.

"Snuck up on you, didn't I? Told the lady you were soft."

"Don't judge me harshly," I said. "Been having a bad day."

He laughed. "My mates are about. Got you, I did. Too, too good, you are, they said. Best of the best. Tough as nails. Quite the trophy. Shit. It was too easy."

"What?"

"You're Caine?"

"Yes, but—"

"John Caine? The detective?"

"Yes."

"You're sure?"

"What—"

"Can you prove it?" Got some ID? A driver's license? Something with a photo?"

"What?"

"*Yes* or *no?* Can you prove you are John Caine, the Honolulu detective, former SEAL?"

"If I have to—"

"It would just save us all some time. A courtesy. So I can collect."

"Collect?"

"The fee. For killing you."

"Wait a minute. You want to kill me? Not her?"

"Right-o, chum. Missed you the other day. It happens."

"Not the woman?"

"Her, too. But only because she's here."

"Care to tell me why?"

He laughed. "You know? I don't think so. Let's keep you in the dark."

I dived off the bridge as he pulled the trigger, knowing the bullet would be faster. Falling, I heard four shots, but didn't feel anything.

Then I hit the rocks.

30

Round river rocks struck me in the ribs, pelvis, knees, and chin. I lay in shallow water, letting the gentle stream flow over and around me, too stunned to move. Even too stunned to lift my head above the surface to take a breath.

"Come on, you big lump." Margo grabbed me under the armpits and tried to lift my dead weight, gave up on that when I refused to help and raised my head above the surface. "You're going to drown and then you'll be even more useless." She looked me right in the eyes, her face close to mine, her hair brushing my face. "If you don't get up and get out of here, John, you're going to be sorry."

I did a slow push-up, got to an upright position, and painfully took stock of myself. Nothing broken, just bruised, and the wind had just begun to come back. I still had my knife and the Colt, and the pistol and the two mini-grenades I'd taken from the dead commando. I still hadn't fully understood what Fenn was talking about. They wanted to kill me, not her. What the hell had I done to deserve that? Who would want to send a team of killer commandos after me? For a fee?

"Come with me. You're no good now. Maybe if you recover from that stupid stunt, you'll think better. You came flying off the bridge like you thought you were Superman.

Just follow now. Don't think. Just move it." She splashed off downstream, not looking back.

"Okay," I said, and got to my feet. My sandals had vanished. Walking on the smooth stones wouldn't be too difficult. My soles already were toughened. The old Hawaiians hardly ever wore shoes. That was before the missionaries imported the thorny bushes and trees in what may have been an attempt to make the natives dress like the good New Englanders that they weren't.

By the time I got my body moving, Margo was already out of sight in the fog, only a vague splashing sound somewhere in the dark.

I hurried to catch up.

She was correct. As I moved, I gradually came out of my own fog, following her trail. Within a hundred yards I caught up with her and waded along behind her. The strong sense of inertia overcame me again, and I just wanted to follow and not make any decisions on my own. I wanted to lie down and go to sleep, something I knew was not a good thing to do, and something that indicated a possible concussion. I fought it and moved along briskly, keeping up with the woman. As I moved along, the exertion aerated the brain tissues, and I became more conscious of my surroundings. As I became more conscious, I noticed that Margo carried the Glock I'd given her, the one I'd borrowed from Chawlie, the same one I'd taken from her ex-husband so many months before.

"Are you shot?" she asked when I moved up beside her.

"Not . . . no. Just banged."

"Keep moving. Don't slow down."

"Where are we going?"

"This way."

"What happened back there?"

"I saw him while you were on the bridge, but I forgot I had the gun. When I remembered it, he had that red light on you. What's that, a laser? Anyway, I aimed at him, got him in my sights just the way Chawlie taught me, and started squeezing the trigger. I wanted to hit him in the head, because Chawlie always told me that was the best place to shoot somebody.''

I gave her a look but she ignored it.

''I had to wait until you got out of the way so I could shoot that fucking Australian. They're the ones, you know. The ones from the café. They sat right next to us and you bought them a round of beer. They were watching us while we tried to get the attention of the Colombians. And you didn't pick up on them? You didn't know who they were?'' She sighed, shaking her head. ''So you just stood there like a lump, talking to him as if you were two old buddies. Then you suddenly just jumped off the bridge so fast I almost flubbed my shot.''

''You shot Fenn?''

''Who?''

''The big, tall Aussie. From the café. Please tell me you shot him.''

''I don't know. Maybe. He moved too fast to tell. He didn't shoot you, though, did he? Keep moving.''

''No.'' My feet kept slipping on the smooth rocks, but I managed to keep up with her. She was setting a pretty good pace. I wondered where she was headed. I wondered if she knew.

Then I heard something behind us. ''Wait!''

''Now wha——''

I clamped my hand over her mouth and whispered in her ear. ''The deal was, I lead, you follow. I got fuzzy there for a minute or two. That doesn't mean I'm done.''

She wriggled and tried to bite my hand.

''If you want to live . . . shut up.''

My warning went unheeded. She continued to struggle against my grip, even tried to get the pistol up. Then she bit me, got a good grip on my wounded hand and chomped down hard on the swollen tissues. I broke free and backed away.

"Jesus," I said, my eyes watering from the pain.

"Keep your hands off of me."

"Okay. But you have to listen to me or I'll abandon you right here."

Margo stood quietly. "You can talk like a gentleman. You know how. You don't have to manhandle me. You're a big man. You're scary. You don't just walk up and grab me. Don't you know what kind of an effect that has on people?"

"Listen!"

Another splash joined the one I'd heard. Then another. And another. A fifth and a six splash followed at regular, purposeful intervals, the sound of bodies jumping into the water. It was disappointing not to have heard an explosion. I had hoped to cut down the odds by at least one more, but these guys were too competent to fall for something like that.

She looked at me, her eyes wide. She knew what I knew.

"They're coming," she said.

31

Margo followed. Probably easy to do. My knees hurt from the fall, my feet began to form blisters on their soles, and my head throbbed almost as much as my hand. I hobbled along like an ancient.

The Aussies, coming up behind us, made no noise. We tried not to make any, either, but our actions failed to match our intentions. We had to get out of the river or they would be on us in minutes. We needed to create more decisions for them, more opportunities to make mistakes.

We needed something to slow them down.

The river began getting rougher as the gradient increased. We slid down a couple of small waterfalls and I noticed, as well as I could in the misty darkness, that the canyon sides had begun getting steeper and higher. The water's voice matured from a gentle burbling to the deeper, throaty roar of a fully-developed river the lower we went, and the volume of water increased as more streams joined ours.

Wading became more difficult. Hopping from rock to rock was unreliable. Remaining in the river, even along the sides, would not be an option for long. I looked for a trail.

Feral pigs inhabited this remote part of the island. All of their trails led to water. Finding one of their pathways took longer than it should have, and I wondered exactly how far behind us our friends really were. Fenn had sneaked up on me so easily the first time, it frightened me to think of it. Had he not wanted to demonstrate his abilities, to show himself superior to me, he could have readily killed me where I stood. Now that he had failed—twice, if you count the bungled shot at the marina—he would be under no such compunction. This time it would be in earnest.

It was so dark along that stretch of the river that I walked past it and Margo found the trail. "Here, John. Here!" she called to me.

When she shouted she might as well have put up a neon sign, advertising our intentions. I got angry. Then I got an idea.

The trail was animal-made, but made by large animals. Not tall, but big and heavy. It seemed more like a tunnel through the brush, four feet high at the peak, four or five feet wide. Some big old porkers inhabited this island, some of the big boys got up to five hundred pounds. It looked like the habitat of the king of the oinkers. I hoped we wouldn't meet him coming the other way. Wild pigs could get mean as hell, and we already had enough trouble.

"Get going." I pointed to the brush tunnel. "Get up there as fast as you can. Get away from the river. Get away from this spot. Don't stop until you come to a fork in the trail. Wait for me there."

She ducked and vanished into the jungle. As long as she thought I knew what I was doing, she took my orders as advice and worked with me. Once she didn't trust me, she went her own way. I shrugged. Couldn't blame her for having a brain.

Feeling exposed, I studied the entrance to the tunnel, scuffed up the mud along the shoreline, enhancing Margo's tracks and adding some of my own. I didn't want them to miss where we had gone. Then I searched the river for a flat rock, found one about eighteen inches across and moved it so it lay just under the surface, a stepping stone, a natural footfall.

I took one of the two grenades and pulled the pin. For this to work it had to be wedged under the rock so that the spring handle would only fly if the rock moved. I checked it, lying down full-length in the water, sticking my best eye under the rock to see. It looked fine. The weight of the rock pinned the spring, and the mini-grenade was round like a baseball and would roll if someone stepped on it. When that happened, the device would explode. Ockham's Razor. Least amount of moving parts. Simple and effective.

If they wouldn't bite on one booby trap, they might fall for another. If it worked, it would take out one or two of them here. Probably one. I doubted these guys would bunch up, knowing their training. But its presence would slow them down, for they would look for more. If they found and disarmed it, the grenade's reality should be enough to make them think, and that would slow them down also. It was a win-win for Margo and me and a lose-lose for them, and that's what we needed. Time was our only ally.

I stepped over the rock and scurried into the brush, trying to catch Margo. I found her twenty yards above the river, crouched at an intersection that reeked of pig dung. She looked tired. Her hair hung limply in tangled strands, her clothes were streaked with mud and blood. One black bra strap had slipped down her right arm. Seeing the strap reminded me of another trap that might work if they discovered the first two.

"Give me your bra."

She looked uncomprehendingly at me for only a second, and then slipped her arms under her blouse and removed her bra. Without removing her blouse, she pulled the brassiere from below the hem and handed it to me.

I took out my Buck knife and began slicing up the material into long, thin strips. When I cut the wires from the cups I twisted them into hooks. We didn't have much time, so I hurried, but I needed some stout dark string or line. The line I had packed had been in my gear bag, blown up in the trunk of the convertible.

Margo sat on the muddy trail like the Indian maiden on the butter wrapper, silently watching what I was doing, absorbing the detail. Now her head turned and she looked down the way we had come, as if she had heard something out there in the dark.

"They're coming."

"We're going to slow them down. This won't stop them, and it will make them angry, but what the hell, they're going to try to kill us anyway. Why not hurt them a little?"

She gave me a look that told me she thought I was full of crap.

I put the Buck away and tied the strips together to make a long, thin rope of material, a lightweight rope. "Which way do you want to go?"

"Why ask me? You're the big man out here. You decide."

"Crawl up that trail to the right, the one in front of you. Go up there about a hundred feet or so. Wait there until I reach you. If you hear an explosion, or if you hear shooting, keep going. Don't look back. Don't come back. Go until you get to the road and then run downhill until you find a house or a town. Call the police. Try to reach Kimo. Tell them everything you saw and everything we did."

"You'd better not screw up," she said, and crawled away on her hands and knees, disappearing into the pig tunnel.

This was an effective technique I'd learned a long time ago when Uncle Sam had paid me to travel into harm's way. Old Sam had even provided a grizzled old marine named Bailey to teach me how to make improvised booby traps, a man who had survived the hand-to-hand fighting on Iwo Jima and other tropical hellholes during the Second Big Mistake. Bailey made us go through each drill a hundred times before he was satisfied with the level of our skills. He wanted us to know

how to assemble these traps so well we could put them together in the dark.

Well, old Bailey, my long-gone teacher and friend, we'll
see how successfully you taught us on this dark and foggy
night. If the Aussies gave me two more minutes, I'd have my
trap completed.

I started giggling. Using a bra to make a booby trap. I wondered if old Bailey had ever considered that, even on his best
day.

"Shut up," said the little man in the back of my head.
"You're a fool, and you've got little chance. Laughing now is
just plain stupid." He crossed his arms and settled back. "And
the joke wasn't even that funny. Proves the pressure is getting
to you."

Taking a deep breath, I got control of my center and con-
centrated on the task at hand.

This was the last of the mini-grenades I'd taken from the
dead guard. The others had so far been wasted, except to buy
us time. I had no illusion that the team wasn't close, or that
they had missed my pitiful attempts to booby-trap rocks and
Jeeps. My only hope now was that they would be mindful of
the danger of rushing after us, and that the mines would slow
them down.

If these exercises succeeded in achieving that, I'd be happy.

If I was able to feel any kind of emotion at all.

This kind of trap worked best if it had two leads, but I didn't
have enough brassiere or enough time to make two thin
ropes. The brush tunnel was low and dense and one should
be sufficient. I hoped so. I hung the grenade in the canopy
above the tunnel. The foliage was so thick the grenade would
be invisible even with a light shining on it. Without one, it
didn't exist. I ran the cup wire lead from the pin to a point
near the ground, and from there across the trail at shoe-top
level and tied the end to a sturdy branch. Fishing line would
have worked better. This lash-up wasn't totally invisible, but

should be easily missed in the dark. If I could get them running, it would work. If this one worked, the blast, at near head height, would be devastating.

Once I was satisfied with the trip line, I reached up and pulled most of the pin from the grenade. I left just enough shaft inside the pin socket to prevent the arming mechanism from springing. Barely enough. It was a hair-trigger device. A strong breeze would detonate it.

I double-checked the trap, keeping a respectful distance. It would work or it wouldn't. Nothing I could do now would improve it. I backed away from the grenade, knowing the kill radius was plus or minus eight yards, possibly a little less in such lush jungle growth. I didn't feel truly safe, however, until the trail rounded a corner and picked itself along the rocky face of a sheer cliff.

The explosion came sooner than I would have expected. I stopped in my tracks and tried to determine which trap had been set off. The second blast came immediately after the first.

Impossible.

A third explosion crumped in the jungle some thirty yards away. I flung myself to the ground and tried to get as much cover as I could before the next one came. I knew what they were doing. I'd have done it myself. Their blooker man was lobbing 40-mm grenades into the jungle, trying to get lucky.

They were using an old technique called reconnaissance by fire, trying to flush us out.

It seemed likely they had discovered my mined rock at the entrance to the brush tunnel and disarmed it, probably by tossing it up the trail, thinking it portended an ambush. They had been slow in coming, slower than they should have been. Either Margo had wounded Fenn, or my reputation, whatever they knew about me, probably kept them back, expecting more than I had been able to deliver. But they were here now, and they were ready to play.

They had to get it done now. They knew all about the time

restrictions. Few people live up here, but there are a few, and this kind of thing creates a racket that tends to make people reach for a telephone, if only to complain.

The blooker man lobbed a few more grenades into the brush, causing consternation to the bird population but no other damage. By now they would have expected a response and we hadn't given them one.

My job now was to get them to come up the trail, and to come fast. If they ventured cautiously, they were good enough to find the last mine and to know that I had no other grenades. Then they would come with less prudence than before. Whatever had held them back must have been the knowledge of the grenades. Once accounted for, they would come on the run, and they would catch us, and we would be dead.

The only way to get them to come fast now would be to expose myself. I crawled back down the trail to the dark intersection, drew the Colt, stretched out on the ground, and waited, a black lump against a dark background, conscious of the danger before me, and the grenade hanging in the trees behind, and of the trip line. My plan was to fire on them as they came up the hill and then let them see me flee up the mined trail.

I hoped they would concentrate on the fleeing figure in the dark. I hoped they would concentrate so hard on the running man they would miss the fact that he jumped over the trip line as he ran up the trail. I hoped the fleeing figure would be at least eight yards ahead of them when they set off the grenade.

I hoped for a lot of things. One of the things I hoped for most was that I would not stumble at the critical moment and set off the damned thing myself.

32

They came low and fast in groups of two, leapfrogging the teams, pausing only briefly to be sure of their coverage before advancing. They were surefooted and sure of themselves, like predatory raptors sniffing the wind. I knew how a gazelle felt, stalked by a pride of lions. And that's where the metaphor broke down. If I had the speed of a gazelle I'd have been on the other side of the island the first time I saw these guys coming my way.

It bothered me that they were after me and not Margo, something Fenn relished, but wouldn't reveal. It bothered me that I might never know.

The lead pair were the only ones visible in the misty black. We were in a brush tunnel in a canyon in the fog in the middle of the night. Visibility approached zero. Only movement showed in the darkness. Only sound directed the senses. Lying in jungle growth at the edge of the trail, I was invisible. Had the point man not been ten yards away and moving I wouldn't have been able to see him at all. The others were there—I could hear them—but I could see the dark shape of the point man effortlessly duckwalking up the trail, feeling the ground and looking ahead, his teammate poised to counterattack any ambush.

Watching the expert teamwork I knew I'd misjudged the situation once again. The grenade hung in the brush behind me. I should have been behind it, not in front. The plan was for them to see me scurry up the trail. But that wouldn't work with these men. I couldn't retreat over the trip line if they could see me. If I could see them, they could see me. And if they could see me they would shoot me dead. It was time for Plan B. But there was no Plan B. I was stuck with what I had.

Trapped, I aligned the front sight of the Colt to the center of mass of the leading Aussie, waited until I couldn't wait any longer, and closed my eyes in the millisecond before I squeezed the trigger.

As soon as the pistol fired I turned and scurried up the tunnel, keeping to the side of the tunnel, careful to step over the trip line, dancing to the impact of bullets chewing up the foliage overhead and to my left. I slid into the brush and settled in about ten yards behind the grenade, and turned to confront them again.

Their response was for two guns to open up on full automatic and spray the brush tunnel. The others waited behind, unable to fire. The trail was so narrow not all of them could engage, and the pig trail turned just behind the grenade site, so their bullets plunged harmlessly into the jungle. A narrow trail was my advantage, but these guys were too good to let that stop them. In no time they'd figure that out and simply dive into the bush to surround me.

I hated closing my eyes when I fired, but it was the only way I knew to preserve my night vision. They hadn't had the luxury of knowing when the gun would go off. Their eyes would have fixated on the flash, the bloom burning a bright image in their minds, and their retinas would carry that flash for a few seconds. Those few seconds kept me alive.

This time.

They came again, slowly but certainly, leapfrogging the teams as before, seemingly unperturbed that I'd attacked them, acting as if my actions had no effect. I didn't know if I had hit the point man or not, and if I had, if I had hurt him. Like all jungle warfare, it is sometimes impossible to know your level of effectiveness. Sometimes you have to wait until the sun rises to count the bodies. Unfortunately, the only ones who get to do that are the victors. And sometimes, not even the victors survive.

I didn't think there would be many victors in this contest. My job was to keep these guys occupied while Margo ran for her life. I depended on her to get to a phone and call for help. If I could stay alive for a few more hours, it was a win. By then, the local cops would come and they would stop the commandos. It would be bloody, and it would be expensive, and the Kauai cops might have to send in the marines before it was over, but the outcome would never be in doubt. Like those two idiot bank robbers in L.A. a couple of years back who dressed in armor and brought AK-47s to the party. They kept the entire Los Angeles Police Department at bay for a few hours, severely wounding a couple of good men, walking back and forth with cop bullets bouncing off them like Superman. But the end was certain the moment the first round was chambered. You can't fight an entire force of trained, armed men. Not alone.

"Now you're talking," said the little man from his easy chair. He was sweating. He looked defeated, as if he'd tried everything and nothing he did or said would work. "That's you, fool. Now let's get out of here!"

Ten yards down the path, their point man approached the trip line. I centered my sights on the man, aimed at what I believed was his upper thigh, aiming to wound, not to kill, closed my eyes again and fired two rounds. He fell, screaming agonal cries of pain.

"Help! I'm hit!"

I rolled to the side of the trail, but held my ground, waiting. For this to work I needed them to charge my position. They were too professional and too seasoned to charge on their own. I had to give them a reason.

"For God's sake, man! Help me!"

It was one of the dirtiest things to do in warfare, but it worked when you were outgunned and outnumbered. I had learned it from the Viet Cong, who, when cornered, had shot to wound, leaving the casualties out in the open, knowing that the wounded would attract others to help. And when they came, blow them away, one by one, until the forces were neutralized.

Help came, two of them. One slithered on his belly up the trail, past the wounded companion. The second was a large dark shadow that merged with the writhing shadow on the ground. For a heartbeat, all three became one amorphous lump, and then the belly crawler broke away and continued crawling up the trail toward me.

I heard the sudden spring of the grenade arming itself, followed by the quiet hiss of the fuse directly above the belly crawler.

"Grenade!"

I covered my ears and opened my mouth and pushed my face into the ground and flattened myself lengthwise toward the blast that I knew was coming.

33

The explosion split the night with a flash and a roar. Too close to the grenade to avoid getting holed, I dug my fingers and toes into the sodden jungle floor, trying to disappear down into the muck. I was only partially shielded by the thick canopy of foliage from the blast; the shock wave blew up and out from its point of origin, most of it blowing over me. Most of it. I was outside the kill zone, but not outside the wound zone.

Two small pieces of jagged metal found the back of my bare right leg, digging twin ragged furrows across the flesh. Like a scythe, they sliced my rugged old hide and passed on into the night.

Those within the center of the kill zone weren't so lucky. I could see about that far down the path. The explosion had blown a hole through the canopy of foliage. The fiery path of the grenade's missiles had killed the advancing crawler where he lay. The wounded man and his would-be savior lay like tossed bundles of discarded rags. Nothing else moved. No one else appeared. But I knew they were there.

To show the others I was still in the game—more as a victory dance than a challenge—I fired a couple of quick shots down through the dark tunnel into the black maw at the other end, then scurried up the trail. Now was the time to put some distance between us.

They would have something to think about. I had no more grenades or tricks up my sleeve, but they might not know that, and they might be treading cautiously now. I'd cut down the opposition by at least half, but it wasn't over. Not yet. My right leg bled freely. It hurt like hell, but no tendons were cut, and the slices were nothing more than an inconvenience.

I wondered if this trail found its way to the road. It seemed to be heading in that direction. I also wondered if I could make it before they collected themselves and came after me. For the first time since the cow exploded, I began to think of survival. It had been six or seven to one before. Now it was more like three to one. And Fenn was either hurting or dead, depending on what Margo had done to him with that Glock. It might only be two to one. If so, the remaining two might turn tail and bug out.

Fat chance. As pleasant as it sounded, I doubted these fellows would give up easily. Even if it came down to one of them against me, whoever was left would still believe he would win. It was as much in their blood as in their training. Men like that don't go into special ops believing they will lose. And those that make it through the training just don't give up. Not ever. Not even when all of their teammates are dead or dying. As long as one is still standing, the fight's still on.

A figure suddenly rose in the darkness from the side of the trail, reaching toward me. I brought the big Colt up and nearly shot Margo through the head before I recognized her slight figure in the dark.

She lunged and clung to me, holding me tightly.

"Let go, Margo," I said, prying her arms from around my neck. "We can do that later."

"I thought they'd killed you."

"Not me. I thought you'd run down the hill to get help."
I took her arm, gently but firmly, and guided her up the trail, mindful of the threat that still lingered behind us. Her failure

to follow directions could get her killed, and her presence now could get us both killed. I was not happy with her staying here, but I wasn't going to complicate things by starting a fight.

"I couldn't leave you. I thought you might need help."

"Yeah," I said, remembering her blistering attack on Fenn, saving me from a certain death. "You're not bad. But I thought you weren't up to shooting people."

"I can, when I'm scared enough."

I wondered what Kimo would say if he heard that. She hadn't said "I could." She had said, "I can," implying experience. I wondered if that included only her most recent experience, or if she had done it before.

"Good. You're here. I'm scared enough for both of us, so you will be, too." We moved quickly up the trail. It was hard work, demanding that we bend over and jog at the same time, a punishing way to get around. I kept looking back, listening for the commandos behind us.

"Those men from the bar. They're Australian? Why do they want to kill us?" Margo asked, her voice a soft whisper.

"The one you shot. That Fenn? He said there's a reward if they kill me. A price on my head. He wanted a picture ID to prove it."

"Like when you write a check?"

"Easier than taking my head back in a sack like they used to do in the bad old days. He wouldn't tell me why, but he said it was me, not you."

Light flashed in the trees ahead of us, then abruptly vanished, swallowed by the foliage.

I jumped off the trail, dragging her with me through ferns and philodendron. I found a spot deep inside the vegetation and shoved her down and lay on top of her, the Colt tracking the forest by the trail. Margo didn't make a sound, but she squirmed under me.

I put my face next to hers so she could see me, my finger to my mouth. She nodded, but kept squirming, and I finally understood that she was trying to get something from her purse.

I rolled off her and she came up with the Glock.

"Caine, you old fool," the little man inside my head scolded me. He'd lost weight. He looked exhausted from his efforts. "Stop thinking of this woman as a liability and start thinking of her as an asset. She is, you know. She's already proved that. You're only still breathing because of her."

"Yeah," I answered, little more than breath between my lips.

"What?"

"I was talking to myself," I said, embarrassed.

"Can't you do it quietly?"

The light flashed through the trees. Someone was coming down the trail from above.

"Did you go any higher? Is there a road up there?"

"No."

The light flashed again. It panned across the vegetation above us, focusing on the trail. It wasn't the commandos. Like me, they would never use a light in the forest. Not at night. Not under combat conditions. Whoever it was wasn't a party to this fight. Whoever it was was walking into the middle of a war.

"Hey, brah! We got us a pig, here!" The singsong voice of a local pig hunter filtered through the bush. The hunters followed the trail. From the location of the light, it looked as if the hunter might have found traces of our tracks running off the road.

"What you got?"

"Tracks. Leadin' off the trail. Big one. Fresh track. Must've been comin' up the trail when we was headin' down."

We had left no tracks in mud, because the ground was covered with a layer of dead and freshly fallen leaves where we left the trail. We must have scuffed enough of the top layer to disturb the pattern, leaving sign. Our passing must have resembled that of a large animal.

"Bring the shotgun!"

"Oh, shit," I said.

"What are they going to do?"

"These guys are going to pepper the bushes around us. They might even hole us. They want their pig, but they don't want to go into the bush for it. Can't blame them. Feral pig can be meaner than hell."

"What are you going to do?"

"Stop them," I said, easing from cover. "Stay put. I'll stop him before he starts shooting."

She nodded, keeping the Glock trained on the light. In a way I felt sorry for the pig hunter. Totally unaware, he had Margo training a gun on him, me crawling through the brush toward him, and an angry commando team climbing up his backside. He didn't know it, but if he lived through the next few moments, he was about to learn the definition of shit-scared.

Probably cure him of coming into the jungle at night for the rest of his life.

"Come on, man. Bring that shotgun down here." He shone the light near me and I froze.

"Something's right there! Something big!"

I heard the racking of a pump gun. Being pig hunters, they'd be loaded with double-aught. Or even slugs. I didn't want to be shot with it, but I wanted that gun. It would keep me in the game.

"Right there?" Another voice asked the first one.

"I'm shining the light. Right there!" The powerful light passed over me and rested on a log lying at an angle to the trail. Its rough gray surface made it look like the flank of a big hog.

Any self-respecting feral pig would have been over the next ridge with these clowns shouting at each other through the trees. They were silly drunks, not serious hunters, out for a lark on a foggy night. Probably got the idea while drinking, thinking of fresh pork, and got to talking and talked themselves into the trip. Probably didn't really mean to find one. Probably trying to scare each other into thinking they'd actually found a pig.

I wondered what they'd do if a real pig came along.

"Hold the light still, brah!"

"I'm holding it. It's right there. You can't miss."

"That's not a pig, that's a tree!"

"Oh?" The man with the light moved forward until his sandaled feet were within reach of my grasp. But I didn't want him. I wanted the shotgun.

"Yeah. Come here. Lookit!"

"I'm taking a leak." Shotgun, the other voice, had moved away, to the far side of the trail.

"When you're through, come here. There's real track."

There was the sound of a zipper and then Shotgun came over and looked, close enough that I could count the hairs on his toes.

"You wanna go in there and meet up with that pig yourself?" he snorted. "That's plenty big pig, brah. That's plenty big trouble, it find you first."

The barrel of the shotgun dropped vertical next to the man's leg, pointed at the ground. It was now or never.

Rising, I grabbed the shotgun, reversed and twisted. By the time I stood in front of the man who had held it I had it trained on his face, my finger on the trigger.

"Aeyeeeeeeeia!" The other man dropped his light and did something I'd never seen a human being do before, wasn't even aware the species was capable of it. He dropped down on all fours and ran backward through the bush on his hands and knees, disappearing into the mist, screaming as he went.

"You want to live, you'd better follow your friend."

Shotgun nodded, his eyes round and white, illuminated

by the filtered yellow light of the discarded flashlight. He sank to his knees in front of me. "Please don't kill me."

"When you get home, call the police. Tell them you ran into a wild man. Tell them he stole your shotgun. Tell them you ran into a war up here. Tell them to come. Understand?"

He nodded again, never taking his eyes from the shotgun pointed at his head.

"You're not going to kill me?"

"You got any more shells for this thing?"

He reached a shaky hand into his shirt pocket and brought out a handful of plastic shotgun shells. Awkwardly, his hand closed the distance between us as if it had a will of its own and offered them to me.

I snatched them from his hand. "This all you have?"

"Uh-huh."

"Then go. Go now. And call the police."

"You're letting me go?"

"You heard me. There's things out here you don't want to see. Just call the police, and get out."

"Thank you!"

"Get out of here!" I hissed.

He went, scrambling after his friend, terrified and relieved at the same time. I waited, then dropped to the forest floor and silently crawled back to the fern patch where Margo lay, covered with mud, tracking me with the Glock.

"Where are those killers?"

"Out there. They saw it all."

"How do you know?"

"They saw it and backed off. They don't want to kill any more civilians than necessary."

"What about me?"

"It's necessary. You can identify them. You're with me, so you're no civilian."

She pondered that. "Where to now?"

"We move. Through the weeds. Toward the water again."

"No more bright ideas?"

"No. We just don't sit still. We move. Until we find a place where I can ambush them again."

"It's one o'clock in the morning. There's a long way to go before dawn."

I glanced back up toward the trail. The abandoned flashlight lay like a beacon in the trees. "More reason to keep moving."

"We've got to, I guess," she said.

"What does a rolling stone gather?"

"No moss."

"Momentum," I said. "That's us. We're gathering momentum."

34

Bushwhacking, following the fall of the land in the dark, off-trail, through tangled jungle, is hard work, but we managed to find the river without falling too many times or stumbling into a bottomless pit. That the commandos didn't follow bothered me. I knew they hadn't given up. Far from discouraging them, the booby traps would have made them furious. Small units train together, live together, sleep together, and play together. They become close friends, closer than most people ever experience. I'd taken some of their friends away, killed them in a most brutal manner. That made it personal.

They were out there, they were angry, and they would be looking for us. As long as we stumbled around in the dark it was only a matter of time before we would meet again.

The sound of the river came through the trees long before we ever saw it, the rushing water giving us a goal. Following the downhill slope guaranteed that we would run into water.

I didn't know where the commandos were and I had no way of knowing that. But I could know where they had been. I wanted to find their trail and follow them. I knew I'd feel much better behind them than in front of them. That was my goal. Then it became a question of what to do with the information.

I'd had enough of this defensive stuff. My first priority had been to get away from them. That hadn't worked, forcing me to fight. But fighting when you're outnumbered and outgunned and ignorant of your opponent's capability is a losing proposition. I got lucky. It wouldn't happen again. Maybe the best thing to do once we reached the river would be to go upstream, not down, get back to the bridge, see if we could start one of the Jeeps and get the hell out of there. Let the police handle it. Live to fight—or run—another day.

We found the river at one of its high points, wading into the middle of the stream to cover any sounds we might make. At the center of the stream the water flowed past our waists.

Decision time. Up or down? From what I could see of her, Margo looked exhausted. I'd run her all night. Covered in mud, crusted with cow's blood, wet head to toe with torn and matted clothing, she had not uttered a single complaint. She had saved my life. And this one, after all, was not her fight.

Decision made. Discretion is the *best* part of valor. I owed her. I had to get her out of this mess.

I took her hand and gently guided her upstream, indicating that I wanted her to follow me.

"We'll use our momentum to get the hell out of here," I whispered, my mouth next to her ear.

She turned her head to answer. "I can hot-wire that Jeep."

"You said that. You sure?"

"Yes."

"Then let's go get one."

I started climbing upstream, automatically looking for cover should we need it, but certain that the Aussies still lurked far downstream, trying to find our trail.

We'd always gone uphill. From the very first, our method was to run uphill, away from the threat. They'd know that, and when they tried to think like their prey they would add that to the calculation. We'd moved downhill for the past two hours. It should have thrown them off.

Now we were going uphill again. If they followed us to the river, they would know.

By then I hoped the two of us would be far away in one of the hot-wired Jeeps.

Even in the dark the terrain began to look familiar. We had been moving quickly before, fleeing the pursuing commandos, trying to make sense out of what Fenn had told me. Soon I could recognize familiar landmarks, one after another, and I knew we were close to the bridge.

The fog had vanished, blown away by the night breezes, and by the time we found the base of the bridge, stars twinkled in the sky like old friends. I handed the shotgun to Margo and climbed the rough concrete abutment as I had before, pausing to check the surroundings. Nothing had changed. The two Jeeps remained untouched, the one with the body and the grenade closer to the bridge. Nothing moved. I crawled back to the edge of the slope and helped her up the slippery slide and retrieved the shotgun.

"Careful not to touch the one with the body in it."

She looked at me as if I'd lost my mind. "I won't go near it."

While I stood watch, she raised the hood. A light came on when she did.

"Turn that off."

"I need it to see what I'm doing. It won't take long."

It made me nervous, standing there watching while she worked under the light, but there was nothing I could do. I didn't know how to start the car. I wondered how she had learned.

"How did you learn to do that?"

"Growing up with four brothers. We were a close bunch. They taught me lots of things."

"They teach you to shoot, too?"

"Rifle, pistol, and shotgun. Dad hunted. So we all hunted. Chawlie taught me some technique, too. I pretended I was a beginner with him. Wait a minute." She twisted bare wires in her fingers and a spark shot across the terminals. The engine caught, and then died. "You've got to get in and push the clutch. You do know how to drive a clutch, don't you?"

"Yep," I said, jumping into the driver's seat and engaging the clutch. "Now," I said, not able to see her under the hood.

The engine caught and revved up and down the scale once or twice as she manipulated the gas feed to the engine. "These new models are different," she said, slamming the hood. "But it's the same logic. All the new parts are the same as the old parts, and they're all in the same places."

"Get in."

She climbed into the passenger seat and buckled her seat belt. "They're gone? Those killers?"

"Looks that way."

"Good. I need a bath and a drink, and not necessarily in that order."

I let up the clutch and the Jeep started rolling slowly forward. "I was thinking—"

Five gunshots, fired from across the road, hit my side of the Jeep. One of the shots hit me in the leg as I pushed past Margo, who was trapped by her seat belt. I dived across her, hit the pavement, rolled and came up with the shotgun and fired over the hood back at the tree line opposite the two Jeeps.

Margo slumped over the seat. I couldn't tell if she was hurt, so I reached in, unfastened her seat belt, and dragged her out of the Jeep onto the ground. She was limp and she landed hard.

"Margo!"

She didn't answer.

More shots came from across the road, striking the body of the Jeep like steel rain.

I answered with the Colt, putting four rounds where I thought the last muzzle flash had been.

"Margo!" I felt her head. One of the first bullets had hit her in the left side of the head, carving a long, straight crease across the top of her skull. Her pulse seemed normal, probably better than mine, considering, but she was out, knocked out cold.

My leg throbbed. The bullet had passed through the fleshy part of the calf, boring a half-inch round hole in the muscle. It hurt, just as the two grenade shrapnel slices hurt, but it wouldn't kill me. Not by itself. Letting it bleed was all I could do.

"Hey, Caine!" It was Fenn.

"Yeah?"

"Tough guy, you are, Caine. They said you were tough, and I thought you might not be easy, but you're a real tough one, you are. You killed five of my mates, including poor Barry. He wasn't one of us, you know. But he wanted to help. So we let him watch the Jeeps. He was an innocent, you might say. Nothing dangerous. And you killed him. With a knife. You didn't have to do that."

"You didn't have to come here, Fenn."

"Oh, but I did. It's a million dollars American. For your head."

I knew he was moving. I could tell by the changes in his voice, the Doppler effect, as he moved around. That's why he was talking to me. He was circling one way, his friend another.

"I'm flattered. A million bucks. Somebody must be unhappy with me."

Fenn laughed, moving farther to my right. Soon the meager cover of the Jeep would be gone. Leaving Margo seemed like a good idea. I edged back away from the Jeep toward the edge of the river.

"That's true. You want to know who?"

"Sure."

"I'm not going to tell you." Fenn laughed again.

Something moved in the darkness at the other end of the bridge, beyond the second Jeep. I was not quick enough to see it clearly, but it was there, a dark figure, dashing through a black background on my left, advancing on my position.

"You're going to kill me now, is that it?"

"That's why I'm here. It took much longer than I thought, but that only made the whole thing interesting. We're all winners and losers here. And you're about to lose."

The blood froze in my veins. That phrase. I hadn't heard it in years. Not since I'd sent Thompson to a watery death off Oahu. A serial killer who tortured and raped young girls before killing them, and got it all down on video tape for commercial sale, I had tracked Thompson down and killed him on his own sailboat. But not before he had killed a woman I had loved.

"Thompson?"

Shots cleaved the air beside me. I dived and rolled toward the Jeep, sprawling beside Margo's body. I fired two rounds to my right and one to my left, and rolled her unconscious form under the Jeep, back near the rear tires.

"His brother. His older brother, the one who managed his financial affairs back in Australia. Took his death very hard, did the elder Thompson. And you were to blame. Only you. So he hired us. Told us to kill you. And here we are."

Out of the corner of my eye, I saw the figure closing in on my left behind the other Jeep, less than fifteen feet away.

Fenn was still somewhere out there on my right.

"Okay, Caine. This is it."

I was wrong. Fenn crouched behind me, pressing a pistol to the back of my head. As before, he had approached as stealthily as a cat, unseen and unheard.

"The girl's dead?" Margo lay facedown on the pavement. Maybe if Fenn thought she was dead he'd leave her alone.

"You shot her," I said.

"Looks like I shot you, too."

"That first one. You got lucky."

Fenn laughed again. "You do have a sense of humor. The woman nearly took my head off the last time I had you." I hadn't been able to see him before, but he showed himself, getting in front of me, sporting a welling bullet wound in his shoulder, just above the clavicle.

"Turn around, Caine. Put the gun down. Face the truck."

I obeyed, and he stuck the pistol against the back of my head.

"Chad!"

"Yes, sir." The other commando appeared near the Jeep.

"Fire up the other car. Leave poor Barry here. He's no use to us."

"They'll find you."

"Doesn't matter. We're long gone as soon as this is done."

I wanted to look to see what Chad was doing at the other Jeep, but I didn't dare. I wanted to duck, but I didn't dare. So I crouched next to the Jeep, feeling the pressure of Fenn's pistol grind into the back of my head, wondering what the final instant would be like.

"You're better than I am, Fenn," I said.

"I know. But you're okay. You're just not the best. And you played the best and lost. No shame in that, man."

"Go on. Do it," I said. "I'm cold and wet and tired and hungry. No reason to drag it out. You'll be doing me a favor."

Fenn laughed. "Okay. But you'll forgive me if I wait just a few more minutes. If you're a religious fool I'll give you time to pray. That's more than you gave old Thompson, if I heard the stories right. And it's more than you gave poor Barry." He released the pressure of the pistol barrel and shouted into the night. "Chad. Bring the car around!"

"Sure, boss."

I waited, counting down the seconds. The Jeep started and the commando drove it over to the other side of the road.

"Thought you'd fooled me with that grenade? After the

rock in the river and the one in the trees? Hardly. Like I said. You're okay. You're just not the best."

"That's disappointing."

"Ready?"

"Will it make any difference?"

"Oh, you're a wiseass," said Fenn, and put the pistol against the side of my head.

Margo rolled over holding the Glock and fired three shots up into Fenn's chest before he fell. As he collapsed I scooped up the shotgun and fired across the space between the two Jeeps, blowing the man away from the wheel. He fell out of the driver's seat and lay on the pavement.

I picked up the Colt and walked over to where he lay and fired two shots into his heart. Then I returned to Margo.

"Shit, this hurts," said Margo, struggling to sit up and hold her head at the same time. She still held the Glock in her right hand.

"Lie down. You need to elevate your feet. Don't sit up."

"I listened to you two talk for a long time. I dreamed it at first. I heard you talking and I thought I was dreaming about you. And then I heard him talking, and I was back at the café, and then I was here on the road, with my hand in my purse on the gun. And I knew what I had to do. Were you just going to let him shoot you? Without a fight? You sounded so . . . so defeated. It made me sick."

"Lie down. And no. There's a move I know that might have worked."

"*Might* have worked . . ."

"It was all I had."

"Except for me."

I smiled. "Except for you. That's two I owe you."

She smiled. It looked as if smiling hurt, but then she was tougher than me. Hell, she was tougher than Golda Meir. "Make that two lives you owe me. Neither of which is worth much."

"Sun's coming up soon. You want to wait until it gets light or chance riding in the Jeep now?"

She nodded her head solemnly. "You promised me we'd get out of here as soon as it was done." She glanced around the bridge, the bloody pavement, the bodies, the bullet-riddled Jeep. "It looks done to me."

35

We saw the sun come up together. We had earned the right.

The great golden ball peeked over the edge of the peaceful Hawaiian waters just as we rounded the lazy corner of the highway to Donkey Beach. The beach was deserted in both directions, so I pulled off the road and drove onto the sand, sailing over the little dunes and dodging the driftwood until we rolled along the edge of the surf line. When waves threatened to swamp us I steered back onto dry land and parked so we could share the splendor of the new dawn.

"It's beautiful," said Margo.

"One of a kind."

Tears welled in her eyes as she watched the sun pull itself up from the water's edge, and then she leaned against me and started sobbing.

I put my arms around her and held her close, waiting for the spasms to pass. "You're going to miss the sunrise, you know."

She nodded.

"It's okay if you miss this one. There will probably be another one tomorrow."

She nodded again.

"Might even be prettier."

She nodded.

"Or it might be worse. Might be fog."

She put her hand over my mouth. "Shut up," she said between heaving, hiccuping sobs.

I let her be, alone with her thoughts but hugging the heck out of one John Caine, a man with whom she had spent two very eventful nights. Let it provide whatever small comfort she could get from it. She must be exhausted. I knew I was. As the events finally caught up with her, she had to deal with them. I did, too, but I had my own way, and it wasn't something I was capable of doing with another around. I had to deal with my demons on my own.

"Caine?"

"May I speak?"

"Yes." She nearly smiled, but she was too tired to manage. "What?"

"What do you think of me?"

"I think you're tough. I think you're determined. I think you're one hell of a shot. And I like you."

"Do you think I'm good?"

"Somewhere in there, I think you are. I didn't like you at first. Then I got to know you."

"Do you trust me?"

"No."

She smiled that time. "No? Just like that? You didn't have to think about it? Just . . . no?"

"Yes."

"Why?"

"You steal. You try to manipulate me. You don't tell me what I'm dealing with. You keep things to yourself. You don't do the things you say you're going to do. You do things you promise you won't. You lie about me, and then you lie to me. That enough?"

"But you like me?"

"Yes."

"No second thoughts?"

"No."

She sighed. By talking, by thinking about something else, by sharing her feelings with another human being, she had stopped crying. Tears still flowed down her cheeks, turning the dirt there into mud.

"You are one filthy mess, you know that?"

"You should see yourself."

"No, thanks. I'll get to that soon enough."

"I killed him, you know."

"I was there. Three shots. Right in the ten-ring. Thank you."

"No. My husband. Glen. I shot him."

"Okay," I said. I wasn't the cops, and I had no vested interest in seeing Glen Halliday's killer brought to justice. I'd met the man only once and I broke his arm.

"Do you remember that night? The night he'd ripped my clothes off and chased me down the alley?"

"Of course."

"We'd been out to dinner. He picked the place. He wanted to get back with me. We still worked together. Somehow he had decided that we belonged together. Just like that. I told him no. I told him to take me back to my place and let me out there. He took me to his car, and then he ripped my dress off. When I tried to fight back he slapped me unconscious. When I woke up I was naked and he was trying to . . . to get inside me. I kneed him, jumped from the car and ran.

"He chased me. I don't know where he got the gun, but he shot at me. Then you came out of nowhere and knocked him down and then you brought me into Chawlie's place and I knew I was going to be all right. At least for that night.

"I found it ironic that you took me to Chawlie's place, because we had just eaten there. Glen had deals going with Chawlie, shipping the jewels to him here in the Islands, and they had met earlier to try to arrange the next shipment. That was before dinner. Then Chawlie disappeared. I learned later that he was with you in his back room. I thought at first you were a part of his organization, until Chawlie set me straight. He told me you were his friend. He told me about you, and that if I ever found myself in deep trouble, you would help me. He said you were a sucker for a good-looking woman.''

"He should see you now.''

"Thanks. I learned that he spoke the truth about you. And that the women didn't even have to be good-looking. You know, that Graham woman and her kid? You dropped everything for her. Even me. And went off and found her husband. I thought you were either some compulsive White Knight, or one of the stupidest men I'd ever met.''

"Which is it?''

"I haven't decided yet.''

"So you and Chawlie took up with each other.''

"He provided protection. And he knew me. I was the courier for the emeralds between Colombia and Hawaii. That was my job. You know the story. I stole them. But I blamed the theft on Glen. I called my contacts in Tortola and told them that he had taken them. They said they'd send somebody. I knew they would kill him, so I just waited.

"Once he was dead I planned on running. There was more than three million dollars in emeralds in the package. They would last me the rest of my life, if I sold them carefully. I had no big ambition. I just wanted to be rid of Glen. I wanted to be my own woman. I didn't want to have to depend on a man again. Ever. For anything.

"I asked Chawlie if I could have a gun. He knew that Glen came around and raped me every once in a while, and he knew that he beat me, too, when the mood struck him. Chawlie offered protection, but I refused it. I didn't want a couple of bouncers around the house all the time. So he gave me the pistol you had taken from Glen that night. The Glock. He asked no questions. He just gave it to me. Chawlie knew why I wanted it.

"I carried the gun in my purse everywhere I went, but Glen was nowhere to be found. I heard he'd gone back to the Mainland, and I relaxed a little bit. One night I went home, drew a hot bath, added some bubbles, poured some cold wine, and stretched out in the tub. Life was good. All I had to do was to wait for the Colombians to catch up with Glen, kill him for me, and then I could hide. I'd bought maps and travel books, and I knew exactly where I wanted to go, but I couldn't leave until I knew he was dead. Otherwise they would know it was me all along.

"I lay in the tub soaking in the bubbles and dreaming dreams like some stupid schoolgirl and Glen walked in on me. He had been drinking again, and I knew what he wanted. He pulled me out of the tub and dragged me into the bedroom and threw me on the bed. The gun was in my purse, on the nightstand beside the bed, but I couldn't reach it, and I knew that if I tried to fight him he'd get even more excited and then he'd beat me. It was one of the things he liked to do, you know. So I stopped fighting and let him have his way. It would calm him, I knew that, so I let it happen. It wasn't as if he hadn't been there before."

The harshness of her words shocked me. Not the content, but the bitterness of her expression, the self-loathing, the almost shuddering recollection of the necessity of the event.

"I waited until he got dressed. When he turned around to tie his shoes, the moment his back was turned, I got to my purse, got the Glock, and shot him nine times. I got out of there. I didn't even shower. I dressed so fast I still had his gunk inside of me as I took the gun back to Chawlie. Chawlie took it. He knew it had been fired, and I think he knew instantly what I had done. And why. But he never questioned me. He made no comment at all.

"I returned home and called the police, pretending I had

just come home and found the body. The police came and arrested me, and then my attorney got me released. The next night I saw those men on the beach and panicked. So I ran to you, to your boat."

"So you killed him in self-defense."

"I shot him in the back."

"Doesn't matter whether he's pointed north or south. You had to kill him. Or have someone kill him. That was your plan? To have the Colombians do it for you?"

"Yeah. But they took their sweet time about it. I couldn't wait any longer."

"Hard to get good help."

"I must say I was a little startled when you handed the Glock to me yesterday. I had no idea you had it."

"Chawlie must have liked the balance there. Me taking the gun from your husband, you borrowing it and killing him with it and returning it to Chawlie, me borrowing it back to give to you. It must have made the old man smile."

I thought about the Glock, implicated in so many deaths.

"Give me the gun."

"What?"

I dug into her purse, found the pistol, got out of the Jeep and waded into the surf until it rose above my waist and pitched the Glock far out into the sea. It hit with a satisfying *plonk* out beyond the surf line.

While I was out there I washed some of the muck off me. It felt good to be in the water, to begin to get clean again.

When I was through I returned to the Jeep. "You should try that. It will make you feel better: How's your leg?"

"My head hurts."

"We should stop at the hospital. You have a nasty cut there."

"It took off scalp, but I'll be okay. I'm not concussed. I know the symptoms. But you—you've got a bullet hole!" She touched my leg where Fenn's bullet had pierced the calf.

"I'll be all right. It hurts, and so does the hand. And so does the rest of me. But hospitals have to report gunshot wounds. And somebody will want to know what happened over there on the other side of the mountain. The sun's up now. Somebody will find the bodies and then people will start asking questions. I think we better get going. If you're up to it."

"You know, for the meanest son of a bitch in the valley, you seem to be fairly clumsy."

"I said meanest, not the quickest on my feet."

"Granted."

"And I guess I lost my title."

She wrinkled up her nose and smiled. "I'll have to be the meanest *bitch* in the valley."

"You said that." I shrugged. "I didn't."

36

Ed Alapai met us at the beach. He had been sleeping in the cab of his pickup but he jumped out as soon as he heard the Jeep's tires crunching the sand. He started to run and then he saw us and stopped and stared openmouthed, as if he were looking at something he had never seen before.

"You okay?" I asked him.

"It was you." His gaze traveled between Margo and me, back and forth, his eyes working like Ping-Pong balls inside his head. "I knew it was you. And I knew you'd be the one to come down off dat mountain."

He turned and whistled. The two boys aboard *Olympia* had been watching. One pulled the painter from the railing and they both jumped into the Avon for the short trip to shore.

"What are you talking about?"

"Betta you get on dat boat and get outta here. Otherwise you gonna be pau. Tyler, he gotta head o'steam about you. Kimo's wit' him. He'll cover your ass, but things heated up last night when you didn't come down. You two were last seen walking to your car. People complained about some loud war games the marines were holding up there. Kimo told me a couple of drunken pig hunters got the shit scared out of dem. Somebody stole their shotgun. Thought dat was you. But nobody wanted to go up there until light. They're up there now. Kimo and Tyler and the others. They just found them. Bodies all over the place." He held up a radio unit. "But not Mrs. Halliday. And not you." He looked at the radio in his hand as if it smelled bad. "I'm supposed to radio Kimo if I see you."

"It was self-defense, Ed."

He appraised me, considered my condition. He winced when he looked at Margo's head wound. "You look like you been shark-wrestling. That all your blood?"

"Mostly not." My leg hurt like hell. The wound had gone beyond throbbing. Once the seawater cleaned out the clots it had begun to bleed again. The bottoms of my feet had blistered, then the blisters had been sliced by the rocks.

"You had a bad night, huh?"

"I've had better."

"I can get somebody to come take the Jeep. He'll have it stripped down to parts in a couple of hours." He bit his lower lip, thinking about the details. "I'll make the call as soon as you're gone."

"Thanks, Ed."

He nodded. "You best get on your boat and clear out of here. Go around the Pali, not toward Lihue. Six of one, half dozen of the other for distance, but they'll be out looking soon enough." He thought about it. "Probably best head for the outer islands, up toward Midway. That's a thousand miles or so. Better than going south."

"What are you talking about, Ed?"

"Tyler don't like you. Kimo's sitting on him, but dat don't hold no water here. He'll cover for you, but it'll take some time. You want to sit in the Lihue jail until it all shakes out, you sit right here. Otherwise, I'll tell them you left a long time ago, tell them you sailed off toward Lihue."

He turned and watched the two boys approaching in the Avon, shading his eyes against the bright morning sun.

"Charles and Filipe can go with you," he said, thinking

out loud. "Be good for dem. You got a bullet wound, too?" Ed looked at my leg, the open wound welling dark worms of blood down both sides of my calf, and nodded gravely. "You're gonna get all stiff and sore in a couple of days. Can't run a boat like dat. The boys can work the sails, take care of the boat while you mend. When you don't need them anymore, send them home. Kimo won't mind."

"What about Neolani?"

He smiled. "She's a good woman. She'll understand. She love dat Charles something fierce, but she'll be okay about it. Just don't get him hurt. It's Tutu Mae you gotta worry about. She'll skin you alive, something happens to her great-grandson."

"I'll take care of them."

"What about you, Mrs. Halliday? Are you better off than you look? Do you need a doctor?"

Margo had been silent during my conversation with Ed, arms folded, sitting in the Jeep staring toward *Olympia* riding calmly at anchor. She had lived through a lifetime of nightmares over the past forty-eight hours. The shakes would come later. Right now she was making a heroic effort to keep herself together.

As was I.

I knew because I had watched her tear herself down and then build herself back up back there at Donkey Beach. This was one tough lady. She had been through the fire and she had survived, and she was going to be fine. As long as I could get her off this island and let her fulfill her dream.

"I'm okay, Ed," she said quietly. "It was a difficult night. It was very hard. But John kept us alive. I expect that he will keep us alive out there on the ocean, too. I have no doubt that he will keep us alive anywhere. Under any circumstance."

Ed shook his head. "Promise me, Caine, that you'll tell me the whole story when you come back."

"It's a promise," I said, wishing I knew the whole story. Somewhere out there was a man who wanted me dead. He was willing to spend a great deal of money to arrange my death. It hadn't worked out for him. None of his people were coming back. I wondered if that would put him off or make him even more determined.

I decided that I didn't care. He would keep. I knew his identity and had a good idea of where I might find him. Someday, when I got bored, I might go hunting.

Or I might not.

I was getting to like the idea of live and let live. If they would only let me.

The two boys beached the Avon. They laughed like two carefree teenagers until they saw Margo and me, and then they were suddenly quiet, the way you're instinctively quiet at a funeral, or a hospital.

"Charles," said Ed. "Filipe? You two think you can run the sails on dat boat?"

Both boys nodded.

"You two are going to go with Mr. Caine and Mrs. Halliday until they get to where they're going. It could take a week, it could take a month. I'll tell your father, Charles, and both your mothers. They'll understand. If you need any clothes, toothpaste or toothbrushes, Mr. Caine here will buy it for you.

He looked them directly in the eye. "You okay with dat?"

Both boys nodded. They looked solemn, but I could see them nearly quiver with anticipation. It was a sailing trip to nowhere, every boy's dream. For a week, or a month, it didn't matter. This was a tradition of Oceana, something young men like these two had done for a thousand years. School could wait. They could make up the work. They were both smart kids, good kids. Watermen. It would be good for them, and it would be good for us to have them around.

"Then get going." Ed smothered them with one of his bear hugs. "You stay safe, you two. Don't get sick and don't get hurt. Mr. Caine will tell you what to do. Take care of the boat and Mr. Caine will take care of you. Come back safe and sound, or your mothers and Tutu Mae will have my big old okole."

The boys laughed, knowing it was true.

He shook my hand, and then hugged Margo, patting her back as he hugged her. Ed was a terrific hugger. I wished he would have hugged me.

"You come back whenever, Caine," he said. "Get this lady out of town, and you stay out of town until it cools down here. Probably have to stay out of Kauai for a while. But Kimo will take care of everything for you. As long as you take care of Charles and Filipe."

"Thank you, Ed. Again."

"It's okay, man. You gotta have somebody who loves you," he said.

We crowded into the dinghy and shoved off from the clean white beach fronting one of the most beautiful bays on one of Hawaii's most beautiful islands, and quietly motored out toward my boat. *Olympia* rode high at anchor, looking peaceful and regal in the clear morning light. A slight swell rolled in from the north, a portent of the powerful winter surge that would be pounding this coast within the month. Bright sun reflected off the rollers. The air smelled of the sea, of salt, and of the fresh, clean air that had blown down from the pole, all the way across thousands of miles of pristine ocean, warming as it traveled until it became balmy, until it arrived in Paradise.

Like Adam and Eve, we were leaving Paradise for an uncertain destination. Only Margo knew where we would go. And I had promised I would ask her only when we had cleared the island and were on our way.

I turned and looked back at Kauai. A truly holy place, and we had brought violence to this island. I understood Tyler's anger. I might feel the same, were our positions reversed. But the island would heal itself. It had seen such violence before;

on a scale larger than this. Still, the birds flew through her trees, the opu'u swam in her streams, and clear blue water washed her shining beaches. We had made some rude noises, had bled a little into her red volcanic soil, but had done nothing that would truly change this island.

I watched Ed walking across the sand to the pay phone on the bathroom wall. The Aussies' rental Jeep would disappear. No trace of it would ever surface.

I wondered about what he had said to me. You have to have somebody who loves you. Ed was my brother. He had adopted me after a time of great loss. I guess that made me family, something I had not experienced in a long time. Something I hardly missed until I thought about it.

An offer was out there, too. Unanswered, it would wither and fade away. Barbara's offer of herself was generous and heart-felt. And she was a hell of a woman. A man could do much, much worse. And all she had asked in return was commitment.

An ocean voyage is good for many things. The minimization of your world to the deck and cabin of a small craft tends to focus your thinking. It's good for concentration. That which is important comes to the forefront of your thoughts. By the time you get to where you're going you find that you can think clearly again. Decisions are possible.

This trip would benefit all of us.

For the boys it was a ceremony of sorts, a coming-of-age as ancient as the Polynesian people. A long voyage, an adventure of being useful and seeing the world, or at least another part of it. They would become acquainted with the seafaring ways of the blue water world. School was one thing. But this was life.

Margo would get to where she wanted to go. With enough money she could disappear and acquire for herself a safe, secure existence. If she wished anonymity she could easily purchase it.

And I could heal and relax, and come to some conclusion about my relationship with Barbara. It was due. I knew that I loved her as I had loved few women in my lifetime. And I understood that she loved me, something rare and valuable in this world of flux. But could I give all this up? Why did it have to be that way? Why couldn't we agree to something else?

We boarded and stowed the dinghy. The boys did the grunt work while I limped around and pointed and told. Their excitement showed, and I had to tell them to stay calm, this was going to be a long trip. Save some of that energy for later.

We raised the sails and the anchor and caught a good breeze immediately. *Olympia* shuddered a little with some anticipation of her own, and we were under way, effortlessly gliding along the swells, away from land, out toward the open sea.

I turned to Margo, standing next to me in the cockpit of my vessel, watching the land move away from us.

"You okay?"

She nodded, keeping her eyes on the green spires of the mountains, their tops once again shrouded in pale gray clouds.

"You keep your promises, don't you?"

"It's all I've got to give. You saved my life. Twice. I'll never forget that."

"And you saved mine, John. You're saving it again. Right now. I never thought we would actually sail away from this place."

She finally broke off her gaze from the island and turned to look at the horizon ahead.

"Okay," I said. "Where to?"

She told me.

I smiled. "We'll have to stop to provision once or twice, but we can make it."

She looked at me, expecting more.

"Going to take a month, you know. Maybe more."

She arched an eyebrow.

"Didn't say we couldn't, or that I wouldn't."

She smiled, leaned over and kissed me. It was a chaste, sisterly kind of kiss. On my cheek.

"Just one thing," I said.

"What?"

"You're going to have to learn to take saltwater showers. All the freshwater we carry won't get us where we want to go if you take those long, long showers."

"I'll make do."

"I'm sure you will."

She patted my shoulder.

"There's a lever in the shower. Runs either freshwater or salt. Turn it to salt and clean yourself up."

"What about you?"

"I'll be okay. I washed the worst of it off back there. Later, when I'm sure we're on course, I'll clean up. This is important right now. Go spend some time on yourself. You look like you could use it."

She nodded. "Thank you, John."

"All part of the service," I said, watching the horizon ahead, and then looking back one more time to say good-bye to Kauai, an emerald jewel on a sapphire sea.

37

The poet must have known what he was talking about when he called April the cruelest month. While the weather doesn't really change from one month to another, a Hawaiian April is the beginning of the hurricane season. And April is when the golden plover begins heading home to Alaska.

Resembling a roadrunner, these little guys spend every winter in Hawaii. If you are lucky enough to have one visit your backyard, you can bet that the same bird will return again the next fall. They spend the winter here getting fat, and then, starting in April, they begin to disappear, one by one, flying in one great, nonstop effort all the way back to Alaska. Fifty-two hours in the air. I don't know how the first one figured out that there was a chain of islands where summer never ends down here in the tropics, but one of the great-great-granddaddies of the species managed to make it here and back, told everyone he knew, and the next season every one of them packed up and made the flight.

April found me like the plover, a long way from home, sailing along foreign coasts, visiting ports of call I had never seen before. It would be many more months before I could slide *Olympia* into her slip at the end of the mauka dock at the

Rainbow Marina. April found me alone, free in an alien part of the world, faced with a mission that I would not have chosen, but faced with no choice in the matter. A piece of unfinished business, it had come looking for me, like some reoccurring nightmare that will not allow you a peaceful night. It was something I could not avoid. So in April, when my other business had concluded, while I was far away from home port, I began to think of how the problem could be handled. I went over all of the alternatives until the only answer, rejected at first, remained the only one standing in the process of elimination.

So in April I went in search of my destiny.

Our first leg of the flight from Kauai had been to cruise the outer islands, that line of coral reefs and truncated volcanic peaks that lay strung out over eleven hundred miles of Pacific Ocean from Kauai to Midway Island. These were the oldest Hawaii, ancient mountains that had been worn down to insignificant sea mounds. Once as massive as the sea mounds of the current Hawaiian chain, these former islands now were mere specks on the map, some of them so insignificant they were completely covered at high tide by the northern Pacific.

Long before man appeared on the planet, even before the time of the dinosaurs, some of these mountains had existed with lofty peaks and lovely valleys. Time and the elements eroded them away. French Frigate Shoals, Nihoa, and the others all had an individuality and a different history. Some had evidence of human habitation, some were without any marking of man's passing. The two boys loved every minute of the trip, and we dropped anchor at every place that looked interesting. We climbed the cliffs of Nihoa, searching for the ancient village we had heard would be there. We dived in crystal-clear lagoons and swam with the monk seals. It took us all of a month just to get to Midway Island. We felt no urge to hurry. We had no schedule and we had no agenda except to hide and to heal.

At the old naval installation, the one with a dramatic history of its own, we purchased plane tickets home for Charles and Filipe. They had had the time of their lives. They had worked hard, had explored truly deserted islands, and had learned more in that one long reach than they could have learned in any classroom. More important, they had joined the tradition of their Polynesian ancestors by getting into a small boat and sailing a thousand miles at a mere whim. The Polynesians had skillfully navigated and explored over a third of the earth's surface, traveling most of it in open canoes. Now Charles and Filipe had joined their ranks, although not in a canoe, but in a "woman's boat," as the old ones called our decked-over Western sailing vessels.

They were tough, those old ones.

I liked my comforts, even while on the ocean. To me, there's nothing better than Jimmy Buffett yammering over the mast speakers at sundown, a following sea, a good Cuban cigar, and a margarita over crushed ice. Tough or not, those old boys couldn't match that, even on their best days.

When we reached Midway the boys wanted to go home, and yet they'd had so much fun they seemed reluctant to leave. Margo and I hugged them before they got on the plane and we stood at the edge of the runway and waved to them as the little jet lifted off the historic field. We probably could have made it to Midway without them, but their presence made the healing period so much easier, and so much more fun that I could not have conceived of doing it alone. They were good kids, they had pulled their weight, and I would miss them.

Margo and I ate dinner of fresh-caught mahimahi at the old officer's club on Midway, now a restaurant catering to the sparse tourist trade, and I wondered at the minds of the men who had climbed into their antiquated airplanes to sacrifice themselves against the Japanese invaders more than a half century before. Their spirits seemed to live all around us, those from both sides of the conflict. And they seemed to exist in harmony. Just as their descendants existed in peace, so did the vanished warriors who haunted this place.

From Midway, I took Margo on a direct voyage to her destination, stopping only to reprovision. The weather cooperated. We met friendly customs officials whenever we entered a strange port. People smiled, were polite, went out of their way to help us. It gave me hope for the human race. Without politics, people were always just people, and they seemed to be the same on every continent.

By the time we reached Margo's chosen destination, our wounds had healed. We were both bronzed by the sun, both fit, and we had become friends. At night she kept to her cabin and I to mine. She helped me make the decision that I had pondered, and she achieved the independence she'd lusted for. Without the sexual tension, men and women can be friends, and that's what we became, sharing what was in our hearts, sharing our hopes and dreams and our worries. It was she who forced me to look honestly at my choices. It must have been easier for her, after so recently completing the same reappraisal of her own life's choices. She guided me through my assessment, and helped me make my own conclusions.

When we reached our final port of call and had cleared our paperwork with the harbormaster, I docked and went looking for her and found her already packed. A solitary bag lay on the bunk she had used. Her purse and her passport lay next to the bag. She wore a simple white cotton dress and sandals. She had cut her hair short, shorn to the top of her collar. She smiled when I noticed it, and shook her head, letting imaginary tresses fling themselves about. She was dressed for business in the tropics, and I knew what that business might be.

"Looks good," I said, approving of her new look with a

wink and a smile. "You need any help out there?"

She shook her head. "Thank you, John, but no. I think I can make it on my own. There are some honest brokers here, and I'll only trade enough to get me to my next stop. I don't want to call attention to myself."

I nodded. She would collect enough funds to travel to the place where she could feel free, where not even John Caine would know where she was. Smart lady. Those who looked for her might drop in on me late some evening and use their vicious talents to get me to tell them everything I knew. If they did that, they would only learn where I had last seen the woman. And by then she would be long gone.

"You have done everything you said you would," she said, reaching up and kissing me above my whiskers. "Absolutely everything. I owe you, and there is no way to repay you except with these." She handed me a small cloth bag. "You earned them. Without you I would not have them, or anything else. Even my life."

"I can't take them. Chawlie told me he would give me half if I got the whole shipment from you."

"Half?"

"That's the going rate."

She stood ramrod-straight staring at me and I saw chicken skin form on her forearms as she understood the primary danger of our voyage. Alone, unarmed, with a man who could have killed her and searched her belongings and taken only the stones, sending everything else to the bottom of the ocean. That it didn't happen stunned her. I watched her eyes focus on the distant horizon, and I knew she visualized her own death at my hands.

"You could have . . ."

"I could have done nothing. You saved my life. Twice. You think that's not worth something?"

"Nobody would ever know."

"I would know. I like you, Margo. And I owe you. You've

earned whatever freedom and peace you're searching for. All I could give you in return for my life was the chance to live your own."

She stared at me.

"You saved me."

"I see it as the other way around. You sure you're going to be all right?"

She nodded, collecting herself. "Better than I've ever been. And don't worry about me. When you travel first class, you usually have little to worry about."

"First class."

"From now on, that's the only way I travel."

"Keep a little for later."

"I could travel everywhere first class and still have plenty for later. And I shall. It's mine. They'll have to kill me if they want to take it away from me."

"They will if they find you."

"Then I'll just have to hide so they don't find me," she said.

"You do that."

She hugged me. "Take care of yourself, John. You are the one I worry about."

"I live the hard life, Margo. It's my choice."

"I know. But I can still worry about you." She looked at me, her eyes filling with tears. "I'm going to miss you," she said.

"And I'll miss you."

"You've been a friend. Probably the only man friend I ever had."

"There's more like me out there."

"Where? I don't think so. I think you're one of a kind." And she reached up and kissed me again, this time on the lips. The kiss lasted a long time. She tasted of mint. Her hair smelled of mangoes.

"Are you going to stick with your decision?" she asked, after she'd kissed me.

"We'll see," I said.

She smiled. "I knew you'd say that." She handed me her bag. "Hold this while I try to find a way off this vessel without showing the locals my lingerie."

"Take care. This is the first day of the rest of your life."

She laughed. "I hadn't heard that trite old crap in years."

"For you it's true."

The last time I saw Margo Halliday it was April, and I watched her marching up the quay, carrying nothing but her purse and a small overnight bag, casually strolling from her old life to her new one. I realized that I would miss her. Considering her situation, it was conceivable that we would never meet again. She knew how to find me. If she ever needed me again, she knew I would come. I owed her.

I watched her disappear into the crowd on the quay and felt the loss. It was the loss of a friend.

I spent some time below, charting the course for home. I had one more stop to make. I looked at the charts, computing the distance, calculating speed and wind direction, checking tide tables and calling up weather reports on the computer, and figured that as long as I was in the neighborhood I might as well drop in. My destination lay 2,200 nautical miles to the south-southeast, but that wasn't much of a distance, considering how far I had already come. I had unfinished business there. Like an overdue bill, it would only get worse if I ignored it. Constantly looking over my shoulder was not a habit I wanted to acquire.

When the tide changed, *Olympia* and I slipped our moorings and set sail on a course to take care of the chore that would give me the freedom I sought for my own life.

Chawlie's place had not changed at all since I had last been there. Bright white overhead lights gave the public dining area all the romantic ambience of a Safeway supermarket. The bar at the far end of the dining room, protected from the fluorescent basting by a red-tiled pagoda roof, seemed cool and shaded, and I headed there, knowing my appearance would soon be reported.

No nephew Choy met me at the entry, and Chawlie had not been at his usual orange plastic chair in the foyer. Things had changed as much as they had remained the same.

The bartender was new. When I asked for a Kendall-Jackson, he frowned and said that they didn't carry that brand.

I shrugged and ordered a Tsingtao. That, they had.

The beer lasted about ten minutes and I drank it in solitude. Chawlie didn't come out of his den. Nobody else accosted me.

The waiters all looked like new hires. Only the oldest one, a tall, frail guy with gray chin whiskers and a beleaguered expression, seemed to recognize me. He nodded as he passed and continued on to his table without breaking stride.

The beer gone, I dropped a bill on the bar and got up to

leave. The bartender had not asked me if I wanted another one. He had not inquired if I wanted something to eat. He had ignored me. He made a point of it.

I left a five-cent tip.

At the entry, the orange plastic chair remained vacant. Chawlie was being inscrutable. More so than usual. Maybe he was just being cautious. Perhaps he was ill. Perhaps he had died. Maybe, while I was sailing the South Pacific taking care of personal business, the Colombians had come in late one night and had given him a necktie party. Something had changed, and I didn't know what.

I pushed the door open and went through the foyer out into the hot, still night. Chinatown was crowded with tourists. I crossed the street and walked down River Street to the municipal parking garage on Pier 11, the one just under the Aloha Tower.

I had parked my Jeep at the farthest end of the lot. I needed to walk after my long voyage. I would have walked the eight miles from Pearl Harbor if I thought it practical. I had compromised, parking as far away from Chinatown as I could and still get the benefit of the walk.

I'd been gone from the Islands a long time, much longer than I'd anticipated. This old planet had almost made a complete orbit around the sun before *Olympia* made it back into port. It had been a year of searching a foreign land and, when I found what I had been looking for, watching and learning. It took me months of travel through a dry, dusty country to find my target, more months to find the opening I sought, then making sure that the back door for escape was still in place, confirming the locations of the traps and the blind alleys.

Doing the deed took no more than a few minutes. Getting to the coast took three nights of travel, holing up during the blazing days. Sailing back to Honolulu took four weeks. All the rest of the time had been intelligence gathering. All the rest had been an investment to make certain that John Caine came home in one piece. Otherwise, the whole exercise would have been useless.

In the deserted parking garage I wondered what had gone wrong while I was gone. Chawlie appeared to have vanished.

The two men behind me were quiet, but not totally silent. I heard them approaching before they got to me, a squeak of a shoe, the grinding of a tiny pebble beneath the leather sole on the concrete deck, sounds so soft they had to have been made in stealth. I dived between two cars to my left, scrambled to my feet and sprinted toward the distant concrete wall.

They pursued, silent dark figures, dressed in black.

Another pair of pursuers came at me from the side. I heard urgent whispering behind, and then another pair came from the opposite end of the row of parked vehicles, racing me to the end of the pier.

I was trapped.

Unarmed but for my Buck knife, I turned to face the two closest hunters. They were closer than I realized, and as I turned, one of them clubbed me across the side of my head and I crashed to the greasy concrete deck, fell into the rabbit hole, and was swallowed by the blackness.

You were not to hurt him!"

A familiar voice cut through the haze. Dim lights told me I was indoors and that it was still night. The gentle rolling of my surroundings told me I was on a small craft, somewhere offshore, moving, not anchored. A sailboat, and not my own. The voice told me that Chawlie lived.

"You were supposed to escort him, not kill him."

"He fought us."

I opened my good eye. The left side of my face felt hot and swollen, my eye closed. Only my right eye worked reasonably well. My stomach stirred and fluttered with nausea. That told me my old body was flirting with concussion.

I had found myself in familiar surroundings, the teak-paneled main cabin of Chawlie's junk.

"If he had fought you, you would not be here and he would have been explaining the death of another son."

"Chawlie?"

"Ah, John Caine, you return from the land of Winken, Brinken and Nod."

"Close enough, Chawlie," I said. "Are these guys yours?"

"Good, eh? They took you down like you old man."

"I am an old man."

"Not supposed to be so easy, John Caine. My boys bring you aboard my junk. Keep you safe until you hand over the emeralds."

"I wasn't that easy. There were eight of them."

"Ten, but no problem, yah? Return my emeralds and I can pay the Colombians, and everything will be fine once more."

"I haven't got the emeralds."

"No? But half are yours!"

I sat up. Slowly. Dozens of little devils with pitchforks ran around inside my head, stabbing me with their sharp, barbed points. My stomach rolled and heaved, but I managed to keep everything down.

"I came to tell you," I said, when all my parts found equilibrium. "She got away. I lost her. She took the emeralds and went overboard one night while we were close to shore. She may have drowned. Sharks may have got her. She may have got to shore. I motored around for a full day, looking for her, but nothing, She'd vanished."

Chawlie regarded me with suspicion. Five million dollars is a powerful argument for selling out a friend. And I had sold Chawlie out, although I had done so for reasons he would never have understood.

"She's gone, Chawlie," I said. "So are the emeralds."

"Why you gone so long? Almost a year!"

"I had some other business to take care of. I was in that part of the world, so I took care of it."

The old man's black eyes burned with a silent fire. "Thompson's brother. You kill him dead, eh?"

"I don't know what you're talking about."

"About a month ago, a little more, Thompson's brother, Russell, died from a gunshot wound to the head. Man lived down in Australia, far out in Outback. Big desert. Someone fired at him from a distance of five hundred yards. One shot. Whoever held that rifle was a world-class marksman. And a soldier. He was gone before the sound of the shot reached the body. Expert in the bush, too. They chased the shooter but never found a sign. Only several kinds of men could do that. Ex-SAS. Ex-SEAL. Men like that. Men like you."

"I don't know what you're talking about, Chawlie."

"Thought you might like to know. Man who paid those men to come kill you is dead. Shot by mystery man."

"I am thankful I no longer have to watch my back."

"Except from my sons."

"Except from your sons."

"Stupid boys. Almost killed you." Chawlie regarded me again, inspecting my wound, looking into my eyes. When he pulled the swollen flesh away from the eye and wiped away the blood, I found I could see rather well. "So what do I do, John Caine? I hold the Colombians off this long, but I get very nervous. They know you're gone, looking for their jewels. They wait. They know you're on commission. High commission. Half. That's what keep them interested. I pay half, then tell them, other half come when Caine come home. We wait. So you show up. And you do not have emeralds. They going to be pissed."

"Five million dollars. What did they cost you?"

"Five million even. Retail almost fifteen million. I pay two point five million cash already. Keep them from killing me. They wait for the rest. Not patiently, but they wait. Their boys work in the restaurant. One is the bartender. They see you come in and then they know. He tell them very quick."

"I stiffed him on the tip."

Chawlie smiled, a grim little smile that floated to the surface and then vanished like a gas bubble in a swamp. "Small victory," he said. "And you have no jewels?"

"None."

"Not one?"

"Get everyone out of here."

He turned and barked fast Mandarin at the two young men standing behind him. They turned and left immediately, closing the cabin door behind them.

When he turned to me I looked him in the eye. "She walked away with everything."

"I thought you said she went overboard."

"I lied," I said, watching him. "This is the truth."

"Why?"

"The idea was that if she was dead nobody would come looking for her. That way she's safer. Somebody may stumble onto her, but it would be accidental. If they think she's still alive, they'll never stop looking. The lie provides a margin of safety."

"Why you lie to Chawlie?"

"I did it for the benefit of your boys out there."

"You think they help them?"

"Are you sure they won't?"

He considered that, nodded, and looked at me quizzically. "You helped her get away. With my money?"

"You set it up when you sent her to me, Chawlie. After that you lost control. You could have helped her, but you chose to have someone else take care of it for you."

"So John Caine now Lobbing Hood? You lob from old Chawlie and give to poor Margo?"

"It seemed like a good idea at the time."

"You stole the emeralds from Chawlie?"

"Margo stole them. From her ex-husband, who stole them first, unless the Colombians stole them before they marketed them overseas. I just let her live."

"You going to tell me where?"

"Not a Chinaman's chance. I promised I would never tell a soul. Not even you. And she's not there, anyway. She probably flew out of there the next day."

"You fall in love with her too?"

Chawlie's admission was startling, and my mind stumbled over the concept for a heartbeat or two.

"Nothing like that," I told him. "I'm involved, remember?"

He hawked and spit, lobbing the gob through an open porthole. "Your lady friend came here looking for you a few months ago. She hadn't heard from you. Thought you were dead. Someone told her you had gone sailing with beautiful woman. Nobody knew where. Nobody knew when you'd come back. Don't think you're involved, anymore."

"I've already spoken to her."

"She mad like tiger, eh?"

"She's not like that. I'll see her next week. She's flying over."

"She trust you?"

"She trusts me."

"Chawlie trust you. And now Chawlie out the whole five million."

"Small price to pay for the company of a beautiful woman, Chawlie. Could have been worse. You had your time with her. Onassis once said that's the only thing money is good for, spending it on a beautiful woman."

"So you are in love with her."

"I owed her, Chawlie. I liked her style."

"Same thing. Liking her style. Could mean liking anything. 'Hey, I like your style,' could mean 'Hey, I like the way your sweater swells out to here.' "

"It's not like that. Never was."

He shook his head. "So what do I do?"

"Pay the money," I said. "Get the Colombians off your back. Count your blessings that you can afford to pay it. And be careful who you do business with in the future."

"Chawlie could give John Caine to the Colombians. They could get you to tell them."

"They could try."

He looked at me, his expression far from inscrutable. "You kidding me, John Caine? You really don't have the stones?"

"She's either long gone or she's dead. I say she's dead. I say you tell the Colombians that she's dead. That way, neither you, nor the Colombians, nor me, nor Kimo will ever go looking for her, and if we don't go looking for her, we probably won't find her. Write this one off, Chawlie. Put it down under experience."

"Experience very expensive."

"I knew a guy once who told me that the biggest difference between the Harvard School of Business and the school of hard knocks is that Harvard is cheaper."

"Your friend right. I send sons to Yale, anyway. Harvard full of sissies."

"You can pay it."

"Difference between not paying and paying is that paying is cheaper."

"The woman earned a second chance."

"With my money?"

"Like I said, Chawlie. You set it up. You knew what I would do."

He looked at me for a long time and then nodded, mostly to himself. The old man turned and left the cabin, leaving me alone in his stateroom. I heard him barking orders, and the rhythm of the sea changed and I knew the junk was turning and we were heading back to port.

I fell asleep in the cabin of my old friend, knowing that I

had stretched that friendship to the limits, and that whatever he had felt he owed me had now been shifted to the other side, and that someday he would come to collect. And when he did, I would pay up. Not in money. It's rarely money between us. There would be a favor to be done, a hard deed, something no one else he knew could achieve. And he would come looking for me, or he would wait patiently until I ambled into his restaurant, seeking something for myself, and he would hand me what I wished in exchange for what he wanted. It was his way.

And I knew, too, that I had done exactly what he had wanted me to do this time. In my own way, making the decision on my own, I had achieved what he could not. In his mind I had set the woman free. But that was not what I had done. Margo had set herself free. It had been her show all along, and Glen Halliday and Chawlie and John Caine and the Colombians and even the Australian commandos had all been bit actors, dancing on her stage, playing to her starring role.

As consciousness fled I wished her well, hoping that somewhere, wherever she landed, Margo found the peace that she sought, knowing in my heart that she deserved it.

39

I watched the woman working in the field of flowers, bending and digging, pruning and cutting, making endless trips to and from a growing pile of weeds and grassy clumps of red earth at the edge of the field. She worked unceasingly, pausing only to drink water from a clear plastic bottle that sat in shade at the end of the row she worked.

Already lean, she had become brown and sinewy, her skin baked to a golden tan from days in the tropical sunshine, her muscles sprung from constant physical labor. She had even become tougher, if that was possible.

The field of riotous color stretched to a shining galvanized chain-link fence that looked new, the white steel running the perimeter of the property on the leeward side of the island, enclosing most of two acres. An automatic irrigation system kicked on across the field, showering the flowers with a fine spray. The woman looked up from her labors when the hissing started, looked at her watch, nodded to herself, and returned to her chores.

I waited for her to finish her work before I approached. She looked happy, the way people do when they achieve goals. She looked as if she felt at home, too. Even though this was not her birthplace, she seemed to have claimed a part of the land as her birthright. Her field of flowers looked nurtured and I wondered about the child.

I got out of the Jeep and walked across the road and down the old rutted lane beside the houses. Kimo's land. He had not wanted me to know where he lived. But I had found it. Like he said, it's a small island. And besides, his son had given me the address, inviting me to visit at my convenience.

She met me halfway up the lane, carrying a basket of weeds and clumps of red volcanic soil. It looked heavy. She had not seen me, and when she did she stopped still, like a fawn caught by predators in the middle of a field, and I realized that she probably did not recognize me.

"Hello," I said.

"Mr. Caine!" She dropped the basket and ran to me and threw her arms around my neck. "Mr. Caine! I never thought I would see you again!"

"How are you?"

"What happened to your face?"

"Had a disagreement with an old friend. How are you?" Up close she looked wonderful. All of the sag had gone out of her face and she looked her age, a young woman in her mid-twenties, full of vigor and power. All of the old worry lines were still there, etched by years of living with Billy Graham. They would never go away. But there were new lines, now. Smile lines, laugh lines, and squint lines from the sun. "How's Julia?"

"She's fine. She's at school. Preschool. There are tons of kids around, and she found some friends, and she's just fine."

"And she remembers . . . ?"

"She remembers everything, but I think she just put it down to adult stupidity. She doesn't ask for her daddy anymore. He served six months and went home. We didn't see him while he was in jail and he didn't try to find us when he got out. He didn't have the chance. Kimo took him from the jail and down to the airport and put him on a plane and told him not to come back."

"You don't miss him?"

"My divorce was final last week. He's history, Mr. Caine. I've got a new life, now."

I nodded. "You look terrific."

She smiled. "Don't I? All this sun and nice weather? I'm pretty."

"I was thinking the same thing," I said.

"Isn't it nice? I'm growing flowers for the hotels. I love flowers. I love the scent of them, when you're right in the middle of the field, and the breeze blows across them and they just, well, they just almost overpower you, they're so sweet and wonderful. And they're happy. They're so colorful and pretty. They make me happy, working with them."

"Is this your land?"

"Kimo's family loaned it to me. I pay rent. We live right here on the property. Just like members of the family. Kimo paid for the fence and the sprinklers and I'm paying him back a little at a time. The business is just getting started, but in time I know we'll do fine. There are more acres back there that they'll let me use, but I have to take it small and just work what I can. I don't have the money to expand. I'm extended right now, and just getting by. But," she said, smiling and thumping herself on the chest, "I am getting by. When I'm not working the flowers I deliver them to the hotels, and when I'm delivering, I bring free samples to the ones not on my route. Last night I got another order. If I get any more I'll have to hire some help."

"I'm glad for you."

"Did you just come by to see how I was? That's sweet."

"Do you remember Margo Halliday?"

"Your client, the one with all the problems. People said you took her and hid her someplace where nobody will ever get to her again."

"People?"

"Kimo said that. He said that you were gone so long you probably took her to Europe and helped her vanish."

"He say anything else?"

"He said she probably didn't kill her husband. He thinks somebody else did it, from South America."

I nodded. I wondered if Kimo really believed that.

"Margo gave me something for you. She told me to give it to you as soon as I came back."

"She wanted to give me a present?"

I nodded. "She bought a little freedom for herself, and she thought that you might need some, too."

"I'm confused."

I reached into my pocket and pulled out the cloth bag that Margo had given me and handed it to her.

"What's this?"

"It's a lot of things. Could be working capital. You could call it freedom."

She opened the bag and looked inside. At first she didn't understand what she saw nestled in the folds of cloth. I could tell when she realized what she held in her hand. "Are these real?"

"So I've been told."

"I've never seen anything like this before. These are . . . ?"

"Emeralds."

"Emeralds."

"Enough to get you started, pay off your debts to Kimo, keep the wolves away from the door, and pay for Julia's college education. She could go to Punahou when she gets to high school, if she works hard and keeps her grades up. She could go to Yale or MIT or anywhere else in the world when she graduates from Punahou."

"Why?"

"Because Margo thought you deserved it."

"Hold me." She reached out and hugged me, burying her

face in my neck. We stood there for the longest time, letting the cool ocean breezes fold around us. I held her until she was ready to let me go. Then I stepped away, gently placing my hands on her shoulders, and looked her in the eyes, holding her attention.

"You'll have to sell them carefully. And you can't tell anyone that you have them. Not Kimo, not Julia, not anyone. Especially Kimo. Do you understand?"

"How . . . ?"

"I'll help you. There's a man I know in Chinatown. He'll get rid of them for you. It will be a surprise at first. He'll laugh. I promise you he will laugh when you show him what you have. It is a very big joke on him, too. A kind of humor that only he will understand. But he will help you when he stops laughing. And he will not cheat you. He's a bad man. But he's not evil."

"I don't understand."

"Do you have a safe place for these?"

"Yes. I know a safe place."

"Then take them. Hide them. When you need some money, let me know and we'll go down and see this man I know and listen to him laugh."

"I don't know about these things, but there's a lot of money here, isn't there?"

I nodded. "A king's ransom. You're a rich woman."

"But why?"

"Why not?"

"I'll have to think on it. Somehow it just doesn't seem fair."

"Life is not fair. But sometimes the ball rolls your way."

She grinned. "I know what you're saying. When life hands you lemons, you make lemonade. But when you've already got a glass of lemonade, why not just drink it?"

I didn't understand what she said, and I doubted that she did either. She was giddy. I watched dreams well in her face, her eyes focused on her new possibilities. It was a pleasant thing to watch.

"I've got to go. Take care of yourself."

"Thank you, Mr. Caine."

"Give Julia a kiss and a hug for me, Karen."

"I will."

I turned to go.

"Mr. Caine?"

"Yes."

"Would you care to come to dinner with Julia and me tomorrow night? Kimo and his family will be here, too. We're getting a fat paycheck from one of the Waikiki hotels, and we were going to celebrate anyway. We're having a barbecue. Hamburgers and stuff. You're welcome to come join us."

"What time?"

"Seven."

"You don't think Kimo will mind?"

She shook her head. "I think he will be happy to see you."

"I'll bring the milk," I said. "In case it gets spilled."

"And bring some wine."

"I'll do that."

"And take care of that eye!"

I walked down the lane and climbed into my Jeep. I didn't feel like going home, so I turned around and drove all the way to the end of the road and parked in the little lot near the concrete bathrooms at Yokohama Beach, and then hiked out to the end of Kaena Point. It took me over an hour to get there, huffing and puffing over rough trail, until I reached the sand dunes and the bird sanctuary where albatross laid their eggs in season and raised their young until they could fly far out into the Pacific and support themselves. I followed the trails through the dunes until I found the jumbled string of smooth lava boulders that lined up all the way to the end of the world.

Ancient Hawaiians believed that the souls of their dead left the temporal world at this very spot. Kaena Point is an arrowhead of rock that extends way out into the Pacific. It's difficult to get to, and it is worth the hike.

I found a boulder that looked comfortable, raised it up, and lay back against the warm black stone to watch the sun set. The conditions looked right. It had been clear all day, and anything seemed possible.

The sun warmed my face as it descended. Through closed eyes I could feel its power. I tried not to think. I just listened to the sound of the waves striking the rocks around me, the cry of the birds, and the mournful sound of the wind as it came scurrying in from across the sea. I tried not to think, and the white noise of the surf helped, and I lived in the moment and appreciated the world around me.

I tried not to think, but perched on a lava boulder at the edge of the sea is always where the thoughts I try not to think come to me. I lay back and let it happen.

The sea and the world had been here a long, long time before me, and would be here a long, long time afterward. There would be nothing to mark my passing. Few will shed tears when I go. In months I will be forgotten. Like the rich and powerful and the poorest of the poor, my time here is short, and the imprint I make is fleeting. We build statues to ourselves and the wind and the rain wash the features away. We build stately mansions, and they are sold and subdivided, the foundations covered by the lives of others. Countless millions have been here and have gone away leaving no trace of their passing.

I counted myself lucky that I had lived a life in this place, in this time. I had no memory of what was behind and no knowledge of what lay beyond. Like the Roman philosopher Titus Lucretius Carus, I suspected that nothing lay beyond. I hoped for something, but accepted nothing. I sought what Lucretius apparently searched for—*vivere parce aequo animo*, "The real wealth of man is to live simply with a mind at peace."

I dug into my pocket and pulled out my remaining, thrice-stolen emerald, a fat twenty-carat stone in the classic emerald cut. I rubbed my thumb over the flat surface to polish it and put it to my eye, viewing the sun through the precious green lens. It wasn't the same.

I examined the jewel in my hand. I didn't know why I had kept it. Perhaps as a souvenir, a reminder of my year. I might give it to Barbara, but I understood that part of my life was over. She would come soon, and we would have our talk, and she would confirm her decision that she did not want this kind of long-distance relationship with long silent absences. I could not blame her. If we could part friends it would be best for both of us. I would like to remain her friend.

I was certain we could not remain lovers. The relationship was not growing and had shifted into neutral by the great distances and differences between us. I knew it. And somehow I sensed that Barbara knew it as well, that she would come to Hawaii with a mission and would leave with a new life and a new sense of purpose, and without attachment. I sensed the parting would be cordial, without recrimination, and we would both act like two civilized people who had inexplicably found themselves in bed with each other and had to dance to get out unscathed, discovering once again that situations are easier to get into than out of.

We had met at a particularly stressful time, and the mutual attraction had been partially a place for both of us to run to from a mutual friend. I had never known if Barbara started the whole thing by trying to rescue me from Claire, or if it had simply been a contest between two powerful competitive females to see who could bed me first. Call it the Stockholm syndrome. Call it the trophy syndrome. Call it anything you like, but what it was not was a love affair.

I wished her well.

I put the emerald away, saving it for a rainy day or a rainy-day woman, and closed my eyes and thought about being in love. I had been truly in love before and I knew the symptoms, and knew that I did not suffer from that particular disease.

There had been Jayne. Had she lived, my life would have been vastly different. And there had been Kate, her life cut short by her association with mine. But there was another one. And to the best of my knowledge she did live, somewhere out there in the world.

The emerald sparked memories of a woman who had been born in May, and I wondered if she still existed in this uncertain world. Her world, especially. When I met her she had lived on the other side of the old Iron Curtain. And I wondered if she prospered in the new Europe. Or even if she remained there.

It might be fun someday to track her down and watch her briefly from a distance, not to stalk her, just to see how she fared. If she had a relationship, or if she did not need me, I would fade. I'd travel to Venice and spend my days walking the cobblestones along the canals and spend my nights in the hotel next to the Doge's Palace and eat pasta at eleven in the open-air cafés. Or I'd travel to Florence, and then Rome, and then go for a walking tour of Scotland, where I could get Scotch Eggs for breakfast and allow the loneliness and the chill of the moors to seep into my soul so I would have to return to Hawaii to thaw. And all of that would be fun to do with her if she had nothing else to do.

It would be worth the trip, just to see Ildiko again.

Or I might just stay here in Paradise and continue my search for the emerald flash of the setting sun.

It had been a year of extremes. I felt good and fit. My wounds all had healed. I had gone up against powerful enemies and had vanquished them all, including the one who had ordered my destruction.

Now it was over.

And so was this fine day. I opened my eyes to watch the ending of it.

The sun had nearly disappeared into the deep blue Pacific, pausing like a timid bather to catch its breath in the cold water before plunging in. It slid down a few more notches, and then, with only the final degree of arc remaining above the horizon, a brilliant emerald flash of pure green light blossomed and bloomed and then vanished with the sun.

And the day was done.